THE NEW NORMAL

THE MADELINE JOURNEYS BOOK 2

P. A. WILSON

FREE EBOOK

Claim your copy of Obstacles of Magic when you use the QR code to sign up for my newsletter and learn more about Madeline's history with magic.

"*M*adeline, my dear, you must bring your focus to bear." Blu pulled his shawl tight around his tiny frame to avoid the draft as Madeline's spell opened windows rather than moved the sheet of paper on the table.

Madeline couldn't help but feel a little pride at the fact she could blow windows open with magic. Even if she needed a lot of work with control, a year was not that long for this anyway. She'd gone from lawyer to mage in what seemed like the blink of an eye. In fact, she'd made more changes in the last ten months than she'd made in ten years back in her old world. Here, in Cartref, she'd won a vicious fight and found a husband, and friend, and made a place for herself. Now all she needed to find was a purpose. Learning was interesting, but she needed more

She sighed and looked around the room for an image she could hold in her mind, something that would help her to achieve inner focus so she could cast the stupid spell. The walls were made of heavy dark wooden posts between which white plaster gleamed. The shutters banged, and she rose to close them. The scent of pine and wood smoke filled her lungs before she pulled the windows closed and drew the tapestries. The air was chill.

Fall was only days away. It was invigorating. Unfortunately, nothing in sight made her feel calm or focused.

Turning to face the monk who had become her teacher, Madeline said, "Blu, maybe we can try something else. I think twenty failed attempts are enough to break anyone's focus, don't you?" She tried to keep the annoyance out of her voice because it was annoyance at herself not at Blu.

"It is true some students excel only in one specific area, but if you do not learn to persevere when you fail, you will not achieve any mastery of this." Blu gestured for Madeline to sit across from him. "Even so, let us try a summoning spell instead."

"I don't want to summon a devil." Madeline hoped there were no devils here, the actual creatures inhabiting the world were scary enough.

"I do not know what that is, but I suggest you try to summon a small object. I am hungry, perhaps a muffin. I saw the cook baking before we came up here." He waited until she nodded. "In your mind, find the place of quiet."

Madeline pulled her curls back and tied her hair into a knot to keep it out of her face. Closing her eyes, she started to construct an image from memory. The image built from her imagination as a tickle of fine grains of sand, a slight smell of dustiness and salt, the sound of water advancing and retreating.

A sigh slipped from her lips. This time it carried contentment, not frustration.

Blu's voice floated to her. "Now, visualize a muffin sitting on a table. It will have berries."

Madeline smiled; Blu loved sweets. On her beach, she imagined the long table that the cooks used to hold food before serving. She added the smell of warm muffins, a little sweet and a little brany. Her mouth started to water.

"Do you have the image?"

Madeline kept focus on the sight of the single muffin sitting in the middle of the table and nodded.

"Now, you must gently replace the table with the one in this room." He waited again until Madeline nodded. "Very good, Madeline, now reach for your power and command the muffin to exist here."

In her old life, this was when she would turn to another interest, abandoning a hobby when it became work rather than fun. This was not a hobby, though. This was her passion, so she reached for the power she felt as heat in her skin, just enough to move the muffin, no flash, no fireworks, just a pastry.

She tried to control the heat of her magic, visualizing a thermostat, and working to maintain the measurement low on the scale. The image of the sandy beach faded, and her world focused only on the table, then the table faded, then the muffin.

"That is perfect, Madeline."

At the sound of Blu's praise, Madeline felt a flush of pride. Then a heat storm of magic poured through her body. Something shifted, and the spell drained the energy that roared in her blood.

She opened her eyes to see a charred muffin smoking in the center of the table.

"I'm sorry." She tried to slow her heart. "I don't know what happened." She bit her lip, knowing exactly what happened. Despite Blu's assurances that all she needed was confidence, here was evidence that she didn't know what she was doing.

Blu shook his head, and then rose from the chair. "Too much power," he said. "Let us use a more practical way to gather our lunch."

---

*M*adeline wandered past the fireplace in the great hall. She had just begun to think of it as their fireplace, not Jode's alone. He had corrected her in the beginning, reminding her that it was her house too, her grounds, her people. Then he stopped, seeming to know that she needed to come to it herself.

When she'd realized Jode was alive after the attack from the Scree woman, Madeline knew her life was here, not back in the law firm. Marriage followed within six weeks, and she had been happy every day since then.

The lawyer in her still looked for logic and consequences in everything, but she was coming to accept the fact that contracts here were honored because of honor, not because of some threat or legal requirement. She was grateful that she had magic to learn, and hopeful that when she achieved, perhaps not mastery, but at least some control, she could help people in some way.

All she really needed was a goal; a clear purpose to aim for. Maybe some peaceful reflection would help her get over the muffin incident. If she knew what went wrong, maybe she could fix it.

"You look happy," Simon's voice broke her musing.

When Blu and Arabela pulled them into this world, he seemed to come home. He had no second thoughts, and his purpose was clear almost from the beginning. He was still lean, but now his pale skin was touched by the sun. Madeline thought the women were attracted to his blue eyes and infectious grin, but it could be that he was the father of the music industry.

"I am," she replied. "Everything feels right today. Well, except for the disaster in my lessons this morning. But that's par for the course."

"What does it feel like? When you do magic."

"I didn't know you were interested."

He laughed. "I didn't know I was either. I'm looking for some inspiration for an opera. It's time we brought high drama in song to the people here."

"You are getting bored then?" she asked.

Something had been bothering Simon these last few weeks. Madeline thought it was about her secretary, Callisra Tallhouse. It was clear to everyone they had feelings for each other, but Simon was not ready to settle – well, he didn't realize he was ready was probably more accurate.

He dropped into one of the chairs by the fire. "No. Well, not bored exactly, not challenged, I guess. I need something to learn, or to teach. You must understand that, with your magic and all."

"I know what you mean," she said. "It's not like I can't find something to do. Just running this household could be a full-time job, but it doesn't have meaning."

"Have you thought about starting a family?" Simon asked.

"No." Madeline realized she hadn't thought of it at all. "But that's not the type of meaning I am looking for. What about you? Have you thought of settling down?"

Simon burst out in a guffaw. "I'm far too young to retire."

Madeline gave up the idea of solitude and tried to answer Simon's earlier question. She sat and closed her eyes, trying to bring up the right images for him. "Like fire and champagne bubbles. When it works right, I feel warm inside, then it gets hot, and just before it gets too hot, I feel like I've been dunked in a bath of champagne, the bubbles tickle the heat away." She opened her eyes and let the feeling slip from her.

"Wow, that's... um, incredible." Simon made notes on a sheet of paper. "Did you ever feel that way about the law? You know. When you won a case?"

"No, I felt satisfied, but nothing like magic. But then I never felt so exhausted when things didn't go well, either. With magic, I feel as though I've let down the whole world. Like some important opportunity slipped away. When a case didn't go the right way, I just felt disappointed in me."

He raised an eyebrow. "Really? Even when Lee made sure everyone thought it was your fault?"

Madeline waved her hand in dismissal. "She just irritated me. Lee Marshall thought making me look bad would stop the partners looking at her mistakes. I learned to ignore her early on."

Simon leaned forward. "It didn't look like you were ignoring her. Your face would get all red and you would stomp out of the room."

"Ignoring her and not being pissed off are two different things." Madeline shrugged off the memory of the woman who had decided they were enemies at first sight. "One really nice thing about being here is that Lee isn't."

"Yeah, there are a few people I'm glad are back on the other side of that summoning spell." Simon stood and moved his chair to the side. "I'll see you later. You've given me something to think about."

"Join us for supper." Madeline would invite Callisra too and see how Simon reacted. If she couldn't do real magic, maybe a little romantic magic would work, and he would see that settling down was far from retiring.

3

---

*L*ater that evening, Madeline watched Simon talking with Callisra. He was civil, if a bit cold, when he spoke to her. But when Callisra turned her attention to Jode or Madeline, Simon would steal glances at the tall beauty. Callisra's straight fall of raven hair was hanging loose tonight. Her green gown bringing out the emerald tones of her eyes.

It wouldn't take much to make Simon realize he loved her, Madeline thought, but it would take a lot to get him to admit it. Perhaps he would bend a little tonight.

Callisra turned back to Simon. "I find myself entranced by this idea of opera. How do you propose to write such a thing?"

Simon shrugged, none of his usual enthusiasm showing. "I haven't thought about how yet. I need some story to tell. If I have a story, I'm sure I'll figure out how to write it."

"Why do you not simply recreate one of the stories from your world?" Jode asked.

"I need one for this world." Simon pushed his empty plate away. "The theme must resonate with people here. There must be deep emotions going on somewhere, or some old legends I can rewrite."

"Love has always been a great theme for opera," Madeline said. "Perhaps you can tell a love story, something joyful rather than tragic."

She and Jode had planned how to keep Simon talking if need be. Her handsome husband – all blond hero of him – was more than up to the task of matchmaking. "About time," he had said earlier. "Simon needs a good woman to give him some direction. The man cannot simply drift through life forever."

Madeline's attention was drawn back to the conversation by Callisra's laugh. Not the delicate titter that Madeline expected when they first met, Callisra's hearty deep laugh always made Madeline join in.

Callisra put her hand on Simon's arm. "You think, Sir Simon, that here there is no jealousy? No plotting of revenge?"

"Not that I've seen." Simon looked at Madeline, hoping for an ally, or perhaps a change of subject. "People here seem so clear headed."

Jode chuckled. "I thank you for that, a complement indeed. I think, perhaps you have not been meeting enough people."

"I can tell you many stories of people behaving poorly to each other," Callisra offered. "Some are tales from legend, some from personal experience. Perhaps I can provide the inspiration?"

"Be my muse?" Simon swallowed. Madeline mentally scored one for the matchmakers. This would be perfect.

"If a muse is someone who inspires artists, then yes." Callisra poured more wine for them. "When shall we start?"

Simon straightened in his seat. "Tomorrow, I think I will need a good night's sleep before hearing these stories."

Jode raised his glass. "To the birth of a new art form."

Madeline silently added *and to love* as she raised her own glass.

Servants arrived to clear the dishes and replace the wine bottle with a sweeter darker vintage. Dessert wines were one of Madeline's favorite ways to end a meal. The cook's assistant placed a plate of pastries and nuts in the center of the table. Madeline thanked whatever fate had given her magic. Spell casting burned calories almost as fast as she ate them; keeping her figure was not a problem.

Simon had gone to join Jode in a chair by the fire. Madeline sat next to Callisra at the table. "Simon, come and tell Callisra more about the opera."

He shook his head and started talking to Jode. Madeline sent her husband a glare. If he was interested in helping to match-make, perhaps he could stop monopolizing Simon.

"Callisra, let's join them." Madeline saw that Callisra was reluctant to move, and decided to ease up on the cupid business, for a while. "It's fine, we can stay here."

A scuffle from the front hall interrupted the mood of the evening. A goblin ran into the room shouting. "You must hear me."

"Urr, what's going on?" Simon waved away the footman who was trying to keep the goblin from the room. "It's okay; he is one of my musicians."

Urr panted out, "I have news. I need to tell you."

Madeline handed him her glass. "It will wait a few minutes, surely. Take a drink and catch your breath."

Urr gulped down the entire glass and wiped his mouth with the back of his hand. "Thank you, Lady Madeline." His face split into a grin that would have looked fearsome had Madeline not known it was a sign of happiness. "I am ready now. I am passing you the news from a friend who witnessed this."

Jode refilled Urr's glass and said, "I know you would not have come so late if the news was not important. Do not worry, we will ask questions if we have any, but you can tell us directly."

Madeline felt a rush of heat across her skin. The itching that meant something important was going to happen.

"This morning someone appeared in a clearing of the forest to the north." Urr looked at them and waited. When there were no questions he continued, "My friend said that this person was dressed in clothes like Lady Madeline wore when she came."

"What do you mean?" Madeline resisted the urge to scratch as the itching increased.

"A woman. She appeared. She was asleep, or perhaps unconscious."

Jode stepped toward Urr, taking over when Simon and Madeline were unable to ask more. "What happened to the woman? Can you lead us to her? We will ensure she is safe."

"Choi happened." Urr shuddered. "They came and took her."

Madeline found her voice. "Choi, what are they?"

Jode touched her arm. "Beings who live beyond the mountains. If they took this woman, they have a purpose."

Simon helped Urr to the table and offered him food. "What did this woman look like, did your friend say?"

"Very tall, like Sir Jode. Yellow hair and skinny."

Madeline looked at Simon before saying, "Can we speak to your friend?"

"He is waiting for us. He was going to come, but his horse is no match for Goblin speed." He grinned again. "We are very fast when we need to be."

"Is there anything else your friend said?" Jode asked. "Anything which might help us rescue this woman?"

"Yes, I forgot." Urr dug around in his pocket for a moment. When he withdrew his hand, it held a bracelet. It was silver with a single charm hanging from the clasp; an anchor with a diamond set in the center.

"Lee," Simon gasped. "Speak of the devil, and the devil appears."

"What have I done?" Madeline recalled the feeling of another object moving during her disastrous spell this morning.

4

*J*ode stoked the fire in their bedroom. "You must not fret. Until we are able to speak to this friend, you cannot be sure of what happened."

After delivering his message, Urr had taken a plate for supper and gone to the wing where all the musicians lived. Madeline had run to Blu's room as soon as they settled the goblin, but the monk didn't answer when she knocked. His door was locked, and she knew better than to disturb him so late in the night. They would talk in the morning.

"I suppose you're right." She sighed. "Tell me about the Choi. I really must get better informed about all the people in the world. I'm afraid my lessons are getting too tightly focused on my own capabilities. I should try to find some time to study the other types of magic."

Jode sat beside her on the bench and ran his finger down the side of her cheek. "You should trust Blu in matters of your magical training. But I will tell you what I know in the morning." He kissed her earlobe. "Let us talk of something more pleasant. We can sort out the world later. Let us talk about sorting out our

P. A. WILSON

small world here. Simon and Callisra will be well matched, I think."

Madeline threw her jewelry into the box. She wasn't in the mood for waiting. "How can you expect me to discuss that when someone is clearly in danger? We need to work out what to do."

"We do not know that she is in danger." Jode sighed and started changing for bed.

Madeline turned to look at him. "Oh? By the reaction on your face at the news, I think we do."

"There are things we do not speak of at night. You know better than to feed problems with energy while they are still weak." Jode handed her a nightgown. "Come to bed. In the morning, Blu can help you with this problem."

"Why don't we speak of some things at night?" Madeline let herself be distracted from the problem at hand, for now. "In my old world, we had similar beliefs. Blu says there is power in the quality of light, or absence of it. But he won't tell me more than that."

"Because some things gain power at night and feed from the fears of others. And at night fears are magnified." Jode pulled back the covers and raised an eyebrow at her. "Are you coming to bed, or will you spend the night chewing this over?"

She remembered earlier warnings about casting magic without protection. The first spells Blu made her learn were about casting wards. She was able to control those and cast them almost without thinking. Why were they different from other spells? "Do the Choi gain power at night?"

"No, other things do. Now that is all until the sun rises." He climbed into their bed, a plain wooden structure that stood three feet off the ground.

Madeline climbed her own steps to join him. "Very well, I won't sleep though."

"I'm sure we can find something to do to tire you out so you are fresh in the morning when you have to solve all the problems of the world." Jode drew her close.

"Not the whole world," Madeline said. Then she giggled as Jode nibbled on her earlobe.

JODE SLEPT SOUNDLY, an occasional grunt revealing his active dream. Madeline was tired and should have been able to sleep because Jode was an expert lover, but her mind would not let go.

She was sure that Lee was here because of what had happened with the muffin spell. She was determined to get information. If Blu was not available, perhaps Arabela would give her news. False dawn had lightened the sky and she hoped that was enough to make it safe to talk.

Sliding gently out of bed, Madeline took her scrying glass and picked up a blanket that was warm from the fire. She glanced at Jode before leaving to go to the hallway outside their bedroom. Her husband grunted, and then rolled himself in the bedding.

Arabela always rose before the sun these days. Her new baby was an early riser, so she had no choice. Madeline spread the blanket so that she could sit on it and wrap some of it around her shoulders. The air was chill and she didn't want to shiver and break the scrying. She sat with her back to the wall, bundled in the blanket, leaving only her hands and face free. Balancing her glass on her lap, she recalled her sandy beach, and breathed on the surface of the glass as soon as she felt calm.

"Arabela," she whispered. "Are you awake?"

Nothing.

Madeline widened her spell. If she could scry through Arabela's house, perhaps she could find someone awake who could help. In the glass, she saw the house and the grounds inside the walls of Arabela's home. Things were peaceful in the court-yard, the grass dark gray in the pale light. The sight brought back her first days in this world. Then, she spent all her time arguing with Arabela about everything and anything. It was hard to believe they had become such good friends.

Madeline focused and moved the view inside to the hall. Someone moved just out of her line of sight. A servant? Perhaps they could get Arabela to answer the call. Madeline chased the movement and brought the woman into focus; a long housecoat, and a mess of tangled black curls. The woman's shoulders slumped as she paced back and forth.

"Arabela," Madeline called a little louder.

The woman tilted her head and turned to stare directly at Madeline. "Good morning. I hope you had a better night than I did. This child will be the death of me." Madeline knew Arabela couldn't see her but was answering where the voice had come from.

Now that Arabela had spoken and the spell was complete, Madeline could hear the wails of Tadric, the heir to the Summer Lands. "He has strong lungs."

"Wait while I go to the pool so I can see you." Arabela moved away and Madeline made the focus follow her. The wails had started to change to hiccups by the time Arabela sat in front of a pool of water. "Ah, you look tired. What is it?"

Madeline brought her friend up to date with the news. "So, I need information about the Choi."

"You always need knowledge. I wonder if you will ever know all that you need to know about this land."

"True, but this time..." Madeline was going to say it was important, but it always was.

"Never mind." Arabela kissed her son's head and smiled. "I will tell you what the Choi are, but I cannot tell why they need your friend."

"Far from friend." Madeline tried to keep the bitterness out of her voice. How cruel did fate need to be that it brought the biggest pain in her ass over here?

"I see. Well, the Choi are a race of magic beings. They speak to beasts; I have seen them call a wild cat from the hills to take sheep from a farmer who scorned them. They use blood in their magic. Usually from animals they breed for the purpose. Occasionally for special magic they take a human or eldman."

Madeline's stomach turned. "So, they are evil?"

"No, they are Choi." Arabela shifted the child to her other shoulder. "You must remember that beings are not evil because of who they are. Their actions may not be as we wish, but that doesn't make them evil."

Madeline had heard that argument before and it didn't sound any more convincing this time than the last. Anyone who takes blood for power was evil in her book. "Okay, so what else? What do they look like?"

"Much like you or I, but they are very delicate and tall. And their skin is the color of the roses in my garden."

Madeline remembered the patch of beautiful pink roses Arabela cultivated. "Is there anything about them I might use to my advantage? I think no matter what happens, I'll need an advantage."

"They are very greedy creatures. Perhaps you can use that." Arabela yawned widely. "It seems that Tadric is sleeping so I must take the opportunity to rest as well. There is a book in the library here. I seem to remember it was about all the creatures of our land. It is in a very ancient language. You must ask Blu to read it for you."

"I will. Sleep well. We will visit soon." Despite wanting to push for more answers, Madeline broke the spell and the image in the glass faded away. "I hope Blu is willing to speak this morning," she muttered before slipping quietly into her bedroom. Madeline returned the glass to its holder and climbed back into her warm bed.

5

After eating breakfast, Madeline reported to Blu's room for her regular lessons. The tiny monk opened the door and smiled up at her as if nothing was wrong. Perhaps he had not heard the news.

"Good morning, Madeline. Are you ready to learn the correct way to move objects?"

She went to her seat at the table before answering. "Have you been sequestered all night, Blu?"

"I have not, but I did not want to hear gossip. I would hear the news from you." He sat across from her. "I would know what you think of it."

Madeline clasped her hands in her lap. "I think I made a mistake yesterday, a bad one. I need some information."

Blu sighed. "Always quick to ask for answers. Tell me what you think happened."

Madeline told him about feeling the surge of power just as the spell went wrong. "I must have brought Lee here with that spell. I don't know how, but now she seems to be captive. Why would the Choi want her?" She realized her hands were hurting, looking down she saw that they were clenched tightly into fists. She relaxed her fingers.

"It is possible that you did not cause her to transfer worlds. That is a difficult spell to cast by accident." He waited for her to respond.

Madeline tried to give up the idea that only she could have brought Lee. "Would the Choi be able to do it?"

"Yes, the spell is within their capabilities. In fact, it is within most beings' capabilities. They need only learn it."

"That's a relief." Madeline ignored the niggling doubt. "Do you know why they might have brought her here?"

"It is also possible that you may have caused her to come." Blu was infuriatingly calm with his words.

Madeline tried to read something, anything, into his expression, but it was blank. "Blu, what do I do here?"

"If you must ask, then there is a story I do not know. It is odd, is it not, that you know this woman?"

"Oh, I know her all right." Madeline sighed. "She worked in the same firm as I did before I came. Maybe there's a connection with the building?" She looked at Blu hoping for a nod, or something to give her optimism. "Or perhaps not."

"Tell me why it makes a difference to you. How will you act differently if you were not responsible?"

Madeline tried to get her thoughts in order. It felt like there was too much to tell. "When we worked together, she always tried to make me feel like a failure. I don't know why she got under my skin, but she did. When I won a case, she would either tell people I could have done better, or that I was taking credit for someone else's work."

Blu nodded. "This does not sound like a pleasant woman. Why do you think she behaved this way?"

"I don't know. But if I didn't bring her here by accident, then someone has a plan for her." Madeline felt a flash of hope. "Perhaps she is here for a quest, just like I was. Maybe the Choi need her for something other than her blood."

"Perhaps. But if we knew that she was not here for a quest, would that change your feelings?" Blu asked.

"Are you saying the Choi would only want her for something bad?" Madeline really wished Blu would simply tell her what was going on, tell her how to find out why Lee was here.

"Bad and good do not matter. The Choi are known for taking sacrifices. If they brought her here, they mean to use her for power. If they found her because you brought her here, they mean to use her for power. What is the difference to your actions?" Blu crossed his arms and waited.

"If I brought her here, I would feel obligated to rescue her. If I didn't..." She realized how selfish she was sounding. "I guess if I knew she was in danger and I could do something about it I would have to. But can we know for sure?"

"That is a good question. I would also ask, can you simply let someone be in danger, someone unused to our world?" Blu's words made Madeline think of her first days here. How confusing it was and how much she had learned about surviving here.

"I spoke to Arabela this morning." She tidied the cloth on the table, not looking at Blu. "She says there is a book in her library you may be able to read. It might tell us more."

"Do you wish to know more?"

"I suppose." Madeline looked into Blu's eyes. "Yes, I do want to know more. I want to know why the Choi need her, or why they took her from whoever brought her. I need to know if I should try to save her."

Blu nodded and waved his hand to motion her to stop messing with the cloth. "We should travel to Arabela's home. We should learn what we can from this book."

She let go of the tension weighing down her heart. "We can

leave tomorrow. I will have things prepared after we finish this lesson."

"You must do one thing also." Blu placed the sheet of paper back in the center of the table. Madeline started to prepare herself to move it. "You must search your heart. You must decide what matters to you."

"I will. I promise." Madeline hoped they would find a benign reason for the Choi taking Lee, and proof she was not responsible for the woman being here.

"Now, please calm your mind and move this paper to the window ledge; without flames, without moving the chair."

Madeline raised her eyes and saw Blu jiggling in his silent chuckle.

---

 kye Greatmother, leader of all the Choi clans, powerful
wizard, held aside the opening of the captive's tent.

The woman was sleeping, or perhaps simply unconscious. She lay on the rug limp, and bound. Her blond hair tangled and matted with sweat and blood from the spell casting. Skye had to bend low to enter, this tent made intentionally small for the discomfort of prisoners. For this captive, the height of the tent would not be a problem; she only stood as high as Skye's shoulder.

Lowering herself to sit on the only cushion in the tent, Skye prepared a translation spell. Taking a small blue vial from her pocket, Skye pulled a plug of black wax from the top and tipped a few drops of blood into her left palm. She carefully stoppered the vial, returned it to her pocket, and then used the nail on her right index finger to draw the blood into an intricate pattern. When it was complete, she raised her hand and breathed a single word across the blood. It glowed briefly. Sky reached over and rubbed half of it on the captive's ears and the remainder on her own.

"Wake, woman, I wish to speak with you." Skye's voice rasped into the silence of the tent. The captive didn't move. She reached over and shook the woman by her shoulders. When that did not work, she slapped her face – hard.

The captive's eyes flew open – deep green, powerful magic in that color.

The woman gasped. "Why am I here?"

"Do you have a name?" Skye did not wish to keep thinking of her as the captive, or the woman.

"Do you?"

Skye slapped her harder this time. "Do not be insolent. If you answer my questions, it will be better for you."

The woman seemed to consider her options. "Lee Marshall. Why am I here and where is here?"

"Lee Marshall, an unusual name, at least here it is unusual." Skye paused, thinking one more time about her actions. Yes, she would give Lee the answers to her questions. The fear would enhance the power they drew from the spell. "You are here to save my people. Here, is another land, another world from yours."

"What other world? You are speaking English, so how different could it be?" Lee struggled unsuccessfully to sit up. Skye noticed she was shaking despite the bravado.

Skye laughed. "No, I speak my own language, but the spell makes it possible for us to understand each other."

"Oh yeah, magic spells. What is this? I'm in Never Neverland?"

"I do not know where that is. You are in my world. Now, I must tell you how you will save my people."

Lee struggled against her bonds. "I don't believe in magic. I can't save your people. Untie me and I'll just go away."

"No, you must stay. It is, however, important that you believe. Let me prove this to you." Skye reached across to Lee and scratched her arm, blood welled in beads. "Watch carefully, you do not want me to have to do this twice."

Lee winced but kept her eyes on Skye.

"Watch your arm, not me." Skye waited until Lee's eyes were focused on her own arm, and then she gently smudged the blood while speaking the words of power.

Lee gasped as a row of flowers bloomed on her arm. The plants grew until one petal touched her face.

"You feel the flower?" Skye asked.

"Make it stop, I believe you." Lee's voice was high and loud.

"Good, fear will make you more valuable." Skye reached through the foliage and wiped the blood away. The plants disappeared.

"How..." Lee stopped to clear her throat. "How can I help you save your people? Will you send me home when it is done?"

"I do not believe you will need to go home when we are done." Skye smiled, knowing her pointed teeth would not reassure the human. "You will be with us until the time when the season changes."

Lee licked her lips and Skye reminded herself to make sure the woman was given food and water. One of the slaves could feed her.

"How long is that?"

"Nine days."

The woman paled. "And what happens in nine days?"

Skye enjoyed the sweetness of fear in Lee's scent. There would be enough power for both of her goals. The one that will save her people for the next fifty years and the one that raises her lover to be her equal. When it was done, they would be together in public, their love apparent to every Choi in the tribe. It would bring an end to the shameful secret they lived every day.

"Please." Lee's voice was shaky. "What happens in nine days?"

"We will sacrifice you to release the power I need to save my people."

Lee moaned and struggled against her bonds.

"Yes, keep fighting us. It will be much better if you do so. But do not break bones." Skye inhaled the scent of fear, intoxicating. She would send her lover to feed from it.

The captive slumped against the restraints. "Is there something, anything I can do to stop this?"

"Stupid woman. I am disappointed. If there were, why would I tell you? Nothing would be better than your sacrifice."

"Please, why me?"

The whine in Lee's voice irritated Skye. "Because we have found your world brings great power and because we found you with our spell." Skye, tired of the conversation, rose and turned to leave. "Because we could."

7

"*I* saw you with Callisra Tallhouse," Gren, the bass player, said as Simon passed the sheets of music out. "You look good together."

"Yeah, we had dinner with Madeline and Jode last night."

Simon worked his way around the room which was filled today with band members, ex-band members and hopefuls. He liked to keep teaching new techniques to anyone who showed interest because there was plenty of demand for music and no way he could satisfy it with just the New Questers.

They had a great rehearsal room in Madeline's house, down a long hallway on the same floor as the kitchen. That way they could practice without driving people crazy and they could get food when they needed it. "This is the overture to a new opera. I want to try it out."

Gren flipped through the pages, his hair twisting itself into an elaborate braid then springing free to stand on end. "It looks pretty heavy, man. Like you have some big emotions on the page here."

Simon shook his head. Even after a year, he found it disturbing to hear a goblin talk like a surfer bum. Of course, that was easier to take than the hair with a mind of its own. He still remembered the sight of Urr's hair twisting into dreadlocks when they learned the Bob Marley stuff. He handed out the last sheet and said, "That's opera for you, big emotions, big drama, and lots of music."

"Good music to woo a woman with," Gren said. "You must have some big feelings about someone to be able to compose such music."

"Well, maybe we should just try to play it." Simon did not want to hear about Callisra. He knew Madeline was match-making and Callisra was a good choice. She was smart, and pretty, and something about her stuck in his mind. That didn't matter. He was not going to settle down. And, she was not someone he could just have a good time with. Well, not and get away with it anyway.

"Just saying," Gren grumbled.

Simon turned to look at his bass player and noticed that the rest of his group was grinning behind his back. "Great. Look, let's get something straight. I am not settling down and I don't want to hear any more about it. If Callisra hears you she'll get the wrong idea. So, can we get back to music? This will be the opening song when it's finished."

The oboist, Simon kept thinking in terms of the instruments he knew – this oboe was more like a cross between a tuba and a flute – held up his hand.

"Yes, Zora, what is it?"

The eldman smiled brightly and asked, "So, you don't like her?"

"Oh, for crying out loud, yes, she's very nice. Now are you done?" Simon glared at Zora who grinned back. They may be be stubborn, but at least the eldmen looked and reacted like humans. It had been so much easier to connect with Zora than say the Fay or the Sylph members of the band.

Zora nodded before turning to Gren, "Okay, put me down for ten silvers on three months."

Simon spun back to face Gren. "Three months? What does that mean?"

Urr looked up from his copy of the music and answered while Gren made notes on a scrap of paper. "We are betting on when you will marry Callisra. I have my money on six months; I think you will want a long engagement."

"Stop that right now." Simon could see the humor, but it would be better if it wasn't about him. "You shouldn't be betting on something like that. Callisra deserves more respect than that."

"Make that twenty silvers," Zora shouted. "Now about this music."

Simon rolled his eyes and decided to pretend it wasn't happening.

THAT AFTERNOON in her private study, Madeline was practicing reading the ancient language of magic. She had managed to translate four pages in the hour she'd been sitting alone. It was an improvement. Blu might be impressed. But she could understand why people didn't know much about how other species worked if this was an example of the research material available.

The door opened and Jode entered with a tray of snacks and tea. "You must be hungry. Are you almost finished?"

"Yes, I've done my assigned pages. I feel like a little kid when I do this, I've been reading for more than thirty years, you would think reading in a new language would be easier."

Jode looked at the fine lines of print in the book Madeline held open. "You know that language is unreadable to most of the people in this world, including me."

"Yes, but that doesn't seem to help." She closed the book and took the mug of tea from him. "It's nice to have this break together. I miss having time with you."

"You are busy with your lessons. I am busy running the estate. It does not matter that we don't see each other much, as long as we sleep together each night."

She smiled at his words and reached for a pastry. "I have a decision to make."

Jode reached over and lifted a lock of hair from her face, dropping a kiss on her forehead. "I know. I will support you either way."

"Jode, I don't want you to do that."

He pulled away.

"No, the kissing, I want. I don't want you to support me blindly. I need you to argue with me and make me better than I am."

Jode chuckled. "What makes you think I can do that?"

She laughed with him and reached over to brush crumbs from his jacket. "You are a good man, and I need all the help I can get."

"No, you don't. You just need time to think things over. Don't be too hard on yourself. Now, what have you decided to do about this woman?"

Madeline wished she could easily say that she was going to rescue Lee. Her head knew that was the right thing to do. But her ego didn't want to deal with Lee's undermining and snarky behavior. "I can't decide. I keep imagining her here, poisoning the atmosphere with her comments. I don't want that."

"I understand, but perhaps she will not want to stay. Perhaps you will be able to send her back to your old world."

"I should be so lucky." Madeline sighed, annoyed at herself. Lee still held some kind of power over her and that didn't feel right. "I think the only thing to do is go rescue her and figure it out later."

Jode nodded. "Have a tart, they're delicious." When she bit into her pastry, he added, "We can leave tomorrow."

Madeline swallowed her bite and chased it down with tea. No need to choke on the food, but she didn't want Jode coming on the journey. She didn't want him in danger, but more, she didn't want him to be near Lee. "I think it would be better if Blu and I with a small force go after Lee. I think it will likely be about magic, not force."

"You don't know that." Jode spoke quietly, but Madeline knew that meant he was not going to move easily off his position. "It would be folly to venture out with too small a force. In fact, it would be better if you stayed here and let me go find this woman. I can leave her elsewhere and you don't need to see her."

"No." Madeline was not prepared to risk Jode alone on a mission that was her responsibility. "You need to look after your home; people need you here."

Jode stood. "Madeline, before we were married, I was a knight in Arabela's service. My household did very well without me for years. I will not allow you to go alone."

"Allow me?" Madeline raised an eyebrow, but she tried not to react, knowing he didn't mean it.

"An unfortunate choice of words. I will not remain here while you go out to face the Choi."

She wished he would sit and start kissing her again, that way she could maybe flirt him into staying. "I don't want to argue. I know you can deal with any danger that comes up, but you can't deal with magic, and I'm not good enough to protect you and rescue Lee."

He took a lock of her hair and twisted it around his finger. "You do not need to protect me from magic, either. I promise not to be a distraction. And I assure you I will follow if you try to sneak out."

She reached out a hand and drew him closer. "Then I would rather you came with us. But do not invite half your guards. We need to move quickly and quietly."

. . .

MADELINE FOUND Blu sitting in the garden. A tree like an oak towered over him as he stared at the distance. Madeline had never traveled south. The mountains were the barrier between the lush lands where they lived, and the desert. She didn't know who lived there, perhaps she should investigate. While she waited for Blu to acknowledge her, she enjoyed the warmth seeping into her skin. When he turned to face her, she said, "It seems I have made a decision."

He smiled and patted her arm. "I see that. And by your unwilling tone, I assume you will be going to rescue this woman. In that case, I will join you on this journey. Something is calling me in that direction." Blu was looking tired. Whatever was calling him was weighing heavy on his mind.

"You knew what I would decide." Madeline sighed. "Why didn't you tell me what to do?"

Blu laughed. "You would have argued. I knew you would rescue the woman; you are a good person."

He gestured for her to look toward the mountains. "What do you feel when you look there?"

Madeline tried to throw her senses out to the range – nothing. "I don't feel anything. Should I be feeling something?"

Blu looked again to the horizon. "Do you see the clouds? They are unusual for this time of year." He shook his head, as if trying to dislodge something. "No, I was hoping you would feel some portent of the journey. It matters not. You may not have that type of power."

Madeline tried to ignore the feeling that she should have been able to sense something from the mountains. But worrying about what she did feel was taking up enough of her energy. "Will you be ready to leave tomorrow? Jode and I will plan the trip. We want to keep it small. To slip out before people know we are going."

"I do not need a lot of preparation. I travel with very little. I can be ready when you need me." Blu gestured toward the house.

"Let us go back to study your translation of the ancient text. If you have progressed enough, perhaps you can assist in reading this book that Arabela has in her library."

Madeline walked with Blu back to the house, sure that her ability to read an ancient language would not be any help in the task ahead of her.

8

*T*hat night when Madeline and Jode were alone in their room, she cast a privacy spell. She walked around the room with the ribbons building a layer of silence as she passed. None of their planning would be overheard, either physically or magically. When they were safely behind her wards, she could get Jode to agree to keep the rescue party down to four or five.

"You do not need to be so careful, Madeline," Jode said. "No one will listen in."

She laughed. "You really believe that? I would be surprised if no one tried. It's part of the normal way of things here. How do you think your servants know so much about what you need? It's not spying, it's efficiency."

"I had never thought about it, but it makes a lot of sense. Are you finished setting the spell?" He started unrolling a map. When Madeline joined him at the table, he showed her where they were on the map. "If we leave at night, we can be at Lady Arabela's within two days. From there we will need to travel over Ale's pass, unless we find the Choi before their homelands."

"How will we track them?" Madeline ran her finger along the

map from Arabela's to the other side of the mountains. It looked like several days as the crow flew, but she had no idea how much time it would take to cross the mountains. When Jode didn't answer, she looked up. He was staring at her, a dopey look on his face. "Oh, for crying out loud." She laughed.

"I will try to concentrate, but you make it difficult, my love." He pointed to a lake on the map. "Lee Marshall was found near here. This path leads to Ale's pass. We will start there."

"Should I look for some tracking spells before we leave for Arabela's? I can probably learn them before we get there." Madeline heard the doubt in her voice. Perhaps Blu was right when he said she undermined her progress.

"We should bring a tracker," Jode said. "We should bring three guards, a tracker and a cook."

"Jode, we can cook for ourselves. I don't want to bring anyone into this if they can't fight." She would figure out how to cook if necessary. "We need to keep this trip quiet and fast. I think a couple of guards are a good idea, but a cook is a luxury."

"A cook is important. We won't be able to fight if we are not properly fed."

Realizing she had two days to find a way to leave people behind at Arabela's, Madeline said, "Fine, I suppose that means we need a wagon for supplies." Madeline waited for Jode to come up with another plan. "And a wagon driver."

"Yes, and two people to help set up and take down the camp." Jode frowned and then gave a curt nod. "That will be enough."

So much for a small group, Madeline thought. "Can eleven people travel fast and quietly enough to get to the Choi before they know we are coming?"

"Perhaps you should look up some spells to conceal us." He started to roll up the map. "Who is the eleventh?"

"Blu." Madeline's skin flushed and she recognized the warning of her magic. "Or maybe not."

Jode slid the map into his pack. He nodded toward hers which was waiting to be filled. "You fill your pack. I'll go and prepare the rest to leave tomorrow under cover of darkness."

9

---

*T*hey had slipped out of the grounds singly to avoid notice in the very early hours of the morning.

Madeline rode alongside the wagon. Barsh the eldman drove the wagon, and Blu sat beside him looking around. She turned to look back at the house; most of the windows were dark. Their plan had worked so far. The cool of the forest was just as peaceful as she wanted. The tang of pine in the air, the shade and the clop of the horses' hooves washed her tension away.

"Should I start practicing to conceal us?" she asked Blu.

He chuckled. "Perhaps it would be better to wait until we are out of sight. Should your spell fail and set off fireworks, we are too close to avoid notice."

"If you want me to be more confident in my magic, perhaps you should display more confidence." She smiled to soften the words, knowing Blu was teasing.

"If you need others to make you confident, then you will always remain uncertain. I know you are capable, but I see the results." He shifted in the seat as the wagon rolled over a pothole.

"I can't argue with results." Madeline reminded herself to listen to the compliment, too. "I will try harder to believe."

"Good, but it would be better if you didn't simply try. If you believed, then there is no trying."

Madeline laughed and suppressed the urge to call him Yoda. She had learned the futility of trying to explain pop references to people here.

The wagon contained the supplies, Mirial the cook, camp tenders Tom and Wint, and Keegan who was their tracker; they all slept in the wagon bed.

Two of the guards, Ridern and Axel were holding the rear and the other, Satra, rode with Jode at the head of the small party. Madeline excused herself and spurred her horse to join her husband.

They rode for a half hour and Madeline relaxed her worry that they had been seen leaving. Despite the nap she had taken yesterday, her body wanted to be asleep and she fought to keep awake and alert. Clenching her jaw to hold in a yawn, she started to listen to the conversation. Jode and Satra were talking about vegetable gardens, which didn't exactly spark her interest. She was searching her brain for a better topic when Jode pulled up his horse and Madeline's stepped quickly to avoid bumping.

She leaned out to see around her husband and saw Simon on his own horse facing her in the middle of the path. "What are you doing here?"

Simon patted his horse and said, "I figured you would need my help when you found Lee."

"I don't need your help. Go back to the house." Madeline thought for a second. "How did you know where we were?"

Simon turned his horse to face in the same direction as the rest of the party. Looking over his shoulder, he said, "You do need me. I hate to think how you'll react when you get her in your hands. She's not likely to be grateful."

"It's going to be dangerous. I want you to be at home so you can take care of things." Madeline realized the party was moving forward again. Was she the only one who thought Simon should go home? "Jode, we planned this with a small group."

"I know, but Madeline, my love, Simon is now here. You have until we leave Arabela's to convince him to stay behind. We need to keep moving forward."

As she started to argue, Madeline realized Jode was right. She would find a way to make Simon go home in the next few days. "So, how did you know we were leaving, Simon?"

"I overheard Jode talking to Mirial about preparing to cook for the journey. So, I left last night because I didn't want to miss you."

Madeline saw Jode flick a glance at Simon and then shrug. She'd figure out what that meant later. Now it was time to think about how she might get Lee away from the Choi. Not that she knew anything about the Choi, but she knew what she was able to do with magic, so maybe –

"Shit, what are you doing here?" Simon's words were accompanied by a second halt.

Madeline had slipped behind Jode and the guard. So, she had to push her horse through the gap between them to see what was going on. The back of an open wagon blocked the road. Facing the party were Gren, Urr and Zora. Two more goblin faces popped up from the driver's bench, Buck, and his wife, Dass waved and smiled.

"We don't want to stop learning the opera," Zora said. "It's good and you need to finish writing it."

"Yeah, man," Gren added. "And we need to get a road trip going anyway. So, here we are."

Simon rode forward and started whispering to Urr.

Madeline looked at Jode who was trying unsuccessfully to stifle a laugh. "I guess we can leave them at Arabela's too," she said.

Simon rode back and the wagon started forward. "I'm sorry,"

he said. "They saw me packing and heard the rumors about Lee, and put two and two together."

Madeline looked around. "Not a problem. I guess six more for a few days won't make a difference, and we can get more supplies from Arabela." She turned back to Simon, "You didn't tell anyone else? They didn't tell anyone else?"

"I didn't. I'm sure they didn't." Simon looked at the wagon again. Gren waved back at him. "I'm pretty sure they didn't."

Madeline shook her head and guided her horse to the side to wait for the other wagon to catch up. Maybe Blu could cover their tracks just in case someone else was following. When his wagon caught up to her, she saw he was in deep meditation – or sleep.

They would just have to make the best of it.

10

A half an hour later, the group was moving slowly, but making progress and Madeline was looking forward to a visit with Arabela. It had been a few months since she'd held Tadric. Seeing him in the scrying glass wasn't the same.

She hadn't been much of a baby person before, but the subject kept popping into her mind at the oddest moments. She slipped a glance at Jode. He would probably want a child, someone to take over the running of the estate, probably a boy. The image of two children tearing through the great hall, red hair – they would likely have red hair – streaming behind them.

Oh. She wondered if it was wishful thinking or premonition. Maybe she would think about it when this adventure was over.

Her musing was broken by the rhythm of hoof beats approaching from behind, someone in a hurry. Turning her horse to see what was coming, Madeline hoped to see a messenger, nothing to do with them, but knew it was not likely. A flash of green skirt confirmed her expectations; Callisra was riding to catch up. Madeline felt a sense of relief, there was no one else left to jump on the bandwagon. "Let her through," Madeline called.

When Callisra came to a stop, Madeline saw her horse packed with two bulging saddlebags.

"How did you find out?" Madeline gave up the idea of sending Callisra back. She just hoped she was right about this being the end of the additions to the party.

Callisra blushed. "Madeline, I'm so sorry. I heard you speaking in your room. I wasn't eavesdropping, I promise. But when I walked past, your voice was so clear."

"You weren't supposed to be able to hear anything," Madeline said, and then turned to see Simon smirk. "Oh, so you didn't overhear Jode."

He shook his head. "Sorry, your voice carried down the hall, like it was projected or something."

"Damn," Madeline said. "I practiced that spell over and over. Okay so you plan on coming, why?"

"I feel compelled to help you, and I have training as a healer." Callisra looked at Simon while she spoke. "I think you will need my services before this adventure is done."

Simon nudged his horse closer. "You should go back. This journey is no place for a secretary."

Madeline looked away so he couldn't see her smile. She thought he was smarter than that.

Callisra urged her horse toward Simon's. "I have camped out for weeks with my father's men as they hunted. I have sewn wounds shut that looked fatal and healed the patient with my own hands. I chose to become Lady Madeline's secretary so that I could sleep with a roof over my head more often than stars. I am not a mere secretary."

Simon turned his horse around and called over his shoulder. "It's still dangerous. This isn't a hunt."

Callisra sighed and turned back to Madeline. "Lady Madeline, do you have an objection to me joining your company?"

Madeline shook her head. "For the time being, no."

Simon glared at her and snapped, "It is not a picnic. I thought you wanted just a small group."

"I did, but then you joined us." Madeline smiled at his discomfiture. "Callisra, you can put your belongings in the supply wagon when we stop."

"Thank you." Callisra guided her horse parallel with Madeline's.

Simon moved closer to the musicians. "I think it's a bad idea," he muttered just loud enough for them to hear.

"I do not care what you think," Callisra said.

Madeline glanced at Callisra and saw disappointment on her face. *If I leave them at Arabela's they just might realize what's going on. And in the meantime, it will be amusing to watch the courtship.*

"Another ten silvers on my bet," Zora's voice rose above the creaks and clops of the party getting underway.

11

*W*hen they stopped for the night, Simon looked across the camp where Callisra was rolling out her bedding. The woman was determined; he had to give her that. She was gentle on the eyes, too. "Stop it," he muttered.

"Stop what?" Gren asked.

Simon turned to his bass player. "I was talking to myself. Sorry, just ignore me."

Gren laughed. "If you keep doing that, Callisra won't be wanting you at all."

"What makes you think she wants me?" Simon shuffled through the notes on the opera he's been writing. "I don't see her pursuing me."

Urr chuckled. "You must be losing your sight as well as your mind. Do you think she's here for anything else?"

Simon looked up at the two goblins. "You think she came here for me? She says she feels a compulsion."

"Ah, Simon, a compulsion for what?" Gren reached for the notes. "Are all men in your world so stupid about women?"

Simon looked over at Callisra again. Now she was walking towards them. "I have to admit, we kind of took pride in it." He thrust the notes into Gren's hands. "Will you give us some privacy?"

Gren chuckled and said, "As much as is possible in the camp, but maybe not enough to let Zora win the pool." He walked away flipping through the pages. Urr grinned, and then followed him.

Simon watched Callisra approach. As she passed people, they greeted her and offered a comment or two that Simon couldn't hear. She didn't stop long with anyone, but kept moving toward him. He tried to think of what to say, but his mind was blank.

"Simon, I was hoping to hear some music. Is everyone retiring early?" Her voice raised a pressure in his chest.

He coughed, to chase away the feelings she spurred. "No, we've just been going through some composition ideas." *Smooth, music geek.*

"Oh. Well perhaps later, or tomorrow." She turned to leave.

"Wait." Simon reached for her arm. He heard a chuckle coming from the other side of the wagon, so much for privacy. "I wanted to talk to you... to say that you should probably stay at Arabela's when we get there. I think this journey might be too dangerous."

She continued to smile, but Simon noticed her eyes narrowed. Even he knew that meant dangerous ground. "Too dangerous for me, and yet not too dangerous for you."

"I didn't mean that." Simon tried to dig himself out of the hole. "I meant if you don't need to be with us, you should probably stay where it's safe."

"When I said I was compelled to come, I meant it." She stepped closer and Simon's heart started to race. "It is clear to me I have a reason to be on this quest. What reason do you have?"

Simon swallowed. This was exactly what he had hoped to avoid. Why couldn't the damn woman just stay at home where it was safe? "I have reason, but I... I think you came so that you would be near me."

She burst into laughter. Simon was relieved at the drop in the tension, but not happy to have amused her with his statement.

Callisra got control of herself and moved away. "You are a very attractive man, Simon, but I did not join this adventure to be with you."

"Well, that's good. Someone did suggest it and I wanted to make sure." He looked around to see if anyone was going to come to his rescue.

She smiled, but it didn't reach her eyes. "Who mentioned it?"

Oh, man, I really need to learn to keep my mouth shut. "It doesn't matter because you have a reason to be here, right?"

"I suppose," she said. Simon watched thoughts flash across her face. A small frown replaced the smile for a second, and then she sighed. "Perhaps under other circumstances we could discuss this more, but I will try to restrain myself." She walked back to her bedroll.

Simon watched the way her hips swayed. Despite her assurances, he knew that walk was designed to get his attention. If she wasn't here just to follow him, she wasn't here just for the quest either.

I'm in big trouble.

12

*S*kye sat in her tent playing with the children who had come with their families on this journey. So few offspring; too many years of too few births. The Choi did not usually travel with their young. This was an exception, but one she considered repeating. In the future, it would be a joy to have these children come. This time, the entire tribe traveled together out of necessity. At the end of the ceremony, every Choi would be anointed. If they succeeded, there would be hundreds of children next year. If not, it didn't matter if the children traveled or not, they would be finished as a people.

The woman, Lee, was proving to be more burden than expected. She found ways to delay their journey at every opportunity. They were now a day behind where Skye expected. No matter, they would still arrive at the temple in plenty of time. Perhaps, they should simply bind the woman and carry her like baggage. But no; it was not worth the risk that she would be too badly injured.

Skye looked up and saw Ophian slip through the opening and said, "Go, children, find your parents." She waited until the tent emptied before smiling and beckoning him to sit beside her.

Ophian sat across from her instead. "It is not safe; there are too many people who might look in." He smiled at her before shaking his head. "It is too soon to declare our love."

"You worry too much about me." She reached to take his hand, but kept her eyes on the tent flap. "But yes, we need to be careful. I do not wish to jeopardize your promotion within the tribe. And, when this sacrifice is done, you will be a suitable lover in the eyes of the Choi. I wish that we could be that today, my love, but you know that the tribe would not allow an apprentice be with the Greatmother."

Ophian sighed, and then glanced at the door flap before pulling a scroll from his pocket. "I have written the ceremony on this. You should study it to be sure I have made no errors. I need to be the power conduit for the sacrifice, and as you point out, I am merely your apprentice."

"Yes, I know this, my love." Skye took the scroll from him. "After all, I was the one who discovered the variant to the ceremony."

"I am sorry to suggest you didn't know that." Ophian looked down at his hands. "I am just very worried. This is important to me." He paused. "And to our people, that was selfish of me."

Skye reached out and caressed his cheek. "I am not angry. Do not worry. This woman will be a powerful sacrifice. She brought power with her through the passage from her world, and she holds that power because she is alien to this world. Sacrificing her will feed our people and they will thrive again, perhaps enough to support more than this one tribe."

He patted her hand. "It will be glorious for you to be the one to save the Choi."

"The tribe will see you as the savior, Ophian. They *must* see you as the savior." She wondered at his hesitation. His confidence was what originally attracted her attention, and her heart.

Ophian looked at her, his eyes hooded. "Yes, they must. When that happens, we can be together."

Sounds penetrated the cloth of the tent. Ophian stood and moved to the doorway before anyone saw him sitting within intimate proximity to Skye.

How kind he can be, how protective of my reputation. The bell at the door jingled. "Come," she called.

One of her advisers stepped inside the tent. "Greatmother, the prisoner has injured a guard."

This woman was proving to be as much trouble as value. It was good that the sacrifice was only a few days away. "How? She is tied up like a bird for the oven. How did she damage a guard?"

Ophian slipped out while the adviser bowed his head. "She rolled herself in front of the tent entrance and he tripped over her when delivering her food."

"Fool. How badly is he injured?"

"A broken arm, Greatmother."

"Send him to me and I will heal him. In the meantime, make sure the woman is secured to something that will stop her from destroying the tribe one broken bone at a time."

"Yes, Greatmother." The adviser bowed low and then left the tent.

When she was alone again, Skye unrolled the scroll and started to read what Ophian had copied. It was perfect, but she would ask him to memorize it. Perhaps they would need private time to ensure he was word perfect.

LEE WOKE up and darkness enveloped her. Relief rushed through her veins. It had all been a dream. Then, the smells registered horses, and musty fabric, and something sickly. With the realization that she hadn't been dreaming came pain, in her arms and legs, where bruises ached, and in her wrists where she was tied by rough ropes.

She was in a tent and this was not the first time she had woken up. She was tied to a barrel, her arms stretched behind her. Lee pushed her back against the barrel and tried to use the leverage to stand. But she couldn't manage more than a deep crouch. The bonds were tight, and it felt as though she was pulling her joints apart. Then her thighs began to burn with the pressure.

"Take a breath," she muttered to herself. "You have been kidnapped. Don't worry about what you remember, there's no way giant anorexic pink people took you. It must be something to do with a case."

She slid back into a sitting position to save her muscles and ease the burn. "Someone will come and find you. People don't just disappear these days." She stopped talking as the memory of Madeline Higginbottom surfaced. *That's exactly what happened to her and to her assistant.*

"No, she just left. No one cared that she was gone anyway. They will care about me." She wasn't convinced of that but didn't pursue the thought.

She ran through a mental inventory of the clients she was handling. None of them were criminal cases. None seemed important enough to warrant kidnapping her. She was winning every case except the Marson one, and Mr. Marson might be creepy, but he wasn't this kind of creepy.

Her thoughts were shattered by a harsh shouting outside the tent. Maybe the rescue was about to happen. Lee tossed her head to get her hair out of her eyes. The darkness had lifted while she struggled and she could see more of her surroundings. She stared at the tent flap determined to catch the first sight of her rescuer.

A slice of sun made her squeeze her eyes shut as the tent flap opened. The shouting had stopped. If this was the rescue, it was a silent one.

"You are awake." It was the tall pink woman. So, that hadn't been a dream either.

"What do you want with me?" She pulled at the bonds and winced as the ropes pinched her already painful wrists. Realizing she sounded weak, Lee decided to try to get a little control. "You never did tell me your name."

"All in good time." The woman strode over to Lee and tested the bonds. "Good, nothing life-threatening."

"I would argue that," Lee said. "It feels like you've been beating me for hours."

The woman drew back. "I do not beat guests. And you are my guest."

Lee pulled at her bonds again. "If this is how you treat guests, I hate to see how you treat prisoners. I think a guest would know the name of her host."

She reached out and drew a finger down Lee's cheek. "You have spirit. That will be very useful when the time comes. I am Skye Greatmother of the Choi."

Lee shook off Skye's finger. "What the hell are the Choi?"

"They are my people. It is not important that you know anything else."

Lee let that go. "When what time comes?"

Skye started toward the tent flap, chuckling.

"Don't you walk out on me. The time comes for what?" Lee bit off the next words, afraid they would release sobs if she gave voice to them. *The woman couldn't have been serious before. A sacrifice? What the hell was this place.*

She heard a deep laugh as Skye stepped out of the tent. The flap dropped into place and the tent became dark again.

13

The night had passed uneventfully and no other stragglers joined them. As they set out for the last leg of the trip to Arabela's, Madeline drew up alongside the wagon where Blu sat enjoying the sun.

"We will be at Arabela's soon," she said. "I think we need to talk about how we go forward from there. It would be helpful to try to make a plan."

"It is not always possible to rely on a plan, Madeline. You worry too much about what might happen, and not enough about what is happening. It causes you to question too much." Blu kept his eyes on the road ahead. The only sign that he was distracted was a furrow in his brow.

"Yes, as always." Madeline reminded herself to be confident. "But I want to be prepared for what will happen. We have a saying; a good plan today is better than a perfect plan tomorrow."

Blu turned to her. "This is true. I believe we may have to gather some information before you have to fight. But what would you do if the Choi appeared here, now?"

My worst freaking nightmare. She considered. What did she have in her arsenal right now? "I would have to fight them with a sword, or something. I don't know enough magic to try fighting with it." She paused. "Or perhaps I should try a healing spell on them since all my spells so far have backfired."

Blu snorted. "It is good that you have humor. Do you know any healing spells?"

"No, nor do I know any fighting spells." She felt for her short sword. It was still at hand. "I also don't know enough about their magic to counter it."

"You must first master the small spells of everyday life, before you can try stronger spells. We cannot have people dying by accident." Blu pulled his robes closer.

"I'll pick up some throwing knives when we stop at Arabela's. At least I can arm myself. Do the Choi have spells that can stop knives?"

"What I know so far is that they do not have spells they can cast quickly enough to stop a blade. In this book of Lady Arabela's we may find differently." He turned his gaze back to the road.

Madeline glanced ahead, but nothing was there. "What's worrying you?"

Blu pointed ahead. "I do not know what, but something is wrong ahead." He sighed. "I have caught your disease of worrying about the future. Let us talk about blood magic to distract ourselves."

Madeline tried to cast her senses to the road ahead, closing out the jingles of harness, creaks of the wagons, and quiet conversation. She listened for the sounds of forest creatures disturbed by their passing. She pictured Arabela's home in the sunshine. The vision dimmed and heat rushed through her body. Blu was right, there was trouble ahead.

"Madeline," Blu's voice snapped her back to the present.

"Sorry, I was..."

"I know what you were doing. Did you have any success?"

"Not much more than you did. There is trouble, but not until we reach Arabela's at least." She sat higher in her saddle and called a guard to her, telling him to pass the information to Jode. "At least he will be alert. Now I am taking your advice and not worrying. Tell me about blood magic."

"Yes, learning always distracts you." Blu settled back against the wagon seat. "You know there are different types of magic."

Madeline nodded; this was old information. "Yes. Not everyone can channel the magic, but each species does it differently; Humans, from within their own spirit, Scree with chalk and dance, the Fay can see and hear at distances, the Mariai through visions..."

Blu smiled at her recitation. "Yes, there are many paths to the power. The Choi do not possess any magic of themselves. They steal the power of others by taking blood. They have learned to channel this magic."

Madeline thought through how that could be turned to her advantage. "Do they need to get fresh blood? Could speed be on our side?"

"No. But not all Choi are allowed to use magic. I forgot that, interesting." Blu went silent.

Madeline waited for what seemed like ten minutes, she was used to him delving into his memories. Just as she was about to ask, Blu returned to the present. "Only the ruling class of Choi is allowed to carry the vials of blood. It is true that the power fades over time, but they keep refreshing it from captives they take. It may be that you will be freeing more than your friend Lee Marshall."

"She's not my friend," Madeline said. "How will I know who has magic and who doesn't?"

Blu shook his head. "That I do not know. It may be that the information we seek will be in the book. Also, we can hope to find the reason they would bring someone from your world."

Madeline was fascinated by this idea of multiple worlds. "Are there other worlds? Could there be people moving between worlds all the time?" She thought of the Bermuda Triangle, and alien abductions. It would certainly explain a lot.

"We believe there are many worlds. Yours comes very close to ours – it seems more often than we thought possible. We have not found others, yet. I believe it is only a matter of time and need."

Madeline sighed. "I suppose it always is. When you brought me here you really needed me and we didn't have a lot of time."

"Perhaps we will find the same urgency for the Choi." Blu seemed to mull this over. "Yes, perhaps."

Madeline thought through her options, her skills with the throwing knives had improved over the year; she was fairly handy with the sword. Maybe – no, she *would* learn some spells she could use. Then what? "Blu, when this is done, when we have freed Lee. Can you send her back? To her world?"

"If this is what she wants, yes. But, Madeline, if she does not want to go, I cannot force her."

I might be able to. "We'll cross that bridge when we come to it. Look, the forest is thinning. We'll be sipping wine in Arabela's home within an hour." *And maybe while we're there, I'll actually get a plan in place.*

14

*M*adeline, Arabela, and Blu sat in the library late that evening. The travelers had arrived at Arabela's home in time for lunch, but the day had been filled with settling in. Now, supper eaten and the tapestries closed over the windows, they studied the book.

The sound of soft music floated up the stairs. Simon and Jode had remained in the great hall with their feet up in front of the fire talking about music, hunting, and other pastimes. Madeline had instructed Jode to tell Simon about the comforts of being married.

Callisra had retired early, claiming a need to restore her energy in case someone needed healing. Madeline was sure that she was exhausted from bickering with Simon all day on the trail. Someone needed to get those two kissing before they killed each other trying to avoid the attraction they felt.

Madeline's mind returned to the book. It had been much easier to translate than she expected. Perhaps the practice had been worth the effort. The information was unexpected, but complete; the Choi were in danger of extinction. They needed a powerful sacrifice to survive.

"Sobering information." Arabela tapped the book. "I'm not sure this problem can be solved easily."

Madeline didn't see a problem all. "I don't know what you mean? If we rescue Lee and any other captives, the problem is solved, and more permanently than we thought. It says without Lee to sacrifice; the remaining Choi will fade and there will be no more within a generation."

"Yes." Blu sat back in his chair, arms folded. "This means you must find a way to save your friend and the Choi."

"She's not my friend." Madeline was getting really tired of saying that. "Why would we want to save the Choi? They take people's blood for crying out loud. That's evil."

Arabela sighed. "Madeline, there is no evil, the Choi are what they are. This world works on balances. I am beginning to suspect your old world did not. If the Choi are no more, then another race will wither. You must save them. But that doesn't mean you have to help them thrive. A single tribe of Choi is plenty."

"I think that may not be the case," Blu said. "To be safe, to honor the balance of peoples, you may have to help the Choi conduct the sacrifice successfully."

Madeline had known it wouldn't be simple. Any time Lee Marshall got involved, things got more complicated. "Is there something they will trade for? Some promise, some – I don't know, something." Madeline was much happier with the idea of negotiating the release, but she needed a bargaining chip. "I like the idea of not killing someone to free Lee. I'm not sure she's worth it."

"I trust that judgment to you," Blu said. "It is true some people are only worth so much to the world as individuals. The Choi only wish power. We will need to give them a supply of power."

Didn't it always come down to power in one way or another? "And it will need to be blood, right? They have no other way of accessing magic."

Blu nodded. "Yes, it will have to be blood. And powerful blood, remember they need a lot of power this time to survive."

Arabela picked up the sheaf of paper that held their translations from the book. "Why would this Lee have enough power? Was she powerful in your world?"

Madeline tried to remember if Lee had seemed talented at anything that would hint at magical power. "In my old world, she was very good at undermining people." She sighed. "But no, I don't know that she had any special magic or talent. But then neither did I before I crossed."

"It is possible that the crossing opens channels we do not understand." Blu stood and pulled down another book. "Let me study this some more. It is possible that simply passing from one world to another awakens power. Your power is strong Madeline it is surprising to me that it did not manifest in some way before you came. Perhaps this Lee Marshall is also powerful but does not know."

The door opened and a servant stepped into the room, her eyes wide. "Lady Arabela, I am sorry to interrupt, but you are needed in the nursery."

"Is it feeding time already?" Arabela stood.

"No, please hurry, something is wrong."

Madeline sent the servant to bring Callisra before running after Arabela. As they entered the nursery, she could hear a thin wail. The room, usually cheery and bright, was darkened and it was hot from the fire which had been built so high it was roaring. Madeline had to hold herself back from throwing open the windows to get some air in. She had come to learn that things didn't work the same here. Fresh air was as likely to be fatal as healthy.

The nanny was wiping Tadric's forehead with a damp cloth. She looked up as they entered, relief flooding her face. "It happened so quickly," she said, standing aside for Arabela. "He was as chipper and chatty as ever when I put him down for his nap. Then suddenly he started making that noise."

Blu approached the cot and placed his hand on Tadric's cheek. "Has he been ill recently?"

"No," Arabela said. "He has not had any of the usual fevers or colds." She wiped her eyes. "Please, help him. He is all I have."

Madeline put her arms around Arabela. If she had to choose between rescuing Lee and helping Arabela, there was no real choice. "Let Blu and Callisra see what is going on. Don't upset yourself."

"I can help him sleep," Blu said. "Perhaps that will be enough to let him recover. I will wait for Miss Tallhouse to see to him first. She may need him to be conscious to assess his illness. It is not in my skill to identify the cause."

"It does help if he is awake, thank you," Callisra said, sliding in beside Blu. She placed a small canvas bag on the floor before removing the covers around Tadric.

"No, Miss." The nanny stepped forward. "He cries more if he's not swaddled."

"I will be quick, but I must examine him." She passed a blanket to the woman. "Keep this by the fire. We can wrap him in warm blankets when I'm done."

Madeline guided Arabela to a group of small chairs. They sat, able to watch, but out of the way.

"Is she a good healer?" Arabela whispered. "Will she help him?"

I only found out she was a healer today. "Yes, she's wonderful."

They watched as Callisra peeled back the layers of clothing. Tadric's skin was pale and Madeline could see a smattering of red patches. She hoped it was just a rash, and he would be fine as soon as some ointment soothed his skin. Arabela tensed and Madeline held her hand.

Callisra placed her hands on Tadric's head and stomach. She closed her eyes and Madeline recognized the stillness of someone drawing on magic. As she slipped into the trance, her face took on the patches of red. Madeline looked again at the child and saw the red fading.

Madeline had seen healers work with injuries and the sight of wounds start to close under their hands had amazed her. Now, watching her secretary draw illness into herself, she felt awe. The redness faded from Callisra and she smiled.

A sigh escaped Arabela as she started to relax. Madeline remembered how strong Arabela was when they went to fight the Scree. Having a child changed more than just your figure apparently.

Callisra let the nanny wrap Tadric and came to join the two women. "He is well now, but there is something I can't quite put my finger on, something magical. Blu may be able to work it out."

Arabela stood. "You will be exhausted. Hanna, bring some food for Callisra." She went to stand beside Blu, who was laying ribbons across the crib.

"You are wasted helping me organize the household," Madeline said to Callisra. "Why on earth did you stop healing people?"

Callisra looked away. For a moment, Madeline didn't think she would reply. "You are right. When I make someone well, it is wonderful. But one man I couldn't help. He died." She firmed her lips. "To be a healer you must believe you will be able to help. When that man died, I stopped believing."

"If that's true, why did you come on this rescue mission? Why did you come to heal Tadric?" Madeline didn't want to ask about the man who died, but she did need to know what to expect.

"I couldn't say no. He's just a baby." Callisra shook her head. "I will always come when I'm needed. But I cannot make my living at healing. And why am I here on this journey? Well there are two reasons. First, I am compelled to come. When I think of staying behind, I fall ill. It has the feeling of prophecy."

"Callisra, come here, please." Blu's voice interrupted.

They both moved toward the cradle. "Tell me what you experienced as you healed the child."

Callisra told Blu the same thing she had told Madeline. "I have never felt anything like it."

"No, you would not have, I think." Blu drew them away from the child. "Someone is sending this sickness."

Arabela jerked at the words. "How is someone doing that? Poison?"

Blu shook his head. "Magic."

"How is magic coming through the wards?" Arabela's voice shook. "I thought we were protected."

Tadric started crying and Arabela spun to look at him.

"He is fine. Your voices are upsetting him." The nanny shooed them toward the door. "Go and solve this problem elsewhere and let the child sleep."

Arabela rushed to the cradle and touched her child's head. A smile crossed her lips and she bent to kiss him. "Sleep, sweetheart." She returned to the rest of the adults. "Come, we need to talk outside."

15

*A*s they stepped into the hall, the servant Hanna, returned with a tray of food. Madeline took it and led them back to the study, settling Callisra on a chair. Pouring glasses of wine, Madeline wondered if she should call for Jode and Simon. It seemed the adventure was getting more complex.

Arabela took a long sip of her wine, a little color returning to her cheeks. "Now, how is magic getting into my home?"

"It may be that someone inside your home is responsible," Blu said. "Or it may be that someone has found a way to breach the protections. Although I have checked, and they seem intact."

"Can you reinforce the wards while we are here?" Callisra asked after swallowing a bite of bread with cheese. Madeline noticed the redness had faded completely and wondered where a healer put the sickness when they were done; another thing to learn when she had time.

Blu nodded. "But before I do that, I need to know what is happening. The strongest wards will not stop the problem if it is someone inside. And I suspect this attack is coming from someone inside the household. I am sorry to say, Arabela, it may be someone you trust."

Madeline felt things slipping out of control. "Is there a way to find out what exactly is going on? Do we have to interrogate everyone in the household?"

Blu answered, "No not everyone, but we must take care. We will surely expose our investigation to the person responsible if we charge around asking too many questions. We may lose our chance to capture them. It is better that we take our time and find out not only who, but why."

Arabela ended her silence by slamming her hand on the table. "I will kill whoever is harming my child. Just find them. I don't care why they are doing this."

Blu nodded. "I understand, Lady Arabela. But why is likely more important than who, I think."

Madeline sipped her wine. "I'll talk to Jode. He can go ahead with the guards and rescue Lee. The rest of us will stay here and help."

A moan escaped Callisra's throat. Madeline turned to look and saw the woman bent over grabbing her stomach. "What is wrong? More magic?"

Callisra shook her head and moaned again before struggling to speak, "No, this is what happens when I think of not joining you on this journey. This is what I meant when I said I was compelled."

"Then maybe you should go with Jode." Madeline started to make the compromise in her head. Another healer may be nearby.

Blu held his hand up. "No, you must all continue. The sacrifice must take place at the turn of this season and there is no time to waste. If you are to rescue Lee Marshall, you must continue. I will stay here and maintain the protections until you return."

Madeline started to feel as sick as Callisra. Without Blu, how would she be able to defeat the Choi? "I–"

"Madeline, you can take my scrolls and study them on the way," he assured her. "I will stay and keep the wards strengthened daily and observe the inhabitants of this household. Now that we know it is magic, I can work with a local healer to ease anything that might happen to the child. Or anyone else."

Madeline looked at Arabela. She seemed calmer and confident now that Blu had made his offer. "Are you sure, Arabela? Will you feel safe?"

"Yes, Blu will take care of us. You must go and save your friend," Arabela said.

"She's not my friend," Madeline said. "But I think you are right. If Callisra still feels this compulsion, it is important to continue. We'll be as fast as possible, I promise. When we get back, we will fix this problem."

---

16

*T*he next morning everyone except Blu slipped out of Arabela's gates. Madeline had made no effort to convince Simon or his musicians to stay.

"We should be at the point where Lee Marshall was found soon," Jode said. "We should stop then to eat."

Madeline looked up from the papers she was reviewing. She was riding the wagon this morning taking time to organize her thoughts and notes about the spells Blu had given her. "What clues do you think we might find? I might have a spell to follow the trail of someone by their clothing."

"I do not know." Jode was not usually that abrupt.

Madeline glanced up at him again. "Is there a problem?"

He shook his head, and then looked at her. His expression lifted from a serious frown to a sunny smile. "No, I am worrying about nothing, I think. I am used to being the one to protect Arabela. I must simply trust that Blu will resolve this problem, at least until we return. I shall focus on our journey."

Madeline had hated leaving Arabela, who she loved like a sister, to rescue Lee, who she hated. But it had not occurred to

her that Blu would not be up to the job. "Do children here have...
difficulty getting through the first few years?"

"No," Jode said. "A few babies do die. It is usually by accident,
not from sickness. It would be dangerous for Arabela's people if
Tadric were to die."

Madeline was amazed at how plainly Jode spoke of babies
dying. She had expected him to be delicate around the subject. "It
would be devastating for Arabela. But why dangerous for her
people?"

"They need a leader from Alric's line to keep the continuity. If
his line dies out, Arabela will be only one of the contestants for
control. It may be why the child is being attacked. Or it could be
anything. With the Choi bringing sacrifices from other worlds,
who knows what other beings are doing?"

Madeline put aside the papers. "Who will inherit your lands if
we do not have a child?"

He looked at her and raised an eyebrow. "I have cousins. But
there is plenty of time for us to have a child. There is plenty of
time to practice as well."

She flushed and looked around. No one was in earshot. Or
they were pretending they weren't at least. "We need to talk
about that. I don't have many years left to have a child."

"We can worry about it when we are done here." Jode nodded
to the papers. "Perhaps you should return to your study. If you
are to learn these spells without Blu, it is important that you
focus."

"Did Blu tell you to say that once in a while?" Madeline
laughed and picked the stack up again. "I guess I'll leave the
tracking to Keegan. That's why he's here after all."

They rode in silence until they came to a clearing. In the center
was evidence of a large fire. It was circled with brown blotches.
Madeline assumed they were evidence of the blood used in the spell.
Across from the entrance, the small shrubs that covered the ground

between the larger trees were trampled and broken. Urr's friend, a quiet human man named Rolf stepped from a copse of trees, joining Madeline and Jode as the rest of the party dismounted around them.

Rolf pointed to the clearing. "I was stalking some game when there was a lot of noise coming through the forest. The Choi came through there." He nodded toward a path. "I got curious. Never seen Choi before, just knew about them from stories. So, I hid over there, behind the oak. They set up the fire and suddenly this woman fell through the bushes. See where they are smashed. The Choi leader dragged her into the circle right away. Then the fire was in my way, so I don't know what they did. Then they left. I found that bracelet then went back to camp where I found Urr. He ran to you and I came back to watch in case something else happened. Nothing did."

Simon walked up, Callisra just behind him. "So, what's the next step?"

Keegan was walking around the circle of blood. He bent low and stared off in the distance, through the trees and toward the mountains.

Madeline watched him, wondering the same thing. From this point forward, Keegan would be leading them. "I think we need to wait until, he does his thing. But I do know I don't want to eat here. I'll go hungry until we can move off."

Simon took a sheaf of paper from his jacket. "I'm going to do some sketches. This will make a great setting for the opera."

17

*M*adeline and Callisra waited on the wagon seat for Keegan to decipher what clues there might be in the clearing.

"Callisra," Madeline said. "You said there were two reasons you came on this journey. What was the other reason?"

"I thought you knew." Callisra shifted in her seat.

"I have my suspicions."

Flicking her eyes to the pile of ashes in the clearing, Callisra sighed. "I do not wish to be apart from Simon. I think he is getting close to realizing we are made for each other."

Madeline laughed. "I hope you are right, but don't be surprised if he resists." Madeline looked toward the center of the clearing and saw Jode talking to the others. "Callisra, is there any limit to your healing?"

"It drains my energy, but as long as I am able to keep myself rested and well, I can heal for hours. It is as if the illness or injury flows through me to somewhere. If I do work myself too hard, I will need a lot of sleep and food. Do not worry, if we can find some honey, I will be able to live on that for some time. I just might sleep for the whole journey home."

Madeline felt some of the tension leave her muscles with that. Having a healer who could take on whatever burden the fight would present was a bonus. What nagged at her mind was the discussion about babies. Jode had just brushed off the idea she was too old to have children. "Can you tell if someone is healthy?"

"How do you mean?" Callisra reached out to touch Madeline's hand. "Are you feeling unwell?"

How to broach this without making it seem like a big deal, oh well, just plow in no one else seems to be embarrassed to talk about having babies. "I was wondering if you can tell whether I can have children or not. When I saw Tadric, I started to feel broody."

"Oh, yes. I should be able to tell you this. But why are you worried? You are both healthy."

Madeline looked to make sure no one was listening. "Well, I kind of wonder why I haven't caught yet. I mean it's been almost a year."

"I can check tonight. It is not something you want to do in this clearing, with the Choi magic lingering." Callisra pointed. "Look, Simon and the others are coming back. There must be some news."

Madeline closed her eyes and wished for good news. She figured wishing might work in this magical land.

Jode arrived first. "We have some information. Keegan found this." He held up a red Hermes scarf, Lee's trademark. If the anchor charm wasn't proof enough, the addition of the scarf confirmed that Lee was in Cartref.

"Will it help find her?" Madeline ached to get the rescue over. "Can Keegan use it to determine where they are?"

"No, Lady Madeline, I have no magic. I track by the sign of broken branch and bent grass."

She sighed. "I guess we can give it back when we rescue her." She took the scarf and tucked it into a space between the sacks of food in the wagon. "Do those signs tell you where we should start?"

"They left more than two days ago, but we knew that from Rolf. He saw them go west through the trees." Keegan shrugged. "I don't know more; I will need to scout ahead."

"Is there anything else for us to learn here?" Madeline waited, but no one offered. "Okay, I should do something before I go. I have a spell here that can raise residual energy. Then we'll find somewhere to stop for lunch further down the road. Keegan, would a couple of hours be enough for you to get some information?"

"It depends on what is out there, but I think I should be able to at least confirm their route." He nodded to her then ran across the clearing and slipped between the trees.

Madeline stood facing the bloody circle. Trying to ignore the smell of blood and buzz of flies, she centered her focus on the sandy beach where she could find the calm she needed to cast a spell. She closed out the chatter and Jode's presence, knowing he wouldn't leave her side while she was deep in the magic.

Thinking about the scene that Rolf had described, Madeline imagined it running in reverse, hoping to get some information from before the spell worked with Lee. Perhaps getting a sight of the preparations for the spell might help when they came to undo it.

She imagined the sound of branches breaking as they must have when Lee came through. The light flickered and something blurry crossed her vision before crashing into the brush which healed as it passed. Movement caught her attention back to the center of the clearing. The flickering faded and she was in another time.

Madeline watched it play out ahead of her like a movie, faded against the brightness of the day. The action reversed. A tall thin woman was holding an animal carcass shoulder height and letting the blood drip while chanting. She was naked and the blood covered her belly and legs. Madeline couldn't make out the words, but there was sibilance and shrieking involved. She pushed away the faintness that threatened to break her concentration at the sight of the blood that dripped up into the animal's sliced neck. The oddness of the woman's backward gait was matched by the pale pink skin and fall of long dark hair.

Other similar beings sat inside the circle, but they were clothed in white robes. Then they stood and filed out in a line, backward. The naked woman slipped on a robe of sky blue.

The fire burned down. The wood seeming to regenerate until it became a pile of branches that threw a flaming brand back into the hands of a male Choi.

Madeline tried to slow the action down, tried desperately to hear the words, but the scene was too far away in time and distance, then she realized the words would be reversed. She was afraid to break her concentration by leaning in too close.

In her peripheral vision, she saw branches jump into the hands of the Choi who were unbuilding the fire, but she kept her eyes on the spell caster. The woman was clearly in charge, the others were getting instructions from her – well, getting them after they had carried out the orders.

When the wood was all removed from the fire, Madeline saw that there was a chest in the center. The woman retrieved it and walked backward to the clearing followed by the other Choi. Madeline blinked and the scene faded.

She was standing beside her solid husband, feeling cold and weak from the casting, but relieved that she was back. She turned to Jode and he wrapped a shawl around her shoulders, and then handed her a piece of the heavy nut bread they had packed for travel.

"Do you think we can dig into the ashes," she asked after telling him what she'd seen.

He rubbed warmth into her arms and said, "Yes, it won't take long. Go sit on the wagon. I will bring you what we find."

When she arrived at the wagon, Callisra handed her a glass of water and sat beside her. They watched as a group of the men started shoveling and brushing ashes away from the center of the pile, while others stood watch.

Madeline saw Jode bend to pick something up, something small. When he arrived at the wagon, he handed metal braces to Madeline. "This is all that survived of the chest. Perhaps you can find some information from it."

One more thing she didn't have the first clue how to use. "I'll scry Blu for advice." Madeline looked at the grimy crew who were getting ready to mount. "Thank you all. You look so uncomfortable. Let's try to find a place for you to wash when we stop for the meal."

18

*A*n hour later they found a clearing beside a stream. It was a small run of water, but allowed the fire clearing team to wash their hands and faces. Upstream, the horses were hobbled and allowed to drink.

Lunch was more nut cake, some dried meat, and a glass of wine. They had planned each day to allow them the most travel time, cold breakfast and lunch, hot meals at night.

Madeline took her food into the shade of the trees and placed the scrying glass in her lap. She tried to call Blu to the glass, but he didn't answer. While she waited to try again, she finished the meal and sipped her wine. If they weren't on such a dire mission, she would enjoy this lush peacefulness. Most of the trees were evergreen, but a few of the deciduous ones were showing gold or red flashes in the leaves. When they were done, she would suggest that they take a more leisurely journey around this countryside. A camping trip would be restful and interesting.

She looked across at Callisra who was tending a small injury. Simon was talking to Jode, but his gaze was clearly on the healer. Madeline smiled. *I might get in on that pool.*

Jode waved at her and she returned the gesture. Then,

bringing her peaceful beach to mind, she focused her gaze on the glass. "Blu," she whispered. "I need to speak to you."

She waited a few moments and was about to call again when his face materialized. "Good afternoon. How does the journey fare?"

Madeline brought Blu up to date on the discovery. "Is there some way of getting information from the metal that held the chest together?"

"Fire usually cleanses what it doesn't burn," Blu answered. "I can only suggest you clean it with water first and look for inscriptions. Even if you don't find anything, try to bring the metal back. It may be that we will find a use for it."

Madeline sighed and accepted that she wasn't going to get answers. "How is Tadric?"

Blu's face lost its usual cheer. "He appears well, but something is testing the wards."

"So, it isn't anyone inside the household?"

"I do not know that, but it seems unlikely that this attack came from inside. It is possible that someone was working within the house and has now left."

Madeline longed to be back helping him protect them. "How is Arabela holding up?"

"She copes. It helps that the boy is healthy now." Blu turned to look at something outside the scrying circle.

"You are busy," Madeline said. "Give my best wishes to Arabela. I will call again when I have more information."

She looked up and saw that Jode was beckoning her.

When she arrived back with the group, she saw Keegan had returned and was drinking from a bottle of wine.

Callisra was trying to get a look at a long scratch on his arm. He pulled away and growled, "Get away woman. I need no healing."

"Hey, no need to be rude." Simon stepped between them. "She's trying to help you."

Callisra stepped back. "It does not matter, Simon. It is his choice. I am not hurt."

Madeline saw Callisra smile and thought, *it's only a matter of time, Simon.*

Keegan looked from Simon to Callisra and gave a small bow. "I am sorry. I am tired from searching."

Madeline stepped closer and asked, "What did you find? I hope we don't have to wait much longer to get Lee out of their hands."

Keegan put the bottle down. "They continued through the woods. We will need to follow that way. I was not able to get far enough to find a short cut, if one exists. We will be hard pressed to catch them up." He drank deeply from the wine again.

Madeline put aside her concerns about drunken trackers – people here seemed well able to hold their drink. She looked at the party gathered around. Horses and two wagons, would it work? She asked Keegan what he thought.

He nodded toward a track across the road. "We can start there. The Choi's route crosses that trail about a mile in. It will be slow, but it's better that we keep the wagons as long as we can. I don't know that we will be able to hunt food and track Choi fast enough."

Jode went to talk to the two camp stewards. Madeline hoped they would be able to find a way to manage the camp supplies without slowing them down. She stowed her paper in her saddle bags and went to speak to Callisra and Simon.

"Simon, I think you must go back," she said. "This is going to be rough travel."

Simon looked at Callisra. "Why are you trying to send me back and not Callisra?"

"I've seen how she reacts to that. I'm convinced she has to come." She saw his face tighten and added, "Don't worry. Jode will make sure she's protected. Don't forget we have three guards with us. We're not on our own."

"Why would I be worried about that?" The intensity of his gaze undermined Simon's words. "I'm not going to leave you alone to face Lee." His voice was light, but Madeline knew he was serious. "I'll send the musicians back, though. They have enough to go on with the opera without me for a while, so their excuse isn't going to cut it any longer."

Madeline tried to bring herself to argue him into leaving, but she wanted his company. As selfish as that felt, she was grateful to have him stay. She looked up to see Jode approaching with Zora following behind.

"The stewards say they can pack both of the wagons differently and make it easier to drive them on rough ground," Jode said.

Simon spoke before Madeline could thank Jode. "Actually, we can send one of the wagons back with my guys. Anything we don't need can be packed with the instruments and we can keep most of their supplies." Simon looked to Zora as he spoke. "Sorry, I think you need to go back."

Zora laughed. "We are not going back. There are songs to be written about this and you are not getting to write them all, my friend." He slapped Simon on the back. "Besides, I need to be there when we find out who wins the pool."

he guitar notes wove through the other instruments, building an audible vision of adventure and joy, and something else, that Simon couldn't put his finger on, but was exactly what he wanted.

"It sounds lovely," Callisra said.

Simon hadn't heard her approach. He put down his guitar and the other musicians stopped playing.

"Oh, please don't stop," she said dropping to sit beside Simon. "It was soothing. And I think we need soothing after today."

Gren spoke before Simon could think of a response. "We need much more practice, Miss Tallhouse. We'll give you some privacy to talk." Gren and Zora rose and gathered their instruments, the others followed suit.

She held out her hand to stop them from leaving. "Please, call me Callisra. I think we have all earned the right to familiarity."

Gren nodded, and then led Zora and the others away.

Simon hoped they went farther than the other side of the wagon, but he doubted it. "I'm glad you liked the music," he said. "It's part of the overture for the opera we're writing. It's based on this journey."

"Perhaps a happy ending then." Callisra hugged her arms around her knees. "I feel as though we have reached a point where we are committed to this journey."

"Still feeling compelled?" Simon knew she wouldn't give up, but if he had some information maybe he could make sure she wasn't hurt in the process of saving a stranger.

"Yes," Callisra said. "I think of leaving, believe me, I don't enjoy riding all day on rough roads to an uncertain outcome. But every time I think of going back, I feel cold and as if the world is retreating, then my stomach is torn with agony."

Simon couldn't imagine being driven by pain in his gut, a pain in his ass, yes. Madeline had been that often enough. "Have you felt this before?"

"No." She sighed. "I wonder why you are here, Simon. I know that Madeline feels responsible for this woman, but you seem to be simply along for the adventure."

He chuckled, thinking about the number of times he had calmed Madeline down after Lee had bullied her. "I don't like it either, but this woman is capable of making Madeline do stupid things. If I can keep them from killing each other, I figure I will have paid back the karma I used coming here."

"What is karma?" She smoothed the fabric over her knees and turned her pale green eyes on him.

"It's like luck. I know I'm not getting it right, but it's like if you do something nice you get more good karma and if you do something bad, you get something bad happening to you."

"Interesting." She frowned. "And what do you mean by paying back the karma you used?"

"I came home when I came here. This was the best thing that ever happened to me." She smiled and Simon smiled back. "Tell me what you think this compulsion is about. Maybe it will help us get Lee out."

She looked at her lap. "When I am near Madeline, I feel the pull of something. When I am near you, I feel it too." She looked at him out of the corner of her eyes. "It is not what you think, not attraction. It is something else."

Simon flushed; maybe he had misread the cues. "So, you are not attracted to me?"

She giggled, a sound he would not have expected. "Oh, yes. I find you quite attractive. This is something more protective – that is the closest that I can come to explaining it." She spun to look behind the wagon at the sound of snickering. Simon started to rise, and she pulled him down. "No, it is all right."

Simon shook his head. "No, it is not all right. Let me send them away."

"What difference would it make to have them gone?" She leaned in closer.

Simon leaned in to her for the kiss he was sure she wanted. "A little real privacy would be useful."

"Yes, it would." She leaned toward him, and then pulled back. "But I am not interested in being on the list of women you seduce and leave."

She pushed him away hard enough to make him fall on his back, then rose to join Madeline near the horses.

$\mathcal{T}$he rest of the day was spent following the trail and waiting for Keegan to return periodically with updates. He kept confirming they were on the right track. Madeline felt relief that they weren't lost, but her frustration spiked every time he said they hadn't caught up.

As the light started to fade, Keegan returned and said, "I haven't found them, but you'll be better off camping soon. There's a clearing ahead that will do."

Madeline was riding bedside Jode at the time and she bent to ask, "Can you tell if we are making headway? I don't want to rest if we fall behind."

"We have made good time, considering," Keegan answered. "We have caught up some time, but I'm not sure if it's an hour or so, or a day or two."

"An hour or so on a five-day lead is not good." Madeline wanted to continue through the night. "How rough is the road ahead?"

Keegan looked at Jode before speaking. "It is much the same as we have traveled up to now. But that's too rough to manage in the dark."

"If we carried torches?"

Keegan looked at Jode again. This time Jode spoke for the tracker. "It is not a good idea to do that. The torches will not give enough light, and you will add the danger of burns to the risk of broken legs or axles."

Madeline sighed. "Is there a chance we will catch up before they get to their homeland?"

"There is always hope," Jode said as he turned his horse away. "Even so, we are likely going the fastest way to them, so we must continue unless we get new information." He rode back and Madeline could hear him directing the guards to ensure the camp was protected.

"There is more than hope." Keegan stepped closer to her horse as he spoke. "The Choi have been resting longer than we have. I think we may have caught up more than anticipated. They are a larger party than us. I have passed a camp that appeared to be an overnight rest."

Hope flitted through Madeline. "Are you sure?"

Keegan patted her horse and said, "I may be wrong. But do not lose heart. We are still traveling faster than they are."

Madeline refused to lose the glimmer of hope. "Then we need to make sure we extend our traveling time each day as long as it is safe. We will be up before the sun. Will you camp with us tonight?"

Keegan looked over his shoulder at the path ahead. "Not for a few hours at least. I will range further before I rest. Good night, Lady Madeline."

"You be careful, Keegan."

He nodded and ran along the path.

DINNER WAS A STEW, hearty and made from the contents of one of the sacks from the back of the wagon. No one had needed to hunt, and Madeline was grateful again for the abundant supplies.

78

She looked up from the spells she was trying to memorize. A melody floated from the musicians, something new, a nice change from Simon's vast memory of songs from their old world. Jode was sitting across the fire from her, humming while he ran his sword along a sharpening stone. The sound of his voice warmed her more than the flames.

Simon was sitting next to Callisra who was picking through a box of needles and thread, probably looking for something to match the color of the torn shirt she held on her lap. Simon was pretending to read the pages in his hand – Madeline assumed it was his opera – but he was really watching Callisra. When she turned to look at him, he glanced at the papers. Madeline wondered how he could be so oblivious to his feelings. There must be some way she could give him a gentle push toward making the commitment.

Madeline did her best to look casual when she said, "Callisra, you are very talented." She pointed to the mending. "Is there anything you don't know how to do?"

Her face flushing, Callisra responded, "It is my misfortune to be unable to cook. And I am a terrible housekeeper."

"You'll be fine. Anyone can hire a cook and maid." Simon didn't look up as he spoke.

"What an excellent idea." Madeline saw an opening. "In fact, I promise to hire your cook and maids for the first year as a wedding gift. That is, if you feel the need to leave my employ when you find the man you want to live with, because you are welcome to stay."

Simon scowled, but the women ignored him.

Callisra threaded a needle and picked up the shirt. "I hope that I would be able to stay with you, but if the man I marry has his own estate, I would go there of course. Who would turn down their own household?"

"Well, then all we need is the right man," Madeline said. "Do you have anyone in mind?"

Simon was giving her that look people use when they want you to shut up but can't say it.

Madeline smiled sweetly at him. Then the music changed abruptly, the mellow tones sharpening to almost discord causing the hair on the back of her neck stand up. "Simon, why would you write such harsh music?"

She turned to look at the musicians, but stopped when she saw Jode slowly straighten, no longer humming. The guards were looking around. She realized it wasn't the music that had set her on alert, but the sure knowledge they were being watched.

"Do you have your knife?" Jode's voice was low. Madeline nodded and saw Simon slide a blade from under his chair. Callisra dropped the shirt back onto her lap and pulled scissors from the sewing box.

"Stay here. Protect yourselves if need be." Jode strolled out of the circle and went toward the guards.

Madeline stood, holding a knife lightly between her fingers just in case, and watched as Ridern and Satra pulled someone from under the wagon. Jode returned to her as the guards brought their captive forward.

It was a Fay boy. To Madeline he looked about fourteen, in reality she knew he was more likely to be thirty or older, but still a boy because he had not completely molted immature white feathers. He was also thin, much thinner than could be explained by a growth spurt.

"What do you want me to do with him?" Ridern asked as he stepped into the circle of light thrown by the fire.

Ridern was tall, but the boy stood a few inches taller and Madeline only came up to his chest.

"Let me talk to him." Madeline waved them closer. "Thank you, Ridern and Satra."

The guards didn't move. Madeline smiled. "I think we can take care of him. Please go back to your patrol. We would not want to have anyone slip in while we are distracted."

Satra handed the boy to Jode and looked for permission to go. Madeline suppressed her annoyance, realizing they really reported to him and only one person could command the guards. She looked at the boy who had dropped to his knees before the fire as soon as Jode release his arm. He shivered in fear or with the cold, or both.

Now he was closer, Madeline could see that his feathers were turning from the white of youth to a blue that would make him blend with the clear sky in flight.

She looked to Jode who shrugged. The Fay were not usually so submissive. Perhaps a simple question would be the best way to start. "What is your name?"

The boy looked up at her, his gray eyes wide. "Elight."

"Why were you watching us from the wagon?" Jode's voice startled the boy who twisted his neck to look up.

Elight licked his lips before speaking. "I have information for you. If you are following the Choi."

Madeline touched Jode's arm and shook her head. He stepped away, but she could feel his tension practically vibrating behind her.

"We are." She would not give the boy any information until she understood why he was frightened, and what information he had.

The boy started to stand and then dropped to his knees again as Jode shifted his hand to the sword at his hip. "You are going the long way around. I have seen where they are; you can catch them if you change your path."

Madeline looked at Simon. "Can you get Keegan here?" He nodded and went to the other side of the clearing.

"Why are you so frightened? I promise no one will hurt you." Madeline watched something cross Elight's face. "Are you hurt?"

"It is nothing," he answered looking down to the ground.

Simon returned. "Keegan is still out, but Satra said he should be back within the hour."

81

Madeline drew Callisra close. "Can you heal him?"

"Probably," she said, looking at the trembling Fay. "I think he needs food and water more than healing."

Madeline crouched in front of Elight. "No one will hurt you. Please let my healer help you. And take some food. You look like you are starving. When Keegan returns, we can discuss what to do."

Callisra held out her hand and Elight took it before standing. Madeline saw a cut on his chest and one wing was swollen along the top edge. She was determined to get the story of how he was hurt along with why he was frightened.

A half hour later, healed and eating a bowl of stew, Elight had stopped trembling and was making eye contact with everyone, except Jode. Madeline took the empty bowl and handed it to Wint, one of the camp tenders. "While we wait for Keegan, tell me why you were afraid."

Elight swallowed and Madeline saw the same hesitation, was he thinking about lying? "As your healer said, I was not afraid, just hungry and tired. Now, I am simply tired and I will be able to put that aside until we speak with your tracker. But I urge you to listen to me. I have seen the Choi."

"Do you mean you saw them in a vision? Or are they that close?" Madeline knew that the Fay could see things at a distance. She also knew that just like any vision, what was seen could be interpreted differently depending on the circumstances. "Tell me exactly what you saw."

"The Choi are a large party. It looked to me as though the entire tribe traveled. There were children in the camp. And there were captives."

Madeline thought back to the ceremony she'd raised in the clearing. There had been no children there, and if that was most of the Choi, then they were almost extinct. "Where were they when you saw them?"

Elight flicked a glance at Jode. "They were camping at the approach to Severed Pass. They will cross within two days."

Madeline looked at Jode. "Is that where we were going to cross?"

"No." Jode frowned. "The Severed Pass is dangerous. It is difficult to believe that the Choi are attempting it."

"Is it faster?" she asked.

Jode scratched his chin. "No, this is most confusing. If they are going to the closest Choi village, it would be better to go through Ale's pass, where we planned to cross. But if Elight is correct, and the whole tribe travels, perhaps they are not going to the village."

Madeline glanced up as movement caught her attention. "Good. Here's Keegan. Perhaps he can interpret this news."

Keegan sat next to Elight and listened as they updated him. Then he spoke to the Fay boy in low tones for a few minutes, before turning to Madeline. "I found evidence today of two parties joining together. I do not know why the Choi would choose this path, as Sir Jode said, it is very dangerous. I know that we are certain to catch them if we keep following their trail. But if they really are headed for Severed Pass, we can take a short cut."

Madeline realized they were looking to her for a decision. She let Keegan go to his bedroll and asked Wint to find Elight somewhere to rest. A decision was going to be difficult. Too many unknowns, and she felt like no matter what she did, she'd be guessing. If she guessed wrong, people would be hurt.

Callisra drew Simon aside. "Come explain the opera to me." They drifted toward the musicians leaving Madeline and Jode alone.

"So, do you have any advice?" Madeline asked her husband. "Any hidden knowledge of the Choi homeland?"

He wrapped his arms around her and kissed the top of her

head. "No, I wish I did. Perhaps Blu will know something. Can you scry him?"

She hugged him and then wiggled free. "I will, but not yet. He is busy and I want to exhaust our knowledge before bothering him. It would help if I could ask him some specific questions. You know he won't tell me what to do."

Jode looked around the camp, and then settled on his bedroll. "I've sent Ridern to ask if anyone has knowledge of the Choi homeland, but I expect if someone did, they would have spoken up by now."

Madeline sat and poured tea from a jug. "Tell me about Severed Pass. By the name, I suspect it is risky. Maybe we can find a way to make it less so."

Jode accepted the mug of tea and waited until Madeline had her hands wrapped around her own before speaking. "It is named that because two caravans of merchants were found dead. This was many generations ago. It is something of a legend."

"So," Madeline said. "Severed Pass because their lives were severed?"

"No, because everyone in the caravan was torn apart."

Madeline felt her blood drain and fought faintness. "Do people think the Choi did it?"

Jode put down his mug and wrapped an arm around her. "No, there were Choi in the caravan. They met the same fate."

"Has it been used since?" Madeline couldn't imagine anyone attempting a crossing with that history.

"Only a few times. People choose to use it only when there are no options and when they can reasonably expect to complete the journey in daylight. We will not be able to do that. If we use Severed Pass, we need to be sure it is the only option."

"I find it hard to ignore what Elight has seen. What if there's a ceremonial site at the other side of the pass. If we follow them and still have to cross that pass, then we've wasted the time we could save by heading there directly."

"I wish I could help you, my love, but this is your rescue. You must decide."

He sat drinking while Madeline tried to find a way to make both choices. Her gut said they should listen to Elight. Her head said to find a reason to take such a risk.

Keegan hadn't helped her to decide, but maybe she should ask him again. "I'll be back." She walked across the small campsite to where Keegan sat on his bedroll.

"I thought you might be asleep." She sat on the ground beside him.

"I am worried about this new development." Keegan rolled a cigarette and lit it with a burning twig that he threw back on the fire. "I have been trying to think of a compromise."

Madeline inhaled the warm smell of spice. Here tobacco was used as pesticide or poison. The cigarettes and pipes were filled with herbs often used as medicine.

She pulled her knees to her chest and laid her head on them. "Me too. I feel as though we should follow Elight's advice but there's nothing that supports that feeling."

Keegan grunted. "What do you need from me?"

Madeline liked his directness. "If we continue as we are and the Choi are heading for this pass, how much more time will it take?"

Keegan drew on the cigarette and didn't respond. Madeline glanced at him and saw concentration crease his brow. Eventually he answered, "I think it will cost us two whole days to stay on this path and follow the trail. If we are truly headed for Severed Pass, we can cross easier land and perhaps the Choi will not know we are coming."

"And if we head directly for Severed Pass and it turns out the Choi are not going in that direction?"

"We will lose three days backtracking." He drew again and blew smoke rings. "I would advise that we cross at Ale's pass regardless. It would be safer. The risk is that there will be no trail to follow if the Choi are not going to the village. It concerns me that the boy saw what he thinks was the whole tribe."

It was comforting that she wasn't the only one who saw all the options. But she needed to make a decision.

"Thank you, Keegan. Please get some rest. I will figure this out."

21

*M*adeline turned to see Jode waiting patiently for her at their fire. Their camp was small, but each group had made their own little private space with a campfire. Being so close to each other meant privacy was more an agreement to pretend you didn't hear what was going on rather than actual privacy. She had learned to keep her voice low.

As she approached, Jode smiled and she wondered at how that still made her feel safe, trusted, and loved after a year. She bent to kiss him before grabbing her saddle bag. "I'll try to scry Blu, can you make sure I'm not interrupted, please."

He nodded and patted the ground beside him. "Do it here; I will keep watch."

She placed the glass in her lap and called for Blu as soon as she settled. The sound of the camp intruded. "Damn," Madeline muttered. She closed her eyes and breathed out slowly. Looking into the glass she stared past her reflection and brought the sense of warm sand running between her fingers. A quiet cough floated into her imagined world, but she allowed the sigh of waves to smother it.

When she felt the beginning of drowsiness, she focused on the glass. "Blu," she whispered.

There was no response. Madeline calmed her reaction knowing it was late and he might be sleeping. She changed the focus from Blu's room to Tadric's and saw a fold of saffron colored robe. "Blu," she said a little louder than before. He turned and she knew he heard the call.

She watched as he crossed the room to face the small mirror on Tadric's wall. "Madeline, I did not expect to hear from you so soon."

"I need your advice. Or, actually, I think I just need to talk this through and if you have advice... well, that would be welcome."

"I am ready to listen." He looked at her, expectation on his face.

She gave him a summary of the news. "I don't know how to decide, and I don't think I can just pick an option and hope for the best. I feel like there is something I'm missing."

Blu nodded. "If the Fay saw them camped before Severed Pass, then there is no doubt the Choi are crossing there. But you are right. There is something missing."

Madeline felt relief. She had worried that she was just avoiding a decision. "Please, just tell me. I am stuck and we don't have a lot of time."

"I can see you are tired. And I can make an exception this time I think." He smiled wider. "You have the ability to scry this woman."

Not the help she was hoping for. She knew better than to press him for a clearer hint, but another question always worked. "How? I don't know where she's being held in the camp."

Madeline felt her mind jumping to solve the problem and Blu's image began to waver until she gained control.

"You have the scarf. You can use that to find her. Now I must go."

"Thank you."

"Remember this when next you struggle to find an answer. I will not always hand you information on a platter." He chuckled and waved goodbye.

Madeline broke the spell and heaved a sigh of relief.

"That sounds as though you have an answer," Jode said.

"Not yet, but I think I might have one very soon."

Madeline dug out the scarf from where she had tossed it. Then she pulled a blanket from the bedroll and wrapped herself against the rising chill. She waited for the distraction of the chill to fade and then centered herself. She searched her mind to find the knowledge of using possessions to scry. Then she thought about the details she knew that would fill out the vision. The Choi were traveling with a large group and were camped before a pass.

Basing a scry on a vision, I wonder if there's a problem with that. The calmness of her beach shattered.

"Damn," she snapped.

"What is wrong?" Jode was sitting across from her now. He had gone back to sharpening his blade.

"Nothing. Well, nothing that wasn't avoidable, don't fret." She decided that she should do her research thinking before dipping into the magic. It was too hard not to question the validity of her assumptions while she tried to be confident in her abilities.

She looked at her husband again. He might be able to help her think it through. "Jode, what does the approach to Severed Pass look like? If I can imagine that, I might have an easier time finding Lee in the glass."

Jode put down the sword and whetstone. "It will depend where they are. Let me get Elight and you can ask him what he actually saw."

Madeline nodded and Jode strode across the camp to bring the Fay boy. While she waited, she recalled the process of scrying with a possession. Blu's voice whispered in her memory. *Find the magic, or if no magic, the essence, is there a scent, a color? Now look with your senses for that same thing. Follow the trail and you will find your object.* Unfortunately, last time she had tried, she learned that if the subject had spent a lot of time anywhere, that's where the magic would lead. At least with Lee, it was simple. The only place she had spent time was with the Choi.

She lifted the scarf to her nose. Ah, Chanel No 5. That should be easy to follow.

"You have questions?" Elight's voice cut through Madeline's thoughts.

She nodded while she placed the scarf under the scrying glass. "Tell me what you saw in your vision exactly, please."

Elight sat. "I saw tents and horses gathered in a camp. It looked like a temporary camp; three tents and rings of bedrolls surrounding them."

Madeline closed her eyes and tried to picture the scene. There were too many variables if she tried to bring up the whole camp. "I am trying to scry the prisoner."

He nodded quickly. "As I understand it, if you do not have a good picture of the subject, you can scry the area and then focus on the subject."

"Yes, that's more or less correct." Madeline had forgotten that different kinds of magic were a mystery to creatures in this world. In fact, she really didn't know how the Fay could see over a long distance. "How do you find what you need to see?" she asked. *Maybe she could have Elight scry and describe... no.* Madeline knew that to make this decision she needed to see for herself.

"Often the vision is sent when a great magic is cast. That is what happened this time. I was studying the winds considering a flight when the world around me changed." He smiled at her. "When we have time, it would be interesting to discuss our different talents."

"Yes, I look forward to that." Madeline still didn't have what she needed. "What about when you look for things rather than have visions sent?"

"I cast my sight in the direction. I see the world pass rapidly below me and when I arrive at the place I wish to see, I slow down." He shrugged. "Is that of help?"

Madeline felt dizzy just imagining what he had described. "I need to focus on some detail and then I am there. Is there anything you can remember? Something unique that I might use?"

Elight closed his eyes and began to gently sway. After a few minutes, he opened his eyes again. "The tents are still there. I imagine they will remain until the sun is up so they can attempt the ascent in the light. Here is what I see." He smoothed the dirt at his side. Madeline leaned closer. Elight drew three circles in a line then squiggles surrounding them. "This is the overview of the camp."

Madeline nodded and Elight smoothed the dirt again. "I think the large tent belongs to the leader. It is brightly colored and patterned. The next tent; Choi are walking in and out, food, or something else I think." He looked at Madeline who gestured for him to continue. "This smaller tent is guarded, that could be where your friend is held. Or, it could be where they keep the other captives."

"She is not my friend." Madeline pictured the tents. If she looked for the three tents, then used the scent of Chanel No 5 to draw her to Lee... it might work. "Thank you, Elight. That will help considerably. Please, go back to your rest."

Jode watched Elight walk away. "It seems odd to me that he didn't give us those details earlier."

"He is young, and he was exhausted. I think he was just concerned that we would know what he saw on a big scale. If he was older, perhaps he would have thought that we would need more detail." She settled herself again and drew in a breath of the perfume as she pictured the camp in her mind.

22

She closed her eyes and the Choi camp sprang into focus. Startled, Madeline struggled to hold the vision.

She saw a dusty campground laid out exactly the way Elight had drawn. There were twenty rings of bedrolls around the main tent, which was a lot more Choi than had been at the ceremony.

She focused on the bright tent in the center of the camp, thinking she might as well try to see who she was up against. As she approached, the noises of the camp rose to meet her, people calling to each other, the ringing of a blacksmith, the snorting of horses. The swoop of her focus came to a crashing halt a few inches from the canvas, and then started to slide down the side of the tent. Some kind of trap?

Madeline pulled outward with her mind and the whole camp came back into focus, not a trap then, a barrier. Mentally crossing her fingers that she hadn't set off an alarm, Madeline turned to the smaller tent. This time following a very faint trail of perfume, she slipped her vision through the fabric of the tent.

It was dark inside.

Madeline waited. She knew that Lee, or something Lee had worn was inside. If she was patient, the balance of light between them would change and she would be able to see more clearly. As she waited for the gloom to lift, she heard something scuffling in the corner. It reminded her of the sounds just before the Dray kidnapped her last year. She sniffed again, no stench of sour milk, no Dray. She moved her focus toward the scuffling and saw Lee bound at the very edge of the tent.

"Lee," she called.

Nothing happened. Well that just meant Lee had no magic. Unfortunately, all that left for Madeline to do was observe and assume, not the best way to make a plan. She moved closer still and saw that Lee was struggling against her bonds. Good, she was still alive and well enough to fight. Madeline hoped she would stay that way. If Lee was not able to walk out under her own power, it was going to add another layer to the already complicated rescue.

Lee wore the clothes she had crossed in. The lightweight wool suit was not made for rough handling and hard travel. The seams were parting on her sleeves and she would never get the stains out of the rest of it. *Great! Now I'll have to find something for Lee to wear when she goes back.*

The sound of canvas slapping against canvas broke Madeline's attention. She felt herself being pulled away and fought to stay.

She watched as a guard carried a bowl of porridge and a jug.

The guard cackled. "Stop fighting, you stupid woman. We prefer you whole, but a few bruises and broken bones won't make a different when we sacrifice you."

Madeline's last glance as she slipped back through the tent was Lee's green eyes blazing murder at the guard. She felt a surge of pride that someone from her world wouldn't be cowed, even if that someone was Lee.

MADELINE SURFACED back to reality with a gasp. She was not used to scrying this way and really wasn't prepared for the energy drain.

"Welcome back." Jode's voice caught her attention.

"It's good to be back. It's good to see you too. Wow, that took a lot out of me, do you think you can find me something to eat?" Madeline folded Lee's scarf and placed it and the scrying glass in her pack, she was glad she'd put the pack on the ground before she started because she wasn't sure she should be trying to stand right now. She expected Jode to leave and was surprised when he passed her a slab of fruit bread and a mug of wine.

"You are as pale as death. I suspected you would need sustenance," he said.

Madeline tried to be ladylike, but her stomach wanted food now. She washed the bread down with the wine and felt her strength rising again. "Thanks, that's much better."

"Did you learn what you needed?"

I learned something, was it what I needed? "I saw Lee, and I met resistance at the many-colored tent. The only real thing I know is I saw what Elight did before I found Lee." She described the terrain around the camp.

Jode nodded as she spoke. When she finished, he said, "Yes, that is the entrance to the pass. If they are planning to take the whole party over, they will need to move quickly as soon as dawn shows." He looked across the camp. "I'll get Keegan. I think we're going to be able to catch them up."

Madeline listened to the camp as she waited. She must have been in the spell for longer than she thought, because most people were already deeply asleep. She could see the two guards who were watching over them patrol just out of the reach of the light. A movement across the camp startled her until she realized it was Simon heading her way.

When he arrived, he sat beside her. "I heard Jode say you saw Lee."

"Yes, she's in pretty bad shape, but fighting. I guess her tendency to want her own way will be to her advantage."

Simon laughed.

"Jode's getting Keegan," Madeline said.

"Yes, he's giving him the Cole's Notes version. I thought you might want a few minutes to talk to someone who understands before you have to decide what to do."

"Thanks." Madeline pulled her shawl tighter. "You know, when I saw her in that tent, I didn't even think about what a bitch she is. I just tried to figure out how to get her out of there."

"Well, you are in the power position here. She can't undermine you so easily." Simon looked at her closely. "You always were, you know. It's up to you whether she gets under your skin."

Madeline was relieved when she saw Jode and Keegan approach. This was not a good time to get into a discussion about self-esteem. "Maybe, but then maybe I've matured. Stranger things have happened."

Simon patted her shoulder. "Don't do that; you'd be no fun."

Before she could respond, Jode and Keegan arrived and sat in the small circle. Simon started to rise, but Madeline pulled him down again. "I need all the help I can get here."

Jode put a few more thin branches on the fire and Madeline felt heat finally chase the chill from her bones. "Okay, Elight was telling the truth and the Choi are going over Severed Pass. If this pass is so dangerous, how do we know what to expect. Like, how long will it take for them to cross?"

Keegan rolled a cigarette, but didn't light it. "I have been searching my memory for clues. It is true that the pass is dangerous, but some people do cross it. There is trade to be had with the Choi and a small party can cross Severed in one day."

One day, how the hell would they be able to catch the Choi. Madeline pushed away the doubt that rose with the question. "How small a party?"

"If you are asking about the Choi?" Keegan waited for her

95

nod. "They will take at least two days. One day to ascend to the top, there is a resting place there. One day to descend. If there really are that many, the last of them will be across at night on the second day."

"And our party?" Madeline looked around, starting to think about who was really needed. "How few of us must there be to cross in one day?"

Jode did not let Keegan answer. "Madeline, take care you do not exchange speed for too much danger. What are you planning?"

"Nothing. I am just gathering information." She hoped he would settle for the lie. Quarrels right now would delay the inevitable. She would be ready to win that argument when they started the crossing. "So, Keegan, how few?"

"A party of three or four, on foot will cross fastest. The problem with the pass is the steepness and ruts in the road. That's what slows down wagons and horses."

Me, Jode and a guard.

Madeline didn't let her expression show her plans. "And if we stay together?"

"We will cross in two days." Keegan shook his head, reconsidering. "No, I think we will be able to descend in half a day."

"If we were to send some people back," Simon's words were almost a whisper. "Would we need to give them a guard?"

"It depends who." Jode raised an eyebrow, but Madeline didn't respond. "And how far they have to travel. If they leave tomorrow morning, they would easily arrive at Arabela's by dinner if they travel light. Who were you thinking of sending?"

Madeline let them talk. She was considering the same question and was sure that they would still want to take more people than she thought necessary.

Simon looked at the camp before speaking. "Callisra, the musicians and maybe the Fay boy."

"One guard could escort them and then catch us back up," Jode said.

Madeline looked around the camp and realized no one would leave in the morning. Callisra couldn't leave; the guards would only leave if they were ordered to. Keegan hadn't offered, and the musicians were being stubborn about not missing the adventure.

Tired and unwilling to start a negotiation on the size of the party, Madeline interrupted, "Keegan, if we stay together, how quickly can we get to the Pass?"

He looked toward their path as though measuring the miles in his head. "We travel fast as a group. If we can travel all day, and leave before dawn, we should arrive by the end of the day tomorrow."

Madeline nodded. "I think we should all rest, then. Tomorrow we head for the pass. We can continue this discussion on the road."

And then I'll find a way to send as many as possible to safety before we start up the mountain.

23

*S*imon left Madeline and Jode hoping they weren't as wound up as he was. Madeline needed her sleep and there would be few opportunities for rest in the next couple of days. He glanced at Callisra, rolled in her blankets, only a few strands of her black hair lying across her pale cheeks.

When he settled down on his own bedroll, he realized he wasn't ready to sleep. He reached for his sheaf of music, there was enough light from the fire for him to make some notes. As he touched the paper, he heard a rustle and slid his hand for the hilt of his sword. It tangled in the blanket. So he spun, holding his hand ready to knock the intruder down when he saw Callisra standing waiting for him.

"What are you doing? I thought you were sneaking in to attack the camp." Simon kept his voice low, and tried to keep the panic out of it. "You were asleep a second ago."

She moved closer. "I was listening to the conversation. I came over to tell you that you don't need to protect me, Simon. I am going with Madeline, no matter what." Her breath caught before she continued. "I have no choice."

"Woman, why are you so insistent about this? Why are you so

willing to go into danger?" Simon could feel frustration rising from his gut. *Why did he care?*

"Keep your voice down." Callisra drew him to the shadow of the wagon. "I just know I have to go with her. I don't know why. Believe me, I would rather be sitting near the fire at home, drinking wine and listening to you sing."

She likes my singing.

"As would I." Simon sighed, knowing that her compulsion was probably important. In fact, here it probably meant something like a major prophesy was in play. "Can you fight? If we get attacked, can you defend yourself?"

Callisra giggled, and Simon was distracted from his worries. "No, I have no skills for fighting, but you don't need to worry about taking care of me, Simon. Although that is sweet. I will keep out of the way of any danger."

Simon shrugged as though he didn't care. "Make sure you do. Um... could you do me a favor?"

"What is it?" Callisra lounged back against the wagon, arms crossed.

Simon swallowed before speaking. "I know I tried to kiss you, but could you back off a bit on the flirting?"

He saw her put her hand to her face, but it was too dark to see her expression. There was laughter in her voice when she finally answered. "I am not flirting with you. Simon, I am pursuing you. Why do you ask me to stop? You seem attracted to me."

Simon blushed. Why did he feel like an idiot around her? "You are a very attractive woman, but that's not the point."

"Then what is the point?" The laughter bubbled back to the surface.

"The point is, everyone is teasing me about you." It sounded weak to his ears and Simon rolled his eyes. "The point is, I can't concentrate on anything because I keep having to deal with the comments."

She pushed herself away from the wagon and Simon found

himself leaning toward her. She pursed her lips. Simon leaned closer for the kiss, and this time she was clearly giving him the right signals.

He felt heat rising from her as their lips touched, and then she pushed him in the chest hard enough to rock him on his heels. "If you want me to keep my feelings hidden, then there will be no kisses, Simon DiPalma."

She spun away and Simon called after her, "If you don't want me to kiss you, stop trying to kiss me."

"You have no right to tell me what to do," she called over her shoulder before running back to her bedroll.

Simon groaned. *Everyone would have heard that.*

24

*S*kye stood outside her tent gazing at the path through the mountain. By night they would be sleeping in the heights and in the morning, they would descend to the temple. Lee Marshall was doing her best to cause problems, but she was a weak creature and well tied.

The journey had been easier than she feared at the outset. Her biggest fear was the risk of losing her people before the ceremony. Traveling with the entire tribe was a risk. If someone found them and thought to attack, there was no way to protect everyone. But no one had attacked. In fact, no one seemed to know they were traveling until last night. The incident last night rankled. Someone had tested her protections which meant someone knew they were on the road.

The sun had risen and now there was enough light for her to see her servants packing the bedrolls on the horses. Soon they would collapse her tent and the other two would follow. It unsettled her that last night her magical senses rang like a bell as someone – someone strong – tried to enter, but this morning not a sign of interference.

She strode across to the smaller tent. Time to have some fun with this woman; time to spice her blood with fear. It would be a pity when she was gone, such good sport. Skye smiled, it didn't matter, because when she was gone the tribe would allow Ophian to stand in council. He could be her lover, and that was much better than this sport.

Bending to enter the tent, Skye noticed the woman was once again tied to a barrel. There were bruises on her cheek and Skye hissed her anger. If the sacrifice was too damaged, the ceremony would be weakened and her people would fail.

She would get to the bottom of this, but first, "Who was looking for you last night?" Skye tried to make her voice sound kind, but was not sure if she succeeded.

Lee glared up at her. "Who would look for me? I don't know anyone here."

Skye did not correct her. The other woman from her world might be aware of the arrival of Lee Marshall. "Someone came looking. But they will be too late to save you. Three more days."

Lee pulled at her bonds. "If they came looking for me, why didn't you capture them? It seems you are not as smart as you claim."

"They did not come in person, stupid woman. They probed with magic."

Lee spat.

"It is nice to see you have spirit. That will increase your value."

Lee turned away as much as she could.

Skye reached out and touched Lee's face. "Who made these bruises? I do not wish you damaged."

Despite her condition, Lee croaked out a laugh. "You should tell your guards. They kick me when they come to feed me."

Skye put that information aside. She would deal with the guards later. "Are you damaged elsewhere?"

"Why don't you untie me and check?" A grin. "I promise to stand quietly."

"Do not play with me." Skye savored the thought of the power that would come from this woman. It had been genius to call her here. There were only a few people in the land who could supply such strong magic.

Skye cast her senses around Lee. No broken skin, but the woman was covered in bruises. "We will be leaving soon. I will speak to you tonight."

Lee didn't respond, but Skye didn't care. She ducked through the opening and stalked to the first guard she saw. "Why is the woman damaged? Was I not clear with my instructions? She is not to be hurt."

The guard kept his eyes on the ground. "We did not do this, Greatmother. She struggles and throws herself against her restraints. We tie her tighter so there is no slack for her to use, but she finds a way. We filled the barrel with sand and tied her there so she couldn't pull it over."

Skye wondered how he expected her to believe that the woman had bruised her face in the process of trying to break the knots. "When we are traveling today, make sure she is padded. The road is rough and if she breaks her skin, if her blood flows, I will take the lost blood from your veins."

The guard paled, but he nodded. "Yes, Greatmother."

25

*M*adeline saddled her horse by the light of torches. Jode assured her that the sun would be up within the hour, but it was still pitch dark. By the time the sun did rise, she expected them to be well down the road.

It was going to be a long and difficult day. Riding as long as they could without hurting the animals, didn't mean the riders would be comfortable. Eating in the saddle meant dried meat and fruits, and water from skins. The only good news was that they would be camping at the foot of the mountain when they settled for the night.

After a few hours on the road, Madeline was tired of the slow pace, the sight of trees, and the jingle of harness. She was parched from the dust and sore from the saddle. She looked down at Elight who walked between Jode's horse and hers, apparently not affected by the boredom and dust.

She bent and asked, "Will you need to ride?"

He smiled up at her. "No, I will happily walk all day and night at this pace."

She nodded and pulled a piece of dried meat from her bag.

"Will you be able to see where the Choi are when we stop to rest the horses?"

"Yes, it will take me a few minutes to prepare. Would it be better if I were to keep them in sight as we journey?"

Jode slowed his horse so he could see the Fay. "Is this possible? I have not heard of Fay maintaining their visions for more than a few minutes."

Elight looked from Jode to Madeline before answering, and then he spoke to Madeline. "It is possible. I will need to ride if I do that because I cannot focus on the vision and the road at the same time."

Madeline considered. Was there value in watching the Choi all the time? It would be nice to know if Lee escaped, or if the Choi were trapped in a rock fall, but they could find that out with periodic checks. "No, I do not think we need to watch them. Checking their progress when we stop will be useful enough."

She took a bite of the meat, sweet and savory in the same mouthful. Chewing, she looked at the scenery feeling her spirit brighten again. They traveled a dirt road, but it was well packed. Trees lined the side of the road. There were no sounds coming from the woods, only the creak of leather and wagon wheels. A quiet humming came from the wagon behind her where the musicians lounged.

She turned back to the Fay boy. "Tell me about yourself, Elight. Why were you alone on the day you saw the Choi?"

He flicked a glance at her then back again at Jode. "It was misfortune on my part."

"Misfortune?" Madeline heard something in Elight's tone of voice that promised a story, and a story would definitely help pass the time.

"I have the misfortune of being stubborn." He sighed. "I believed I was ready for my first flight. My village elders did not agree."

"A little rebellion from the youth is a good thing." Jode's voice held the ring of experience. Madeline made a note to pursue that when they were alone.

Elight stared at the road. "Perhaps for humans, for the Fay, it is better to heed the elders."

"So, you ran away?" Madeline asked.

"I thought if I could fly back into the village, I would prove them wrong." Elight shrugged and sighed, too like a teenager from her past world for Madeline to believe the elders were wrong. "I wandered farther than I intended. I was looking for the perfect cliff and I found myself far from the village."

"Why didn't you just go back?" Madeline asked.

"My pride kept me looking. Then I had the idea that I should practice my flights so that I would be impressive when I glided into the village; impressive enough to turn some heads. I had only just taken my first leap when the vision grasped me and I fell to the ground."

Madeline remembered some of the stupid things she'd done as a teenager. Mostly because she kept digging herself in deeper rather than admitting defeat. "And now you find yourself moving farther from home."

Elight flicked his wings up a few inches then back again. "I am curious, Lady Madeline. My people speak of your deeds, but not about you. Would you tell me a tale of your old world?"

Madeline groaned at the thought of explaining all the differences between her old life and this new one. She tried to dodge the question. "If you want to go home, Elight, I will let you. I don't want your attempt to fly to turn into something dangerous. Do you want to go?"

He looked sideways at her. "It is not possible for me to return just now."

"Why? I'm sure your elders will forgive you," Madeline said, wondering if culture had any effect on magic. Perhaps her plans of documenting the powers of Cartref would need to be expanded.

"Perhaps, but I still wish to return with proof I am an adult." He grinned at her. "But I would enjoy a story of another world. Are there Fay there?"

Madeline relented and tried to think of a suitable story, one that didn't involve television, the internet, or being a lawyer.

26

Simon was falling asleep in his saddle and that wasn't a good thing. He knew he wasn't a good enough rider to manage a nap without falling. He urged his horse to the side. Letting the wagon full of musicians move ahead while he waited for the second wagon, where Callisra sat chatting with Barsh the driver.

He had been thinking about last night. Maybe he did read the signals wrong. She was definitely interested, that wasn't signals. She'd said she was pursuing him. He was interested too. The problem was he was interested in a fling, but she probably wanted to tie him down to a wedding, and a house, and kids, and everything he didn't want.

He rode alongside listening to them chatter for a few minutes, then Barsh spoke to him, "Sir Simon, I heard your new songs last night. It was very interesting. Is there more to come?"

"A lot more, but probably not for a while." Simon looked at Callisra. She ignored him. "Opera takes time to create."

They rode a while longer, until he built up the courage to say what he had to say. "Um, Callisra."

She turned to look at him. "Yes."

"Last night." He cleared his throat. "I'm sorry that I got the wrong impression."

"Mm." She reached under the wagon seat and came back up with a water skin and took a long drink before answering. "In what way did you get the wrong impression?"

Oh, she was not going to make it easy. Well, two can play at that game. "Well, when you tried to kiss me for instance."

The driver chuckled.

Callisra blushed. "Yes, you did get the wrong impression. I would not have tried to kiss you. I believe I had to push you away when you tried to kiss me, and not for the first time."

"I thought you wanted me to. I thought you were sweet on me." Simon winked at Barsh.

"That is another wrong impression and I would appreciate it if you didn't talk about me in that way."

Had he pushed too hard? "I wouldn't dream of talking about you in any way but complimentary." Simon glanced at Barsh for support, but the eldman smirked and turned away.

"I am not sweet on you, Simon DiPalma. That is for school-girls. I am not a child. I think you are a good prospect for a husband, but that is all."

Her cheeks were now blazing and Simon couldn't tell if it was anger, or embarrassment, or worse, both.

Time to mend bridges. "Please accept my apology then. I did get the wrong impression. And it seems I gave it, too." He rode away before she could respond.

27

*M*adeline felt every jolt of her horse's step in her bones. They had been riding for sixteen hours with only two small breaks. She kept pinching her leg to stop from falling asleep. The other riders were silent, but since sunset, everyone had been alert for danger from the woods.

She needed mental stimulation, so she dropped back in line to the musician's wagon, hoping Simon would be willing to talk. Perhaps she could help him see the benefit of settling down with Callisra. He was obviously interested.

Zora was driving the wagon. "Good evening, Lady Madeline. A beautiful night for a ride, is it not?"

She grinned. "I couldn't ask for more. Is Simon around?"

"No, he rode with the guard a few hours ago, and hasn't come back. Good thing, he's been like a galla with a stone in its paw since this morning."

Madeline looked toward the end of their party. Simon was talking with Satra. Ridern had slipped a little behind them. She turned back to Zora and asked, "Will you grace us with some music tonight when we stop?"

"If there is an opportunity," Zora answered. "It might be a

good idea to have a song before we try to go over this Severed Pass."

"True. Well, I'll see you later." Madeline cringed inside every time she heard the words Severed Pass, but no warning flush came, so perhaps nothing bad would happen to them.

She slipped back to the second wagon where Callisra was in the driver's seat.

"How are you faring?" Madeline asked.

"It is not so bad on the wagon," Callisra answered. "I am glad I rode here rather than the horse. I will have the energy and strength to do some healing before I sleep tonight."

Madeline tried to imagine the feeling of no pain; it didn't work. "Thank you, but don't wear yourself out. We will probably need you later. I'm expecting that at least Lee will need some help. She looked pretty banged up when I scryed." She turned back to Callisra and realized the woman was holding herself very still. "What is wrong?"

"It is nothing." Callisra's back stiffened.

"No, it isn't. I've never seen you angry before. What has happened?" Madeline shifted in the saddle. "Oh, wait a minute, it must be something to do with Simon. What has he done?"

"Nothing." Callisra sighed. "And that's the problem. I thought we were getting closer. Last night we almost kissed and then he just gave up."

Madeline grinned; Simon wouldn't have given up a kiss for nothing. "Do you want to tell me what happened?"

"He treats me as though I am a child. I can't understand why he is being so stubborn."

Madeline looked around to make sure no one was eavesdropping. Callisra was truly hurt, and she didn't want to make it worse. "It's just that he doesn't know he's ready to settle down."

"Why wouldn't he want to start his own family?" Callisra gave a frustrated sigh. "Is this normal for men from your world?"

Madeline suppressed a laugh. "For some men, yes. But Simon is a good man. You just need to give him some time."

"Why should he need time? It seems to me that he returns my feelings. I don't understand." Callisra's words came out on a hiss of frustration.

Madeline leaned over to pat her arm. "He's been single too long and hasn't felt strongly about anyone. On top of it, he's not used to being famous. He's had too many women throwing themselves at him in the last year."

"It must be good for his ego," Callisra admitted.

"Yes," Madeline answered. "And he's not going to give up his freedom easily." Madeline started to plan what they would do when they got home. Perhaps a dinner party or two would help set the mood for commitment. "Be patient. Jode and I will do what we can to help. But you have to let him come to you. If you push too hard, he will run as far and as fast as he can."

"I will try to be patient, but I am not very good at it." Callisra smiled. "Perhaps I can learn."

Madeline laughed. "Well just make sure you aren't too patient with him after you catch him."

Callisra winked before saying, "True enough, someone has to make sure we get a wedding date set. Well we have a long journey and who knows what will happen to throw us together."

28

*T*he next morning, Madeline stood looking at the pass. From her perspective, it looked steep but manageable. But then, it did take that left twist out of sight about a half mile in.

She turned to see a cluster of people waiting for her; Jode, Simon, Barsh, and Keegan. Running to join them were Elight, and Callisra. It was conference time.

"I'm glad it was too dark to see this when we arrived." She pointed at the turn in the path. "What happens after that turn?"

Jode looked at Keegan who said, "I went up an hour ago. At the turn is a narrow crossing over a chasm. It will be tight, but the wagons will pass."

Barsh nodded. "I went with him and he's right. It will help if we offload some of the heavier cargo."

Madeline started mentally inventorying the contents of the wagons. There was very little they could leave behind. "It will take time to unpack and repack the wagons. Will we still make the summit before dark if we do?"

"We might be able to help there," Simon said. "We talked last night, the band and me. If we can find a way of securing the instruments here, we can share the load between the two wagons."

"That would work," Barsh said before looking at the two wagons parked beside each other. "I'd mix it up. Put most of the food in the smaller wagon and most of the equipment in the other. If everyone else rides or walks, we should be okay."

Madeline looked at Keegan, waiting for an answer to her question. He looked at the pass and the wagons before speaking, "It's not a problem. And we will be saving time on the trip up. If we lighten the load now, it will be less to pack and unpack at the difficult parts of the trail."

Madeline turned to the rest of the group. "If you trust my casting, I can hide the instruments. We should probably try to add any other things we don't need to the pile before I do it." She wished they would agree to leave some of the people behind. Then the instruments could be guarded, rather than trusted to her magical skills. *Argh, you are supposed to be confident.*

Barsh left to organize the wagons.

Madeline turned to Simon. "Are you sure Zora and Gren and the others won't stay? I'm not sure we'll need a musical distraction this time."

Simon shook his head. "We're all committed here. I'm not going to leave you to this alone and the band isn't taking a chance that someone will have an adventure without them."

Jode didn't wait for her to ask about the camp servants. "Madeline, the camp tenders will not leave. In fact, I have to tell you now that I have been less than honest with you."

Madeline waited, her heart clenching. Jode had always been open and honest with her. She trusted that. Did she have to start questioning everything he did?

He continued, "When I put the team together, I asked two of my guards to take on the role of servant. I thought it best to have more force on our side."

Madeline sighed in relief. "That's good thinking. We'll talk about why you didn't tell me before, later. I don't think right now is a good time for that." She added a smile to show she wasn't truly angry. It was Jode's job to protect the camp anyway.

Jode smiled back before saying, "I will leave you then to go arrange the party for defense."

Feeling like a general briefing her army, Madeline turned to look at the remaining people: Elight, Keegan, and Callisra.

"Keegan, are you going to scout ahead again?" He nodded and said he'd range only as far as needed and return frequently to the main party until they got to the top.

She nodded and Keegan ran off up the trail. "Elight, can you find the Choi now?"

"I already did, Lady Madeline. They are moving down the pass." He smiled. "We have caught up. That is a good sign."

She thanked him and suggested he find Mirial, the cook. If he was going to walk up the pass, he would need to be fed.

Elight sprinted across the camp toward the only fire burning during the hustle of packing. Callisra and Madeline were left alone.

"You are doing a really good job, Madeline," Callisra said. "I know that you question your skills, but you are doing well."

Madeline grinned. In her old life, she would look for hidden meanings in the compliment. Here she accepted it because no one had given her any reason not to. When had she become so trusting?

"I suppose I can't convince you to stay on this side of the mountain?" Madeline took Callisra's arm as she spoke and started toward the campfire.

Callisra laughed. "I would not miss the opportunity to woo Simon for the world. And I still feel drawn to this adventure. I wish I knew why. I would prefer to prepare myself than just trust to a feeling."

Madeline thought back to her quest last year. "I know exactly how you feel." She hurried her steps; a hot breakfast was a treat after eating trail food all day yesterday. "Perhaps I can convince Mirial to stay here."

Callisra laughed, "Since there are no other cooks, I think I'll work to convince her to stay. It would be worth dedicating a guard to her for the celebration feast she'll create."

29

"*H*eave," Barsh said. Madeline heard the effort in his voice.

She placed the small barrel of salt to the side of the road and watched as the team of horses strained to pull the wagon out of the rut. Four men were behind putting their strength into lifting the back wheels.

"Okay," Barsh called. "One more, we almost made it. One, two, heave."

Suddenly the wagon popped over the edge of the rut and the horses ran a few steps before Barsh pulled them to a stop.

She wondered how they would have managed if she wasn't able to hide half the load under a spell so they could leave it behind. They were two hours into the climb and this was the second time they had unloaded the wagon to make it easier to pass a deep gouge in the road surface.

Madeline picked up the barrel and handed it to Keegan who had just returned from scouting. "How is it ahead?" she asked as he tossed the barrel to Barsh.

"Better. There's one more place we might have problems. But it's mostly just steep and twisting."

She passed another barrel along for reloading, and returned to her horse. Fortunately, the first wagon was smaller and hadn't gotten stuck. She wiped the sweat from her brow and then mounted. Jode came up beside her and pulled himself onto his horse.

He leaned toward her and tucked a stray lock behind her ear. "We should make better time now. I've asked Keegan to look for a space where we can rest the horses."

"Do you think we'll make the summit early enough to see the road down?" She urged her horse to go a little faster, trying to catch up with the first wagon. "It would be nice to get a handle on what we'll face."

He looked out over the side of the road before answering. Madeline couldn't bring herself to ride at the center of the road, let alone near the drop off. Despite the delays, they were high enough that the drop made her queasy.

Jode returned his attention to her. "Yes, unless something delays us considerably, we will achieve the summit in time to set camp and look down the path a way." He started to say something then clearly thought better of it.

"What?" Madeline dreaded hearing what he was holding back, but knew it was better out now than later.

"It occurs to me we have not discussed protection for tonight. We will be camping in the place where others were torn apart."

Oh, just that. For a moment, she had thought he was going to try to convince her to stay behind – but perhaps that was more wishful thinking than dread. Madeline considered some options. "I wonder what the Choi did. Keegan didn't say anything about finding bodies when he last returned from scouting. I'm sure he would have."

"Let's ask him if there was anything there." Jode turned and called for the tracker. "I do not wish to make plans based on the absence of comment," he said.

When Keegan trotted up, Jode asked if he'd seen evidence of any struggle.

"No, there were no bodies. There was some blood, but not enough to worry me," Keegan said. "I don't know about magic. I can't sense it. Maybe there were too many of them and the Reavers didn't attack."

"Reavers?" Madeline didn't like the sound of that.

Keegan waved his hands dismissively. "It's what some people call whatever chopped up those traders. Probably just a bunch of bandits, and we have enough swords to deal with bandits."

Madeline decided not to pursue the idea of Reavers. "So, the Choi were probably not bothered."

"I can go look closer if you like?" Keegan offered.

Jode shook his head. "No, another strong back will be more valuable here if we run into problems with the wagons."

Keegan nodded and ran back to join Barsh.

"We are not as large a party as the Choi." Madeline paused. By the set of his shoulders, Jode had something more to say. "What?"

"No, we are the same number as the parties that were severed."

Great, someone could have mentioned it before now. "I guess I can do the hiding spell. And we'll have to put out guards." She considered. "Did those others put out guards?"

"There is no way of knowing. But it is probable. Although, perhaps they didn't have guards trained by me."

Madeline chuckled and started to review the spell in her mind. It would be harder to hide the whole group, but not impossible.

THEY ROUNDED the next hairpin turn and saw the musician's wagon lurch over another washed out part of the trail.

Madeline guided her horse through the gouge in the road and

said to Jode, "This is the last break in the road we'll have to deal with according to Keegan – at least on the way up."

They sent the smaller wagon on ahead and dismounted, preparing to start unloading the larger one. Barsh held the horses still while the last two riders crossed. Simon and the final guard dismounted and they checked out the gully in the road.

"Callisra and Madeline, stay here." Simon pointed to the horses. "We'll ferry the contents of the wagon here. You take care of the horses and we'll heave the wagon over."

Madeline was happy not to have to lug barrels. "No problem. That will leave Callisra with the energy to heal any strains, and me with time to think about our protections for tonight."

Jode looked at the wagon and horses. "It would be sensible to have more than one person with the wagon team. Simon and Ridern, you manage the horses and give a pull when we push. Perhaps we can make this time easier and faster."

A half hour later, Madeline and Callisra stood together in front of the contents of the wagon.

Barsh was snapping the reins and hawing at the horses. She couldn't see the people behind, but Simon and Ridern were straining at the halters and talking the beasts into more effort. It looked like the wagon was going to cross on the first try.

The horses cleared the gully. The front of the wagon rose above the lip of the washout. The wheels started to grab dirt, and Madeline let out a sigh of relief.

A crack shattered the air.

Madeline stepped toward the wagon as she saw the back-end skew and start to fall.

Everyone started moving.

Knives flashed about the wagon team cutting all the traces.

Barsh leapt sideways as the wagon slid away toward the edge of the path.

Someone grasped her arm and dragged her to the cliff face; Callisra.

Horses ran past them and up the trail.

As it passed, the last horse kicked the bottom barrel in the stack.

The carefully organized barrels shifted and for a moment Madeline thought they would settle back without further incident. Then one barrel tipped and nudged another, and suddenly, like some horrific domino effect, half of the barrels were bouncing to the edge.

Madeline stepped forward to try stopping the avalanche of supplies, but Callisra pulled her back to the safety of the cliff. This time she kept her grip on Madeline's arm. Madeline turned to thank her and saw Callisra's lips moving, but the thunder of the barrels and shattering of the wagon as it slipped away, drowned out every other sound.

When the noise and dust settled, Madeline looked at the supplies, half the barrels were gone. She looked at the group of men gasping on the path below and counted. Relief washed over her as she realized everyone had survived.

Jode rushed toward her and wrapped her in his arms. "I saw you try to save the barrels, foolish woman." He kissed the top of her head.

"I'm fine." She wiggled out of his arms. "I'm sorry. I know it was dangerous, but I didn't think. All we had to do was watch the barrels and now..."

"Everyone survived. That is important." He placed his hands on her shoulders and looked directly into her eyes. "That is the most important thing."

"If it hadn't been for Callisra, I don't know what I would have done." Madeline turned to her secretary. "You saved my life."

Callisra raised a shaky grin. "Perhaps I did have a purpose for being here."

Madeline grinned in response, her heart slowing now the danger was past.

"Callisra?" Simon called as he limped toward them. "Oh,

thank god. You are not hurt." He grabbed her arm and pulled her toward him. "You are okay, right?"

She beamed and threw her arms around him. "Yes, I am now. But you are not. What happened? Why are you limping? Let me help you."

30

*M*adeline still felt her body shudder with adrenaline later that day when they set up in the summit clearing.

As soon as they had caught their breath, the whole group had rushed to load the remaining supplies onto the smaller wagon and head for the camp.

The wagon team was unsuitable for riding, so Tom and Ridern attached rope leads and brought them into camp. They could be laden with equipment and supplies and used as pack horses.

Barsh, mourning the loss of his wagon, trudged beside Keegan and Elight.

Tom and Wint were taking all of the supplies and trying to make some sense of them, falling back into the role of camp tenders. The other guards were working out a patrol shift and Madeline was pacing to burn off the tension so she could cast the spell to hide them.

She saw Jode walk back toward the treacherous path, and went to join him.

She wove her arm around his. "What is it, love?"

"Perhaps nothing," he answered. "Even so, we cannot check it now."

"Check what?" It concerned her when Jode was like this. He could worry something to death if she didn't get him to talk about it.

He gave her arm a squeeze. "It seems odd to me that the wagon should break at that point after surviving so many bumps and potholes along the way."

"It may just have been damaged earlier on the first gouge." Despite her reassurance, Madeline was beginning to share Jode's worries. If this wasn't an accident, then they had bigger problems. "If it was sabotaged then it's someone in our group."

Jode patted her hand. "I know, but I cannot think who might do something like this. And now I have made you upset with no evidence. Let us put it aside and join the others."

Madeline followed her husband and tried to put the idea of sabotage out of her mind. She rejoined Tom and Wint, asking what they had found.

Tom pointed to the barrels. "We have a couple of day's food supplies, but the extra arms are gone. I doubt we can supplement the food with hunting until we cross back."

She hoped to be back across and in the forests within a day or so. "It should be enough to get us back to where we can find game. We'll be hungry, but not starving. I'm more worried about the armor, do you all have some?"

"Yes, we have one set each. Well, Tom here is missing an arm piece but that is not a major problem. We all have a sword. We carried them with us, not on the wagon."

Madeline was grateful that they would still have the protection of the guards. Now that Tom and Wint had been unmasked, there were plenty to patrol tonight. They would stay within the spell boundary, more to protect them against someone who stumbled in through the wards than anything else. If they were very lucky all of the guards would still be with them on the return journey.

She was mentally rehearsing the spell when Tom jerked and said, "Did you see that?"

"What?" Madeline brought her focus back to the reality of the camp.

"Something moved," Tom said, scanning the sides of the clearing.

Wint turned, sword in hand. "Nothing here. Tom, what exactly did you see?"

Tom pointed to the cliff face where the horses were resting. "Like a bit of the cliff moved."

"Like a landslide about to happen?" Madeline asked. *Or something that is going to tear us apart in our sleep?*

Tom scratched the back of his head. "No, maybe it was just the heat and the excitement; nothing there now."

It didn't make her feel any better, but she forced it out of her mind. It would soon be time to cast the spell and she had to work on her calm, and she was having trouble imagining a sandy warm beach right now.

Looking around to see how best to gather people, she saw Jode talking to Simon and Barsh. She turned to Wint. "Can you start setting up the camp so we are close, please? A circle would be best for the spell."

"Yes, Lady Madeline. A tight circle would be best for patrolling, too." Wint bent to pick up a barrel.

She thanked them and went to join the conversation. It was getting animated; Barsh was holding something and gesturing with it.

"It's definitely been sawed," Barsh said, pointing to the bar of wood he was holding.

Jode placed his hand on the wood and stopped Barsh from waving it around. "It does look that way, but I think this is not the best place or time to raise suspicions in our small group."

"So, it wasn't an accident." Madeline reached for the wood. It looked like part of the wagon wheel. She could see where it was cut. A clean cut halfway through, just waiting for the right stress to rip it in half.

"Jode is right. We should keep this to ourselves. It won't help if everyone is looking over their shoulder. Well, more than they already are." She sighed. "Has anyone checked the other wagon? It will be a very different problem if something happens on the way down. At least we didn't have any fatalities today."

"I've already done that and it's sound. I'll be sleeping next to it tonight. was taking the loss of his wagon badly.

Madeline handed the wood back to him. "No, but we can't panic anyone. We will keep an eye on the situation, and I'll see what I can do to identify who it is. But until we are back on the other side of this mountain range, we have to behave as though we are all working together."

"Can you find any clues from the wood?" Jode asked.

Madeline shook her head. "I tried when I held it, but there's nothing. Throw it on the fire tonight."

Simon slapped Barsh on the back. "Come on, let's get settled in. Madeline needs to put on the protections, and we need to get a good night's sleep."

An hour later, the sun was going down and Madeline was sitting at the center of the group calming and focusing her mind. The guards were standing just inside the edge of where she needed to stretch the protection.

Before setting the spell, Madeline sent her senses out to see if they shared the pass with any other creatures. She only felt the touch of simple thoughts. Probably wildlife, the sense of hunger was strong in the contact.

She drew in her focus and started to speak the words that would hide them from anyone who might come looking, or scrying. The spell settled gently, and Madeline relaxed. Just as she tied off the last of the power, she heard a hiss and spit of sound.

Probably a cat hunting for dinner, she thought.

31

*S*kye was sitting in her tent eating her evening meal of grains and berries. She would eat no meat until after the ceremony.

They had arrived at the temple in the early afternoon and now the camp was settling down. Here in an hour or so, the chill would rob the heat from the tent, but for now she would enjoy the feeling of comfort.

A breeze made her look up from the bowl. Ophian entered her tent and bowed low. He was trembling.

She put aside her dinner and held out her hands to him. "Sit, and calm yourself. What has made you so agitated?"

Ophian kissed her cheek as he sat. "We have company approaching. It seems that we were being followed after all. We have had a report of someone crossing Severed Pass. We expect them to camp at the summit tonight. That means they will be here tomorrow. It is too close to the ceremony for me to believe it coincidence."

Skye felt cold fear spread from her stomach, but she was the Greatmother and had learned long ago to hide her emotions. "It is not sure that they will survive the night. Perhaps they do not know how to propitiate the Tryll. Most beings do not even know the Tryll exist."

Ophian smoothed his robes. "And if they do. They will be here tomorrow, the day before the ceremony. I worry that there will be a disturbance and our plans will come to naught."

Skye refused to allow any doubt to enter her mind. "We have sufficient fighters to protect us. Do not fear; you will be raised to leadership and we will be together. No one can stop this."

"I only worry about the ceremony saving our people." He looked away as he spoke, but Skye saw a smile cross his face.

She burned with her love for him. "What details do we have about this party? Do we have any idea who they might be?"

"A small party of mostly humans." Ophian reached a tentative hand to touch Skye's knee.

She patted his hand. "They are weak humans. I do not think this is something to concern you."

"It seems the other woman from across the world barrier is leading them. I worry that she has some affinity with the sacrifice. That there will be trouble. That I will not... I mean, that we will not save our people."

Why did he withhold that information? Skye sighed. "Very well. When you leave, send a few of the men to see who is there, and perhaps stop them." She took his hand and stroked the palm.

If the woman had come to rescue Lee Marshall, it would be better to have her die on the summit.

---

32

*M*adeline glanced around the group of travelers. Everyone was eating breakfast; an odd blend of ingredients that Mirial had combined into a hash. Relief was evident in the laughter that echoed off the mountain. They had survived the night and now were preparing to start the last stage of the rescue. In short order, they would be going down the mountain. By morning, she hoped they would be back at this camp, with Lee and other captives.

She turned to Jode and said, "I think we should send some people back. I know we've had this conversation before, but now we have no food and that makes a difference."

"What difference?" Jode looked at her and shrugged. "If you can convince some people to go, I will be happy."

"If we send everyone except you, me, and Ridern, or one of the other guards, we can move fast. The others can go back to the bottom and hunt while they wait for us."

Jode frowned and then said, "That might work, well on some of them anyway." He called everyone together so Madeline could try to convince them.

When Madeline shared her plan, she was disappointed to see

everyone shake their head. "Look, if you stay with us, you are in danger. I can't be worried about you when I go get Lee."

"Who's going to get between you and Lee if she starts with the sniping?" Simon asked. "You know she's going to say something that will set you off."

Madeline stamped her foot. "I will exercise some self-control."

Everyone chuckled.

Madeline suppressed her own smile and said, "What? I'm not some crazy woman. I can control myself."

Zora was the first to speak. "Simon has been sharing some of the stories. I do not think anyone would have self-control enough to stay polite around that woman. I suspect her first words will be 'why have you taken so long.'"

"She's not that ungrateful." Madeline found it strange to defend Lee, after all Zora was probably right.

He continued, "We will also not agree to miss the epic end to this adventure."

When the laughter died down, Callisra added her comments, "I will be needed. It is unlikely this will be done without injury. I can heal people enough to survive the climb back up here."

"Do you still feel the compulsion?" Simon asked, and Madeline hoped for an ally in protecting at least one of their party.

"There is something drawing me," Callisra said. "But it is not that powerful." Simon started to talk, but Callisra held up a hand. "I am coming. Please do not force me to follow you alone."

"I agree I am not needed," Mirial said. "But I would rather come with you than go back down alone."

Madeline threw her hands up in surrender. "Fine, at least let's leave everything but the horses here. That way we can travel light."

The wagon horses were each attached by lead to a rider, because Madeline was not going to leave anything living on the summit to be torn apart. Blankets provided padding to anyone wishing to ride.

All of the water and wine was poured into the skins everyone carried, and bags of oats were hung on the saddles. All that was left was for a concealment spell, and then they would set off.

"Give me a minute," she said to Jode. "Have everyone move out of the way. I'll do the spell and we can go."

33

*S*imon took a deep breath. He needed to gather his courage before speaking to Callisra. He never thought he would be in this position, but it was time.

He walked to where she was standing, admiring how she could be so poised. Not many women he knew would be willing to spend time on the trail and face danger as though it was just another event in the day. That included women in this world as well as the old one.

I may have been looking for the wrong kind of woman. Simon paused for a moment, still needing to build courage. Then he stepped forward and said, "Callisra, I need to talk to you."

"Of course, Simon, but if you are going to try to convince me to go back, you are wasting your breath. I will not leave just when there may be need for my skills." She smiled at him, but he still felt the weight of her conviction in her words.

"No." He hesitated. Now not sure how to start. *Grow up, man.* He wanted to be smooth, like he always was with women. He just couldn't remember how. It was like high school, when he was the shortest guy in class and no girls would even look at him.

"Well, what is it you wish to say? We do not have much time." She stared at him, and he noticed her green eyes darken.

"I..." He took another breath. "Okay, yesterday, when the horse bolted, I saw them head for you... and I..." He gave himself a mental kick. "I thought you were going to die. It felt like my world was about to end. I want to make sure you know that if we survive, I think we should be a couple."

She smiled at him and all his worries faded from sight.

Putting her hand on his arm, she said, "I have not kept my interest a secret. If by 'being a couple' you mean we should announce our intention to marry, then we can do that when we return to Lady Arabela's."

He felt the words, 'slow down, I didn't say marriage' form in his mind, but then he realized that was exactly what he meant; marriage, kids, growing old together.

Jode's voice calling his name broke through his thoughts. He leaned in and gave Callisra a quick kiss on the cheek. "Yes, we can talk about everything later."

As he crossed to join Jode, Simon heard Zora speaking, "Who won? Did anyone have an earlier date than me? Gren, where is the pool?"

Simon didn't wait to hear the response.

34

*M*adeline cast the spell to hide what they were leaving in the camp. When she was done, she stood and turned to see Jode standing with the guards, something held their attention.

Then Ridern shouted.

Madeline turned to look where he pointed. There was no one there. Unsure what the problem was, she looked for Simon. He was running toward the trail head. She scanned the area, no Callisra, no musicians, no Elight. They had been standing at the entrance to the trail when she started casting the spell. Did she cast too wide?

She ran to join Simon. "What happened?"

Simon ignored her.

She looked back at Jode and saw him run toward her. "Jode, what happened?"

He came to a stop beside her. "They disappeared. After you cast the spell, they suddenly weren't there."

"I can undo the spell," Madeline said. "I must have cast it too large."

Jode shook his head. "No, it was not your spell. They were there when the barrels disappeared. Then they were not."

Keegan approached and said, "There are tracks. A scuffle, and then the tracks show they went down the trail but disappear after a few yards. As if they went onto the rocks or flew away."

"Did you see any other path?" Madeline tried to calm her thoughts so she could formulate a plan to carry out two rescues.

Keegan chewed his lip, a sure sign he was thinking. "No, and I do not know of one, but there may be something if you cross the boulders."

"They did not make a sound when they disappeared. That does not bode well," Jode said.

Simon rushed back from the trail head. "Madeline," he gasped. "We have to do something. I can't lose her now. And my friends. We have to do something."

She wrapped her arm around his shoulders. "I know. We will find them. We'll split up. And we'll find them."

Jode sent two guards to gather the horses. "Simon, we have enough people to form two parties. Keegan will go with you and a guard."

Simon started to run back to the trail, but Jode reached for his arm. "Wait, Simon. You need to wait. Keegan will be the best one to lead you. He will know what signs to look for."

Madeline saw Simon close his eyes and take a deep breath. His body relaxed and color returned to his face. "Please, Simon, be careful."

Simon opened his eyes and nodded. "I will. I promise I won't go crazy. But I just told her I that I was in love with her. I can't just let her disappear."

Madeline gave him another hug and then turned to her mount.

Jode took the reins of his horse. "Double up the horses and we will take them down with us. We will leave the extra mounts at the foot of the path. Those going to find our friends may have to travel where horses cannot."

Madeline felt Simon relax a little as the plans came together. "We don't need all the guards," she said. "We will take Barsh and Mirial with us. You take Axel and Satra to guard you."

Jode nodded his approval of her plan. "We can spare one more guard."

"No, you will need protection when you get to the Choi camp," Satra said. He shifted his sword so that it hung on his back. "We'll move faster as a small party. It will not take long. I'm sure we will meet you at the base of the trail."

Keegan led the four members of the rescue party at a run.

Madeline crossed her fingers that Satra was right and they would find their missing friends within a day.

35

*D*espite Madeline's worry, they reached the bottom of the trail without a major disaster. It was late afternoon and the party was resting in a shallow notch in the side of the mountain, if it had a roof, it would be a cave.

On the way down, Jode had pointed out the mark Keegan must have left for them. He was leading the other team along a narrow track that crossed the side of the mountain. Madeline thought they must have seen some trail to follow, good luck for a change.

As they rounded the last turn in the trail, she'd seen a camp in the distance. A large colorful tent confirmed it was the Choi.

She sat with her back against the cool stone of the shaded side of the notch and looked at the people with her. Mirial and Barsh would stay with the horses and Tom would guard them. The rescue party would be Jode, Ridern, Wint, and herself. If that wasn't enough, so be it.

"How long until it's dark enough to go?" Madeline was anxious to get started because they didn't know if the sacrifice would start at midnight tonight, or sunset tomorrow – just that it would start tomorrow.

"We have about two hours before the sun starts to fall. I am not sure how quickly the light goes here," Jode answered from where he stood at the entrance to their shelter.

She hadn't thought of that. Would darkness fall as the sun fell behind the mountain? Was that west? She had lost track of their direction in the twists of the mountain pass.

"We should take turns resting," she said. "I have a feeling we will need every ounce of energy we can summon to finish this. And I want it done quickly if we can."

Tom waved the others to the shade. "You get some rest. Guarding this space won't take too much, so I'll keep my eye out now."

They arranged themselves to take advantage of the cool stone. Jode sat beside Madeline and put his arm around her shoulders. "We will succeed. I know you are capable of this."

She nestled into him, not feeling the same confidence. "How do you know? I keep telling myself to be confident, but I just feel like it's going to be luck, not skill, if we succeed."

Jode gave her a squeeze. "I know because you have shown how able you are. You saved my life." Jode held up a finger. "You stopped Sayer Goddard from taking the Summer Lands." He held up a second finger. "When it comes to the crisis, you stop questioning and just do what needs to be done."

She smiled at him. "I will keep that in mind. Now, I can't sleep, so I think I'll try to get in touch with Blu. He might have some ideas about how we get through this." She pulled out the scrying glass. "And, I guess I should bring him up to date anyway."

He kissed her and then settled down to nap.

Madeline used Lee's scarf to polish the mirror. Still basking in Jode's admiration, she visualized the sandy beach and started to bring Blu's image into her mind.

She called his name and waited. He would be aware of her call, so he would answer when he was able.

After what felt like an hour, but could well have been only a couple of minutes, Blu's face looked out from the glass. "Hello, Madeline. I am happy to see your face. I have been wondering how you fare."

"We survived Severed Pass. But before we talk about what has happened here, tell me how is Tadric?"

Blu smiled. "All is well. I still hold the wards tight, but it seems that there is no enemy in the household now."

Madeline wasn't sure how to interpret that. "Now?"

"It seems there are three people who have left the household with no notice. It is not unusual for this to happen. But in the circumstances, I think we are justified in assuming one, or more, of them were responsible for the child's illness."

Madeline shook her head. "I thought everyone loved Arabela. Who could be behind this?"

"There are some who believe they should lead the Summer Lands," Blu's voice was regretful. "And there may be some aspect we do not know about."

"If you have it under control, we can talk about that in a few days when I am there," Madeline said.

"Indeed." Blu peered at her. "But you did not call to ask about our problems."

Madeline gave Blu an update and the monk listened intently. He paused before speaking. "So, it seems that something lives at the summit. I think it's possible that the Choi took your companions. They must be aware of your presence."

"Assuming that seems the prudent approach. Do you have any ideas about how I get through the next day?" Madeline mentally crossed her fingers.

"Ideas to help you with the Choi? Or to help find your friends?"

"Hmm." She hoped she didn't have to choose. "You have suggestions for both?"

Blu grinned. "I do not. I was simply wondering what you would say."

She laughed and felt some of the tension leave her shoulders. "I guess we'll figure it out."

"Do you have a plan? Perhaps I can help you with the final details."

Madeline wished he could cast spells over the mountains and save her the anxiety. "I was planning to sneak in and liberate Lee. Then sneak back out."

He tapped his lips. "Do you not think they will be guarding her?"

"Well, I am getting really good at the hiding spell. I thought I would try placing it on us and seeing if we could move within it."

"A very good idea." Blu held up his finger. "Wait. Let me check to see if there is anything in Arabela's library." He slipped from view.

Madeline tried to come up with a plan B while she waited. If the spell didn't work, and she would test it before they left, they would most likely have to capture some Choi guards and force them to help.

Blu appeared again in the glass. "Yes, here it is. You must cast the spell on something that can be shared among all of the people you wish to hide. A piece of paper will suffice. Then you tear the paper and each person carries their piece as long as you need them to be invisible."

Madeline was surprised that he had found something so quickly, and that it was useful. So far, the fates had thrown every barrier they could find in her way. "I may have grasped some of the theory of magic. Now all I have to do is get just as good with the practice."

Blu nodded. "I have told you more than one time that your biggest barrier is inside. Now when you are within the spell, do not allow your companions to get out of your sight. If they do, the spell will fade for them."

"Thank you."

Blu's smile dropped. "How have you planned to ensure the Choi do not fade to nothing."

"I can't think of anything. I don't know their magic." She looked over at Jode, he slept deeply beside her. She lowered her voice to a whisper just in case. "I have not said anything to the others, but I plan to return as soon as we have Lee safe and talk to the Choi about that."

Blu frowned. "That will be very dangerous. Are you prepared to die in this woman's place?"

"No. I will not do that." *Not for Lee Marshall anyway.* "But I can't think of anything else. And, I am trained to negotiate disputes. Do you think I can give them blood from someone else?"

Blu shook his head. "I also do not know blood magic enough to answer that. I do know that you are the first person to travel from your world to ours. So, the last time they worked this ceremony, they did something other than this."

"Good point." Madeline yawned. "I think my best approach right now would be to get some sleep. I will speak with you tomorrow, when this is finished."

LATER MADELINE SEARCHED her bags for something to hold the spell. Lee's Hermes scarf was tempting, but it was too difficult to separate, and it might have to go with Lee when she went back. She found a light scarf of her own and had Jode slice it into four parts. One of the men would carry Lee out of the camp so she would be invisible without having to be convinced to carry a scrap of fabric.

Keeping together and running low, they slipped through the outer defenses of the Choi camp. Madeline was behind the guards and Jode was following her. There were bedrolls laid out in concentric circles with a central building. It looked like the temple to some Greek god – all columns and stairs.

The brightly colored tent stood to the right of the temple, and a small dust colored tent stood on the other side. Madeline hoped Lee was still inside and not tied to some sacrificial stake ready to be bled.

Jode pointed to the tent and then to two Choi standing near the entrance. Ridern and Wint slipped in closer, staying within Madeline's line of sight.

The two guards returned and reported that the Choi were paying attention but not particularly alert. Madeline whispered to them, "I'll go to the tent, stay close." She waited until they nodded. "We can't go through the front, even invisible. We won't be able to disguise the tent opening."

"The back?" Jode whispered. "You can cut a slit and slide in. There is no one there."

Madeline felt the tension in her gut tighten. "We'll need to scout more. I don't like just rushing in."

"We can move closer." Ridern traced a path in the dust with his finger, pointing from the edge of one campfire to another. "If we stop at that wagon, we will have a wide view of the camp. We can see if anyone is heading toward the tent, and if there are any hindrances to cutting the canvas."

Looking across to the wagon, Madeline nodded. "Okay. Keep close."

They moved carefully. Although invisible, they would be found out if someone stumbled, or bumped into a Choi. They arrived at the wagon and Madeline breathed a quiet sigh. Ridern was right. They could see a good third of the camp.

Jode tapped her shoulder. "No one is paying attention. Go now."

Madeline reached into the scabbard at her side and drew out the knife. Looking at it she flashed on the memory of the Dray trio who had cut through the back of her tent last year. They were invisible at the time and hadn't seemed to question their ability.

She reached back and grabbed Jode's hand, giving it a quick squeeze before she left. He squeezed back and let go.

Shifting her weight, Madeline focused on the tent.

Then Jode jerked her back to him. His hand on her mouth stifled her squawk of surprise.

"Look," he whispered, pointing to her left.

Madeline tried to calm her racing heart while her gaze followed Jode's finger. In the light of the fires scattered across the path, Callisra was striding toward the colored tent, two Choi followed.

"What the hell?"

"Hush, love, there must be an explanation." Jode's words didn't dispel the feeling of betrayal that flooded Madeline's heart.

The two guards slid their swords out and stood ready to fight. Madeline shook her head and patted the air to let them know to be at ease. "Jode is right. There must be an explanation. Head for the edge of that temple. I'll be able to keep you hidden and get close enough to listen in."

She didn't wait for them to speak, just crouched low and ran toward the tent.

ee shivered in her tent, cold, and since the light had been sucked out of the world, more alone than she had ever been. The noises outside the tent had ebbed and flowed before, but now there was a pattern, as though people moved purposely to and fro. She had not seen Skye for hours. Was this the time she had been talking about earlier?

She wished someone would tell her what was going to happen. If she knew what was going to happen, she could figure out a way to stop it. "I don't care how weird these people are, no matter what cult they are in, I can talk them out of doing something drastic. Then I'll find a way back to civilization and back home."

Lee sighed as a vision of her home floated through the pain. It was beautiful, on the river and high up. She had a designer come in and create a space just for her, black furniture, cream paint, and white marble. If she concentrated, she could taste a sip of wine from the cellar she kept stocked.

When she got home, she would make sure someone brought these people to justice. They were going to spend the rest of their lives in prison. They were going to be very sorry they kidnapped her.

"I am going to get home." She struggled against the bonds, but they held just as fast as every time before.

The sounds of the camp faded again. Lee could hear her guards chatting. "The feast is going to be magnificent. I hear the last time we went through this, they ate for three days."

Lee was grateful they spoke English – there was no way a translation spell existed. If she'd been stranded here with some foreign crazies, not understanding a word they said, she would have gone mad. As it was, she was starting to lose it. "They must have slipped me some drugs. I must have hallucinated the flowers on my arm." She groaned. "I've never talked to myself so much. That's not a good sign."

The pain in her shoulders from pulling against the ropes, screamed again as she moved. Lee bit back the moan. She wasn't going to give them the satisfaction of knowing how much pain she was in.

She stared at the dusty gray walls of the tent. Her only view for what had seemed like weeks. The campfires had been lit. She recognized the flicker of light on the fabric.

Her mouth watered at the aroma of roasting meats and some kind of aromatic herb. Whatever these people were, they knew how to cook.

If they were preparing a feast, perhaps this would be over soon. As she tried to shift to a less painful position, having given up on comfortable days ago, the tent flap was thrown back and a man stepped in.

"Are you prepared?" he asked.

Lee didn't answer, hoping he would fill the silence. It had worked for her in the past, in court, and at parties.

He simply smiled. "I see you do not understand what is about to happen to you when we perform the rite of Ascension." When she still didn't speak, he bent close to whisper, "You will be dead by the time the sun is half risen. We will kill you, but as your life flows with the blood from your veins, we will drain the precious liquid for the power it holds."

Her breath came in ragged gasps, the shock robbing her of the ability to speak when she wanted desperately to do so. *This is not real.*

"Greatmother said you should not know when it will happen, that the surprise would increase the power. But I think she is growing afraid in her old age. I think your power will be sweeter if you stew in your fear. Only a few hours remain." With the last word, he spun and left the tent.

Lee tried to grasp what he told her. She was going to die. Her body started to shake and she couldn't stop it. The trembling sent new shocks of pain through her joints, but nothing could penetrate the fear that blanked out her thoughts. The flowers on her arm, the translation spell, a sacrifice, it was all real.

She was going to die. There was no rescue on its way, no SWAT team, and no hope.

37

As she approached, Madeline realized she didn't know if the spell would protect her from being silhouetted against the fabric of the tent. It wasn't canvas, like Lee's. It was more like silk; shiny slick and thin. Madeline could make out the shapes of the people inside, so they might be able to do the same.

Looking to make sure Jode and the two guards were close enough that the spell would hold, she crouched and ran the last few feet. When she arrived, she lay on the ground. From that position, she could just place her head next to the fabric and still be taken for uneven ground if she could be seen from the inside – probably.

At first her heart was pounding so loud she couldn't make out any words, just sounds of murmuring. She concentrated on calming herself. Her heart slowed and she was able to make out the individual voices, then the words.

"Let the prisoner enter," a woman's voice commanded. "Let us see if we can gain information before we find another use for her and the others."

A male voice murmured something, but his words were unclear, as though he mumbled.

Something itched at Madeline's stomach. She hoped it was a bug not a spell. She pushed aside the concern, having managed to learn to ignore crawling bugs in the last year.

"Who are you, woman?" the voice asked.

Callisra stated her name and asked, "And your name madam?"

"You have the honor of addressing Skye Greatmother of the Choi," the man's voice snapped. "Do not be insolent."

"Ophian," Skye spoke over the final words. "Do not concern yourself. She will be punished well enough."

He muttered something Madeline couldn't hear.

"You traveled with a band of thieves," Skye stated. "Tell me when they plan to attack, and I will spare you."

"I did not travel with thieves. You captured me and my friends from a peaceful party of traders." Callisra's voice was clear and calm.

Madeline smiled.

"Do not pretend with me. A party of traders would not come over Severed Pass. There is no profit that would be worth the risk," Skye said. "I have felt your mage's touch against my barriers. You have been scouting a way to steal our treasure."

There was no response.

She spoke again, the volume of her voice rising. "Do not defy me woman. If you do not tell me what I need to know, I will sacrifice your friends one at a time, beginning with the Fay spawn."

"I have nothing to tell you, madam." Callisra's words brought a hiss from the tent. Madeline couldn't tell whether it was Skye, or someone near her.

In the silence that followed, Madeline worked out her next steps. If the musicians and Elight were captive here, then it was only a matter of time before the rescue party arrived.

A tickle started in her nose. She pressed on her upper lip to suppress the sneeze. Invisible or not, sneezing would alert everyone that there was more than just a mound of earth outside the tent. She pressed harder as the tickle continued. If she was captured, Jode and the guards would appear as soon as they took her into the tent.

Her eyes watered with the strain of not sneezing. Then it passed as suddenly as it came.

"So, you will not speak." The Choi woman was clearly not used to being thwarted. "Then you leave me no choice. Prepare yourself and your companions. I will be conducting more than one sacrifice today."

Madeline was getting ready to retreat back to the four men waiting for her when someone else spoke.

"Do not overwork yourself my love." It was the one Skye had called Ophian. The words came out as wheedling and Madeline recognized the tone. When she heard it in court, it always came from someone looking for a favor.

"Do not fret about me, Ophian. When we are finished with the rite of Ascension, we will have all the power we need. I plan to save these new ones until I get the information I need."

"You are, as usual, wiser than I am." The voice was so oily and insincere that Madeline wondered why the woman didn't realize he was lying.

Well maybe that's how they speak to each other.

Skye's voice broke through Madeline's thoughts. "I think that woman would make a suitable candidate for your first sacrifice. She will bring much power to you. We will see about the others, perhaps we will hold them."

Madeline slid back into the shadows and returned to the waiting men.

"WE HAVE A PROBLEM," Madeline said when they had pulled back out of the camp to a safe place to talk. "Well, make that more problems."

She told them what she'd heard in the tent. "As I see it, we need to rescue Lee and the others and make sure that Simon doesn't stumble into the middle of a fight to rescue Callisra and the rest."

Ridern looked back toward the Choi camp. "We are already spread thin. Four of us are going to find it difficult to mount three separate campaigns."

"Are we still assuming they may start their ceremony at midnight?" Wint was looking at the sky. "We don't have long."

Madeline considered before speaking. "They don't seem to be preparing for a ceremony. But then, I don't know if they need to make preparations. Damn, I wish I had more information."

Jode patted her hand. "It would not make a difference. Even the best plans change when the battle starts. I suggest we assume that Lee Marshall is in the most danger."

Madeline looked at Wint. He was usually quiet and willing to follow orders, but she knew that Jode's knights were all capable of leadership whether they were acting as simple guards or mounting a campaign. He was looking past them to the camp and then scanning the whole area before turning to look at the mountain behind. It was a minute or two before he spoke.

"I don't see any Choi scouts outside the camp. That might mean they are invisible as we are, but I've not seen any footprints either." He pointed to the sand around them. Madeline saw a clear trail of disturbed sand.

"Have we left a trail behind like that?" she asked.

Jode shook his head. "No, I made sure one of us disguised our trail. We cannot be followed from the camp. This trail only goes a few feet away."

Madeline made a mental note to remember about the footprints next time she had to use the spell. "Go on Wint."

"If there's no scouts we could leave Mirial and Barsh unguarded and bring Tom with us." Wint was drawing a circle in the dust as he spoke. "Lady Madeline, you and Sir Jode can go rescue your friend. One of us, maybe Tom, could patrol the likely path for Keegan to follow and intercept them. Ridern and I can find the other captives and rescue them." As he spoke, he drew points on the circle.

Madeline's heart sank. "But I can't keep you concealed if we split up like that."

"We have the skills to sneak in and out of this camp." Ridern turned and drew their attention to the camp in front of them. "It is not a military camp. If it were, there would be clear lines of sight. The wagons would be used as a barrier or they would be together and well-guarded. See how the wagons are spread through the camp? See how few tents there are?"

Madeline nodded.

Ridern continued, "Callisra and the others will be in one of the tents. It is easier to contain them in a confined space than around a fire. We can use the cover of the wagons and those piles of supplies to get to the tents."

Jode pointed to the side of the mountain. "Simon and the others will have to come down the mountain somewhere. My guess is that they will have returned to the path and Tom only need, patrol this area." His hand swept to either side of the trail. "The rest is too steep for the Choi to have brought captives down."

"There's one thing that worries me," Madeline said.

Jode chuckled. "Only one thing?"

"Well, let's focus on one thing." Madeline suppressed her anxiety. "Somehow Callisra and the others were taken in front of our eyes. Someone is using a concealment spell, and we could be walking into a trap."

"This is true," Jode said. "Do you have a way to expose someone if they are protected in this way?"

"Not that I can think of." Madeline sighed. "Okay, I'll accept that we can't plug every hole. If any of us get captured, then all bets are off. We fight, and hope that is enough."

The three men nodded.

"Since I don't have training in sneaking in and out of camps, I will conceal Jode, myself, and Lee when we have her. I'll need to recast the spell because it's keyed to four people and I can't be sure it will work on just three. Does anyone have something I can use?"

Wint pulled a fine linen handkerchief from his pocket and handed it to her. "This is the first time a woman's favor has actually been of help." He grinned. "Well, help with more than gaining a kiss or..." He waggled his eyebrows.

Madeline shook her head. "I'll be sure to let the lady know." She chuckled at Wint's expression. "Go get Tom in place and then start your part. I'll cast the spell, and then Jode and I will get Lee as quickly as possible. We'll meet back where Barsh and Mirial are hiding."

"Good luck," Jode said, nodding at Wint.

"And to you," the guard responded before slipping away.

38

*M*adeline watched as Wint and Ridern moved closer to the camp. They were heading for the side farther away from Lee's tent. After only a few yards, the darkness swallowed them. She turned to face Jode again.

"Give me a second to work the spell," she said.

She was able to cast the spell almost instantaneously, but she needed time to chase the scattered worries out of her mind so she felt comfortable that the casting would work. She realized that the worries were about Lee and Callisra and all the other members of their party. The usual worry that the spell would fail was gone. She knew she was capable of casting it perfectly.

I can't wait to get back and let Blu know.

She whispered the words and set the spell. When it was complete, she tore the handkerchief into three and stuffed two of the pieces in her pocket. "Here," she said, handing Jode the other piece. "Let's go."

"Do you remember where we entered the camp?" Jode asked. When she nodded, he continued, "You lead. I will do my best to brush our footprints away."

Madeline ran lightly to the edge of the camp, near a wagon that reeked of sour wine.

As she ran, she kept glancing back to make sure she hadn't outpaced Jode. Each time she looked, she saw him running close, dragging his jacket on the ground behind him.

They caught up to each other and paused beside the wagon. "It's busier now," she said quietly.

"Yes, but see, they are all moving between the temple and the supplies." Jode pointed along their path. "It is a matter of timing. Most of the activity is on the other side of the camp. Ridern and Wint will need to take more care than we will."

Madeline watched the bustle of the Choi and saw what Jode meant. Only a few groups of Choi were moving on their side of the camp. As long as they avoided contact, it would be easy. "If Lee is still in the tent, we'll be okay. As long as... well, you know what I mean."

"Yes, but it will soon be done. And then we will have a whole list of other things to worry about."

Madeline covered her mouth to stifle the laugh his words brought. "It does seem like adventure follows us around."

Jode checked the path. "Then we should hurry to finish this one. Go."

The distance from the wagon to Lee's tent was not far, but Madeline felt like she had traveled for hours because she had to keep stopping for Choi who moved supplies to and fro. One instance had her holding her breath and her knife when a Choi walked between her and Jode. She had no idea if the spell would snap. But it held.

They stopped beside the last wagon and Lee's tent was only a few yards away. Madeline could see the guards still at their post. They were chatting now not as vigilant. Madeline felt less anxious about approaching the back of the tent.

She took Jode's hand and said, "I'll go in, you stay outside. If someone approaches, you can come in and get us."

He nodded, and Madeline led him to the edge of the tent.

Madeline tiptoed a few steps and then came to a halt.

Pressing herself as tight as she could to Jode, she sucked in her stomach to avoid the touching the guard who had walked around Lee's tent, his loose clothes flapping in his wake.

She felt Jode tense and gripped her sword tighter, waiting for his signal. Jode didn't move.

Madeline's heart thudded so loudly that she was sure the Choi guard would turn and grab both of them. He walked slowly past them, a flap of his jacket brushing her shoulder. Relieved that he hadn't noticed, Madeline only just pulled her foot out of the way in time to avoid tripping him.

The guard had stopped and turned back the way he had come.

He sniffed the air and looked directly into her eyes. Madeline swallowed and lifted her sword arm in preparation. She felt Jode shift back from her and knew he was getting ready to swing his own weapon.

The guard took a step toward them and sniffed again. He cocked his head to the side and frowned.

He took another step toward her, and another sniff.

Suddenly his eyes lit and his face split in a wide grin.

Moving more quickly, he ran past, missing the point of her knife by an inch.

"Ossah," he shouted as he rounded the tent. "They've started roasting the celebration meats."

"You should stay undercover of the spell. Just don't go anywhere." Madeline didn't hear the response as she let a breath go and heard the tremor in it. Jode gave her a gentle push and she moved to the back of the tent.

She felt to make sure there was nothing leaning against it. It would be a pity to slice Lee open during the rescue. Holding the blade in both hands because she was still shaking from the adrenaline release, Madeline cut a four-foot slice into the fabric and slipped through the opening.

It was dark inside the tent. Madeline squeezed her eyes shut and tried to get her night vision working. She couldn't hazard a light because the glow would definitely shine through the canvas and alert the guards.

She could hear them speaking about the coming feast, excited as children on Christmas Eve. Madeline listened but there was no hint of when the ceremony was going to happen. She knew that it must be soon, so she needed to get going.

Opening her eyes, she saw shapes in shades of dark gray, much better than just a black hole.

There was a heavy barrel in the center of the tent. She could see Lee tied to the barrel. Her head hung forward, hair falling around her face. Lee was unconscious. Madeline dropped the two pieces of linen so that she would be visible.

It might be better that she was. Madeline was sure Lee wouldn't be expecting to see her right now. And that Lee would find a way to make Madeline wish she hadn't come to the rescue

Stepping close, Madeline lifted Lee's hair with one hand and covered her mouth with the other. Then she tilted Lee's head so she could see who was rescuing her.

Lee's eyes opened.

Madeline said, "Don't make a sound."

Lee's eyes went wide, and Madeline felt her gasp between her fingers.

Lee blinked, and then she nodded.

Madeline waited a few seconds, making sure that Lee wasn't going to argue. Then she took her hand away.

"You look like crap, Lee," she said.

Lee chuckled and it ended in a groan. "I didn't have time to put my makeup on this morning." Her spirit was clearly not broken.

Madeline hoped Lee's body wasn't too badly damaged either. If they had to carry her away from the camp, it would be harder now that there were only two rescuers.

Lee blinked again, and then said, "What are you doing here? You went missing a year ago."

"Time for that story when we get you out of here." Madeline felt behind Lee. She was secured with rope, not chain. Things were going her way for a change.

"Are you sure you can get me out? There are a lot of them." Lee shifted so that Madeline could get to the rope more easily.

Madeline picked up her knife and Lee flinched. "Don't worry. I know how to use it. I won't cut you if you don't get in the way."

She sawed through the ropes, keeping her ears open for any changes in the guards' chatter. When she was free, Lee slumped forward then righted herself breathing deeply.

Madeline helped Lee to stand. "We'll get you out. If you can walk it will help."

"I think I can, but give me a minute." She started shaking her hands and rolling her shoulders. "Who's we?"

Madeline said, "My husband and some of his guards. But we have other people to rescue tonight, so we don't have time to catch up."

39

*M*adeline looked Lee over, wishing Callisra was here to heal her a little.

"Can you move?" Madeline asked. She knew Lee would do whatever it took, but the woman had been tied up for days. By the look of her wrists, she'd actually been tied to that barrel most of the time.

"Does it matter?" Lee bounced on the balls of her feet, her face white.

Madeline pushed Lee gently back down before she fainted.

The sounds outside hadn't changed. Jode had not given a hint that they had to move quickly. If they could let Lee recover a bit more, then she would be able to move on her own, as opposed to half carrying her the way she was now.

"Yes, it matters. We need to get out without being noticed. I have a way, but it would be easier if you can move under your own steam."

"They were planning to sacrifice me," Lee whispered. "I don't know where I am, but maybe somewhere in Arizona, or near Drumheller. It's pretty dry and deserty out there."

Madeline started to answer but Lee kept talking.

"I don't know what kind of cult these people belong to, but they've done some kind of body modification. And a weird tattooing that makes them look pink."

"It's not a tattoo." Madeline couldn't think of a better way to tell Lee. "Didn't you notice that you came to a different –"

"Someone must have dropped something in my drink," Lee interrupted. "One minute I'm having a martini at Mulligan's and the next I'm lying in the middle of this clearing in a forest. Then I get dragged through a trail, and over a mountain, and now I'm here in the middle of the Mojave and some crazy old woman is telling me she's going to steal my blood, and then you show up with a machete." Lee's voice started to rise.

Madeline put her finger to Lee's lips. "Don't panic, but you need to believe this. You are in another world. This isn't the Mojave or any other desert you know." She waited to see if Lee would say anything. When Lee just blinked, Madeline continued, "The crazy old lady is not human, she is Choi. They are a magical race that needs blood to raise power." Madeline watched Lee turn white and stopped talking to push the woman's head between her knees.

Lee struggled weakly against Madeline's hand. "I'm fine. You are just part of the hallucination."

"Sorry, Lee. It isn't a hallucination. And we have to get out of here." She pointed to the two pieces of handkerchief she'd dropped near the slit in the back of the tent. "When we go, I'll give you one of those. You'll be invisible while you hang on to it and stay close to me."

Lee opened her mouth, but Madeline kept speaking, "I can do magic here. I put a concealment spell on the cloth. My husband is outside waiting for us. We are going to leave here and then get some help sending you home." She paused for breath and then continued, "You can argue with me later if you want, but can you just follow instructions for a while?"

Lee nodded; a shocked look on her face. "I keep telling myself it's a dream or something and then something happens to make it feel real. First that woman makes flowers grow on my arm, and then you show up. You really are here, right?"

"Yes, and we need to go. How are you feeling? Do you think you can walk?"

Lee struggled to her feet and took a few steps. "I think so. Are you sure we'll be invisible?"

Madeline sighed and picked up one of the linen scraps. She heard Lee gasp, and then dropped it. "Convinced?"

Lee nodded, and the fight went out of her face. "I have to believe it's true. I don't think my mind could have made up you coming here. Since this is all true, then you should know that the woman knows something is up. She asked me who might be looking for me. She said she felt someone the other night."

"It was me." Madeline listened again. The guards were still talking about food. She felt her stomach clench with hunger. "We should go. They might be coming for you any minute. We don't know when this ceremony is going to start, but it will be soon."

Lee took the linen and Madeline pointed her to the slit in the back of the tent.

Jode reached to pull Madeline through and then made the two women wait. Madeline looked at Lee; she seemed steady enough. If they could get her through the camp, she could probably make it to the notch where the others were waiting. She would have some time to rest while Madeline and Jode helped rescue the others. *And with luck, Lee will be able to ride a horse out of here.*

Jode leaned close and whispered, "Look to your right."

She turned her head and tried not to lean too far. Jode pointed again, and then Madeline saw movement. The other captives were moving low and crossing between two wagons, at least that part of the plan was working. Hopefully Tom had found Simon's group and they could all ride out of there.

Madeline scanned and saw that there were no Choi in her line of sight. "Where is everyone?"

Jode leaned in again. "They are at the temple. Some tend the cooking fires, but most are setting up for a ceremony." He jerked his head and Madeline glanced at the building. It was surrounded by Choi carrying bowls and other vessels.

"Do you think they are planning to collect that much from Lee? There's not that much blood in us." She turned and saw Lee staring at the temple. "Don't look. We are getting out of here."

"It is a good time to go," Jode said.

Madeline looked again at the captives creeping between wagons. "I think we should wait until they have reached the edge of the campsite. When they are clear we can move. I think too much movement in the wrong direction might draw attention, even if we're invisible."

Jode nodded and reached to place a hand under Lee's elbow. Lee was still staring at the preparations for the ceremony. He gently turned her head away and checked her eyes. "She is not going to make it, Madeline. I should probably carry her."

Lee shook her head and seemed to regain her senses. "No, I'll be fine, but it would probably be a good idea if we left soon."

Madeline glanced around again and decided she was right. The others were almost to the edge of the camp and the longer Lee had to worry about it, the harder it would be for her. She started to speak when a shout interrupted her.

All three heads turned to the sound. Across the camp, the Choi were staring at some movement at the edge of the light, just past where Zora and Elight crouched in the shadow of a wagon. She prayed that no one would notice them.

The movement that had caught the attention of the Choi came close to a campfire and Madeline swore under her breath. Simon stumbled in front of a Choi spear. Each of the rescue party was marched in, and each of them were covered in blood. They had been beaten, badly. Madeline noticed a darkening bruise on the lead Choi. At least someone had fought back.

"We'll be back," Madeline muttered. She nodded to Jode to

lead them. Lee followed and Madeline brought up the rear. The sooner they left the camp, the faster they could gather the guards and come back to rescue the new captives. And they would, even if they had to cut through the entire Choi contingent.

They had to dodge some Choi who ran from the temple to help with the captives. It's only a matter of time before someone looks to make sure Lee is still there, Madeline thought.

"Stop!" Madeline felt her heart obey.

The voice had been directed elsewhere, she realized. Turning, she saw Ridern draw his sword and start swinging it at the closest Choi. Madeline watched as several Choi launched themselves at Ridern, bringing him down by sheer weight.

"Fuck." Madeline managed to keep her voice low. "Keep going." She touched Lee's back. "We'll have to figure something out, when we get you safe. At least no one is dead yet. And now we know where everyone is."

40

*S*imon walked behind the Choi guards. They had been ambushed as they came down the side of the mountain. He looked and saw crowds of Choi moving toward a central temple. No sign of Madeline, Lee, or Jode. That could be a good thing.

Keegan was beside him. The tracker was looking around keeping his head down and moving his eyes from one side of the camp to the other. Simon figured he was looking for potential escape routes.

The rest of the group was behind him, but Simon kept his focus on Keegan. If he could help the tracker move through the camp without falling, Keegan could keep looking for escape opportunities.

"Turn," their escort barked and shoved Simon to the left.

When he straightened, Simon saw a cluster of people, too short to be Choi. Then Zora moved and Simon realized they had found the missing part of the group. Well, not quite the rescue he planned, but there was still hope.

As he approached, Zora stepped aside and Callisra became visible. Simon felt his heart lift. She looked unharmed.

The Choi guard shoved Simon in the small of his back and he stumbled into the group, just avoiding knocking Gren over. Urr, Buck, and Dass, waved at him from just behind Ridern who was nursing a sore wrist.

"Simon." Callisra grabbed his arm. "What are you doing here?"

"Rescuing you."

She grinned. "Well, thank you. Are we about to leave?"

"A small snag." He kissed her. "I was so worried about you. Did they hurt you?"

"No," she said, blushing. "We were just captives and when Ridern tried to free us, we were caught again. They won't let me heal his wrist."

Zora slapped him on the back. "I knew it. I win the pool. It is good to see you."

"You don't win until they wed," Gren said.

Simon laughed. "Don't count your chickens. What's going on?"

Callisra pointed at the temple. The campfires gave just enough light for Simon to see that all the Choi were beginning to gather around it.

She moved in closer to Simon. "When we were recaptured, the guards brought us here and said we might as well watch the ceremony to see what was in store for us."

Simon hugged her tightly. "What happened on the pass? We didn't see anything. One second you were all there and the next you were gone."

"It felt like the ground rose up and grabbed us, but it was some creature I've never seen before," Zora said. "They just picked us up and ran down the trail."

Callisra shuddered in Simon's arms. "I was afraid that we were going to be found torn apart on the trail. It was difficult to see our captors, but Zora is right. I have never heard of creatures like these before. They blended into the background, changing as the background changed."

"They brought us here," Gren said. "The Choi gave them something. I didn't see what."

adeline shoved Lee underneath the wagon. Choi were rushing toward the action and paying little attention to anything else. Madeline reminded herself that Ridern was capable of taking care of things. Their job was to get Lee safe. When that was done, they could come back and get everyone else out.

Jode pointed behind them. "It is clear if we go this way. It will take a little longer, but my men can hold their own for a while."

Madeline nodded for Jode to lead and grabbed Lee's arm. As she followed him, she glanced at the crowds. There was nothing happening. All she could see was the backs of Choi. She hoped their friends would be able to stand until rescued.

Madeline pushed Lee to follow Jode and took up the rear position. There were still a few Choi on this side of the camp, but they were tending to the meal and only glancing in the direction of the crowd. Only two more minutes and Jode could pick up Lee and run. It would only take ten minutes to deposit Lee with Mirial and Barsh and then return.

Madeline kept her eyes to the front.

A few more yards, and they would be clear. Madeline started counting steps; one, two, three, four, five –

Lee tripped and fell. Madeline heard the groan that escaped and saw the linen rag fly from Lee's hands.

She was visible.

Madeline bent to retrieve the cloth and press it into Lee's grasp, but the damage was done.

"Stop!"

Madeline kept moving. If Lee disappeared, maybe they could still get her out. In midstride something smashed into her back and she fell to the ground. Then a hand scrabbled at her shoulder trying to drag her to her feet.

She didn't know how they saw her. She glanced at Jode and nodded him forward. He could get clear. It would only take one of them to turn this debacle into a success. Only one of them needed to get clear.

He frowned, but then turned and ran for the desert.

Madeline threw her scrap of cloth away as soon as Jode was behind the gathering Choi. When she was visible, someone pulled her roughly to her feet and dragged her to the fire.

Two Choi held them. One was a wizened old man, and the other a young-looking woman. "Get me a rope," the woman said. The old man shoved Lee at her and stamped off.

"I'm sorry," Lee muttered.

Madeline felt a little glow of satisfaction at the apology, then it flicked out. This was not the place to savor any victory. "Keep quiet. Maybe we can get away before they bring someone who is used to keeping people captive."

The old man returned with some twine. Madeline held her hands out in front. "How did you see me?"

The old man shook her roughly. "Saw that rag disappear, knew someone was there."

The woman spat. "That won't hold them long, but it will do. Truss them together. No, behind their backs." She turned and pulled a boy away from the spit he was turning. "Go tell Great-mother what we have."

Madeline felt Lee twisting against the restraints. "Wait," she said, not caring that the Choi woman would hear. "The twine might not be strong, but it will still do some damage if you break it. Let it be."

Lee stopped moving and turned her gaze on Madeline, anger and fear darkening her emerald eyes. "Do you have any more of those fancy knives?"

"Not that I want to mention." Madeline watched the Choi woman. She stood just out of reach. Madeline could see that she had some battle training in the way she balanced her weight and seemed ready to spring forward if necessary.

It was only a few minutes later when the boy came running back. "She says bring them to the temple." He was gasping for breath.

The woman pointed the boy to the fire. "Keep turning the spit. The feast is as important as the sacrifice."

adeline stood in the center of the temple floor. She looked around to make sure she knew where the edges were when the fight started. It was dark but there were fires and torches all around so Madeline could see everything.

She could feel the slight sloping of the floor toward the channel dug into the center of the temple. The floor was granite, polished and sparkling with minerals. Pillars ringed the sides, except where the channel ended in a lip, any liquid spilled could be collected at the edge.

Just to the side of this gap, two Choi held Lee. From her vantage point, Madeline could see the others. They were at the edge of the crowd, appearing forgotten by their captors. As she watched, Jode led Callisra and Elight away. At worst, the night would end with only Madeline and Lee dead. At best, Madeline would figure out how to get away and bring Lee with her and they would all survive.

The Choi had searched her and found all her knives, but they hadn't taken them away, just placed them on the floor around her feet.

The crowd in front of her parted, and a tall Choi woman

strode up to the steps. Behind her was a line of other Choi, men and women. The first woman was dressed in flowing robes the pearly gray of the lightening sky. The others were clothed in different shades of blue and yellow.

"Interfering fool." The woman sneered as she walked onto the temple floor. "Who are you?" Madeline recognized the voice of Skye Greatmother.

Madeline shifted to keep the woman turned away from the captives. If she was looking at Madeline, she wouldn't see Jode at work. "Lady Madeline of the Lower Plains, and you?"

"I do not normally converse with sacrifices, but you have proven yourself more than the usual cattle we use. I assume it was you who spied on us."

"Perhaps someone else is interested in your actions. I asked your name."

The woman laughed. "Very well, I am Skye Greatmother of the Choi clan."

"And what happens now?" Madeline tried not to look directly at what was happening across the camp, but it was impossible. Jode took Zora from the group of captives, and the rest shifted to hide his absence. Now that three of them were missing, it was going to be difficult to hide that the group was shrinking. "Do you just stick a straw in me and drink my blood?"

"No, we need your blood on fire with your anger and your fear. You must fight for your life."

Madeline didn't see any weapons on Skye. "How will you defend yourself? Is this to be a magical duel?"

Skye reach into the side of her robe and extracted a foot of gleaming steel from it. Her sword was short, but she stood two feet taller than Madeline. Skill would be important, and the willingness to fight dirty.

Skye smiled at Madeline. "You have your knives. Can you use them?"

"Yes." Madeline bent and picked up one in each hand. She

brought her focus to her opponent. Jode would continue to rescue the others. She needed all her attention here. "I've killed before."

"Enough talking. It is time to start." Skye took a vial out of her other pocket and sliced the top off with the blade. Pouring a few crimson drops onto the cutting edge, she breathed a few words across it, all the time keeping her eyes on Madeline. Then she poured the rest of the blood on the temple floor, using her toe to spread it into curlicues, and chanting words that Madeline could not understand.

Madeline tested her balance, bouncing on the balls of her feet to loosen the muscles a little. She watched Skye's eyes, blocking out every other distraction. Jode had insisted that she hone her fighting skills and she knew how to prepare for a fight. She had only sparred since the fight with the Scree, but she knew that she was able to kill if the stakes were high enough. And today almost everyone she loved was in danger.

Skye stood waiting. Madeline didn't know why, but she wasn't going to make the first move. "If I win, I expect all of my companions to be freed."

A sneer curled at Skye's lips. "If you win, then yes. I order all the captives freed."

The crowd pushed against the sides of the raised floor. Murmurs rustled around her and Madeline realized that they were chanting. A bell chimed and Skye stepped forward.

"Now we begin the dance of slashes." Skye rapidly flicked her knife and Madeline danced back. No contact this time.

Madeline tried to keep Skye between her and the captives, but found that she was being herded to avoid the flickering of Skye's blade. If she didn't give herself to the fight it would be over sooner than she expected.

She blocked a swipe and flicked the blade in her other hand to nick Skye's arm. The Choi woman hissed and withdrew. One of the men behind her ran up and wrapped the arm before blood did more than bead.

"Don't like seeing your own blood, Skye?" Madeline waited until the man left the temple, seeing no need to bring him into the fight.

"It is not my blood we need to shed. I am impressed with your skill, but you will bleed tonight, Madeline Lady of the Lower Plains."

"Perhaps, but not only me I think." She flicked a glance at Lee. The woman was opened mouthed. *Let's see you find fault with me today.*

Skye was stepping forward again, flicking the blade in her fingertips, making it hard to see and impossible to anticipate.

Madeline dodged and attacked until she started gasping for breath. She managed to avoid getting cut, but didn't manage to do any damage to Skye either. It was getting to the point where she was too tired to keep dodging fast enough to avoid the flicker of Skye's blade when the bell chimed again.

"Stop," Skye commanded.

Madeline obeyed. If Skye was going to let her rest, she would take advantage. Standing still and slowing her breathing, she felt her energy rebuilding.

Skye held her blade out to the side. The same man who bandaged her ran forward to take it. He handed her a blade that was dull and black. It was thin, but about the same length as the first sword.

"Was your sword getting too heavy?" Madeline asked, keeping her voice sweet. "We can take a break if you want."

"No." Skye wasn't even breaking a sweat.

It was probably easier when you knew what was coming next, Madeline thought.

Skye opened another vial. This time she poured the blood from the hilt to the tip then dropped the vial and crushed it under her heel.

Madeline wondered how they kept the blood from coagulating.

"Now is the time for the dance of thrusts." She lunged toward Madeline without warning.

Parrying the lunge, Madeline twisted her body and heard a ripping sound. Skye's blade had sliced through the cotton of Madeline's sleeve. She spun away from Skye and checked her arm. A faint scratch lined her upper arm, but no blood welled. In the second that she took looking for damage, Skye had crossed the floor and was whipping the blade back and forth.

Madeline raised one knife and held the other behind her back. Turning to minimize the target she presented, Madeline parried the thrust and spun away again. As she did, she raised the other blade, pivoted to change direction, and managed to slash Skye's shoulder before they separated again. Madeline felt like a bullfighter without a cape.

Skye hissed again and returned to her original place. Once again, the man put a dressing on the wound. Madeline saw Skye look at him, something warmed in the woman's expression, then was gone. She turned back to Madeline and narrowed her eyes. "That is the last time you will break my skin."

"I don't know how you can guarantee that," Madeline said.

The crowd started stamping their feet, raising dust clouds that floated to the top of the temple stairs. Madeline watched it start to creep to the top of the steps and knew it would cover the floor of the temple soon.

She coughed with the dryness and waited. There was something she didn't understand. Skye could have killed her at least three times already, but had drawn back at the last second, only trying to scratch or slice clothing.

Skye looked at the mountain in the distance and smiled. "Soon it will be time. Until then, let us dance again." She rushed at Madeline, sword raised.

Madeline made ready to parry the Choi's blade; it would be

easy with such a crude attack. At the last second, Skye twisted and changed the lunge into an upward sweep of the blade. Madeline jerked back and managed to turn what would have been a gut wound into a slice at her hip. The knife did not penetrate the leather of her trousers, but she would have a bone deep bruise.

Spinning to keep her eye on Skye, Madeline swung her own blade out and around. Skye hissed as she just managed to avoid the point.

"What happens if your blood spills?" Madeline asked as she retreated to a position across from Skye.

"It does not concern you; my blood will not spill." Skye returned to her handlers as she spoke.

Madeline was beginning to feel as though they were taking part in a bizarre boxing match. They engaged and then they broke away for a rest, only to engage again. She had been trained to fight until the match was over.

"Why did you choose this woman for your sacrifice?" Madeline hoped to hear something she could use to stop this madness.

"When you traveled through the passage between worlds, you gathered great power. I felt it even as far as the Choi village. We simply wanted that power, and you were too well protected."

Skye's attendant took her cloak and now the Choi wore a tunic and pants the color of blood. She took the black sword again and faced Madeline.

"Now we must season your blood with pain." She stepped toward Madeline who backed up.

"I thought you were supposed to raise my fear and anger. You haven't done that."

Skye laughed. "I do not believe you."

Madeline hoped that confirmation didn't show on her face. She was plenty mad because Skye wasn't helping her solve the problem, and she was scared she was running out of time. "I am told that I was the first to come through that passage."

Skye approached as if she were stalking prey. Madeline prepared to defend herself.

"You are," Skye said as she raised her sword as if she was going to impale Madeline.

Thrusting under Skye's arm and across to her side, Madeline twisted and felt the point of her sword catch on something. It was pulled out of her hand. And Skye laughed.

43

*T*he Choi woman slipped away again. Madeline could not believe she had left without taking Madeline's sword. What was the deal here? "I thought you wanted me to feel pain."

Keeping her eyes on Skye, she stepped over and picked up the sword. Her stomach sank. Skye was trading the black sword for a whip.

"Do you understand now?" Skye cracked the whip. Madeline was relieved to see it reached only a little farther than the sword had. If she did this properly, Skye would not be able to do much more damage with the whip. But if she couldn't draw out more information, Madeline feared she wouldn't figure out a solution. Up to now, she'd been fighting defensively. If it went on much longer, she would be fighting for her life, and be tired. As much as she didn't want to kill Skye Greatmother, it might come to that.

"I see you have a lot of toys." Madeline slid her free hand to the hidden sheath of one of her throwing knives. It was still there and ready to use. "Tell me, how did you manage this sacrifice last time?"

Skye started to cross the temple floor, cracking the whip as she approached. "We used a Choi volunteer."

Madeline slashed at the whip as Skye tried to flail her. The clatter and shriek of metal meeting metal surprised her. At closer inspection, she saw that the leather was studded with metal buttons. That would be a good way to make sure someone felt pain, and it wouldn't likely shed blood. Madeline guessed that the actual sacrifice was dependent on some timing. She hoped it wasn't sunset; a day of this would break her.

She dodged another lash of the whip and managed to slice away a good six inches of leather. Now, Skye would need to get within the reach of Madeline's blade to make contact.

"Tell me, Skye, why did you not do the same this time. It seems risky to take a stranger to this world on the off chance she would pull power."

"Can you not tell? She has power shining from her like the sun." Skye stepped toward Madeline and managed to make contact with her ribs. Madeline gasped and stumbled away.

"No, I don't see that," she managed through gritted teeth. "But it was still a big risk."

Skye reached to hit at Madeline's arm with the whip. "The last Choi volunteer was barely powerful enough to sustain this one tribe."

As the fight progressed, Skye seemed to become more willing to share information. Even if she thought Madeline would be dead, it seemed like she had forgotten the others were listening.

Madeline danced aside to avoid another lashing and smacked the flat of her blade against Skye's wrist. The Choi woman dropped the whip and cradled her wrist with the other hand. Her face registered shock.

"You didn't count on all the risks." Madeline was feeling winded and prayed that there would be another break in the fight. "A sacrifice that fights back might be a bit too much for you to handle."

"Stupid woman." Skye's voice rose in a screech. "Your spirit only makes it more right to take your blood to sustain us. We will rise again to a multitude."

Madeline took a chance and glanced to Lee. She was looking better than the last time. Maybe she'd decided to just accept what was going on.

"So, you couldn't get another volunteer?" Madeline asked. "What kind of tribe are you that no one would make the sacrifice to save you?"

Skye seemed to forget herself and reached over to slap Madeline. As soon as she reached out her wrist twisted and she shrieked in pain and stepped back. "That is untrue. If I hadn't made this plan, someone would have volunteered; someone with enough power to sustain us until the next sacrifice. I wanted more than simply sustenance." Realization that Madeline had successfully baited, her dawned on Skye's face. Cradling her arm closer, she returned to her attendant. They whispered and he seemed to be arguing with Skye. Madeline considered rushing them and stabbing Skye, but she still hoped to be able to solve this without death.

Finally, the attendant wrapped Skye's hand and gave her another weapon. Madeline couldn't see what it was, but Skye carried it as though it was heavy.

Madeline glanced at where Jode had been the last time and saw only Ridern and Tom. She hoped he was going to rescue Lee so that Madeline only had to deal with one problem – saving the Choi.

"What are we dancing next?" She tried to see what Skye was carrying. "The dance of death by flower petals?"

Skye laughed and swung her weapon. The woman was incredibly strong. In her uninjured hand, she held a two-foot-long iron bar with a chain attached to the end, and attached to that, a ball of metal.

"Is beating me to a pulp the way you get my blood?" Madeline couldn't see how Skye planned to just hurt her with the flail. If it made contact, it would break things.

"No, it is not yet time for the final step of the ceremony." Skye circled the temple floor following Madeline who was doing her best to stay out of reach. "Soon, but do not worry. I am very skilled with this and will not break your skin."

Madeline ran scenarios through her head as she kept moving ahead of Skye. She couldn't chance being hit by that weapon. It would immobilize her and then everything would go off the rails. She knew Jode was out there with his guards, ready to attack if necessary. He would not do anything until he saw no other choice, but she was certain he would not just stand by and let Skye kill her. *If that happens, we will never get the chance to talk about having kids.*

The only tactic she could think of was to keep avoiding the flail. Keep Skye talking. Find a solution. Sell the solution to Skye. Everybody survives and she goes home to have lots of little babies. Madeline realized that someone was going to have to die. She just hoped it was a volunteer, and a Choi.

"What if I kill you? Do you have enough power?"

Skye laughed again. "I do, but the Greatmother is not a suitable sacrifice. I need to lead my people after the ceremony. If the Greatmother is sacrificed, there is no one with enough power to lead."

Interesting, Madeline thought. "So, you are the only one who can do the sacrifice? The only one who can convert the blood to power?"

"No."

Skye's voice was a little too close for Madeline who had turned away to make sure she didn't fall off the edge of the temple. A sound made her drop to the stone floor and roll to the center. Just as she did, the sound changed to a clang as the metal ball met stone.

She saw a crack appear at the point of impact.

"Are you sure you can hit me with that and not kill me?"

Skye had come to a complete stop, staring at the pillar. "Perhaps not. I will change weapons."

"Please, take your time." Madeline stood and saw Jode out of the corner of her eye; she shook her head and returned to the center.

Skye returned with a new whip. This one had thinner lashes and Madeline didn't see any studs. "So, if I understand correctly, you need to survive and yet, there is someone who can do the ceremony if you can't."

"Yes. My apprentice, Ophian, can perform the ceremony. It would be foolish to not have another who can do so." Skye raised the whip and Madeline countered with a slash that had no effect. The lashes slipped along the blade.

"It does not matter. You cannot kill me." Skye raised the whip again.

"I don't really want to." Madeline was forming a plan, but she needed to figure out how to get a powerful Choi to volunteer as the sacrifice.

Skye stopped in mid swing. "You wish to volunteer to die?"

Madeline took the pause to step back and catch her breath. "No, I don't want anyone to die. But it seems you must kill someone to survive. I'm just trying to figure out how to make that work for everyone."

The growing light started to take on a yellow tinge. It would not be long before the sun crested the hill. Skye seemed to be poised between lashing Madeline and returning to her apprentice.

"Did you ask for a sacrifice?" Madeline suspected there was something more to this than she had uncovered so far. Despite what Skye said, taking Lee was a big risk. There was no way the Choi could know that the power Lee held from the passage between worlds would stay until the ceremony. Although Madeline realized her knowledge of magical theory was way too thin

P. A. WILSON

to rely on that argument. That realization floated a plan into her mind. Perhaps that is what she would do; build a knowledge base for all the different magical powers. But that would mean she had to deal with the Scree and other less than pleasant species. And survive this fight. She forced her mind back to the present.

"We held a ballot," Skye answered the question.

Madeline realized that stress, or fatigue, or both had distorted her sense of time. It seemed like an hour since she had asked. She tried to keep her guard up. Just because Skye was answering questions, didn't mean she was willing to deal, or that she would pause in the attack each time.

Madeline shifted her weight to keep her muscles limber. Not wanting to kill Skye didn't mean she wanted to die. "And what happened? Why did you have to bring Lee here? That must have taken a lot of power."

"It was not possible to use the results of the ballot." Skye's eyes flicked to her apprentice. "And now we are finished talking." She raised her arm to swing the whip.

Madeline was taken off guard despite her determination not to be. The lash hit her bare feet. The pain ripped through her skin to set every nerve ending in her body on fire. A wave of nausea built from her stomach, making her gasp. Her knees buckled. She dropped her sword to save herself from planting her face on the stone floor of the temple.

The edge of her vision faded to gray and then she felt the blood rush to her legs. Then her consciousness slipped away.

44

*T*he world swam back into Madeline's focus with the next breath. The pain faded to a tingle, and then was gone. All of this had taken place within the space of two breaths. Skye was still completing the arc of her swing, and the crowd was just starting a roar of approval. Madeline looked for Jode. He was starting to draw his sword, ready to attack.

"No," she shouted, hoping he would hear her voice over the rising roar. Flicking her eyes back to Skye, Madeline was relieved to see a smile crawl across her lips. The Choi woman thought Madeline was begging for the pain to stop. Jode was still unnoticed just behind the crowd.

Standing, Madeline put weight on the leg and was surprised that there was no damage. She looked at Lee and saw her being led away from the fight by a couple of Choi.

"Why are you taking her away?" Madeline asked. "You promised she would be safe."

Skye glanced at where Lee was struggling against the guards. "She will be taken to a safe point. When the ceremony is complete, we will release her into the desert. What happens to her after that is up to her ability to survive. But perhaps it would be more useful for her to stay and watch." She waved her free hand at the Choi and they returned Lee to where she could see the performance.

If Madeline could keep Skye's attention on Lee, there would be no reason for her to look in Jode's direction. Madeline looked past Skye and saw Jode had sheathed the sword. Not sure where the others were in the crowd, she gave him a look that she hoped he would interpret as 'leave this to me' and turned her attention back to Skye.

"Now, where were we before that mosquito bit me?" She saw a gleam in Skye's eyes, hoping it was appreciation of the joke. "Oh, yes. You didn't want to use a Choi for the sacrifice. Now that strikes me as odd. Do you not have enough magic left to make it work?"

"That is not the case." Skye looked at the crest of the mountain again.

Madeline followed her gaze. The sun was about to rise above the peaks. "Are we going to finish this soon?"

Skye nodded. "When the sun is fully risen, it will bless the ceremony and then your blood will flow into the channel."

As she spoke several Choi ran to the edge of the temple. They waved large fans and Madeline watched the dust clear from the floor. Other Choi followed with brooms and cloths. Madeline realized they were ensuring no dust lay in the channel to soak up the blood.

"So, I guess you are done with the whip?" Madeline figured there was about twenty minutes left for her to find a different solution. "What's next?"

"You are a curious one are you not?"

Skye tossed the whip across the temple and one of the Choi in the crowd caught it. Madeline was reminded of a baseball fan catching the home run ball when the other Choi cheered.

"I always want to learn new things," Madeline said. She moved to draw Skye's attention away from where she noticed the other guards had joined Jode. She didn't know how the crowd would react to the presence of armed guards. "For instance, I would love to know who it was you deemed unsuitable for this sacrifice."

The crowd hushed and Madeline realized they didn't know whose name was drawn. She continued prodding at Skye. "If you didn't like the name that was drawn, why not draw another?"

Skye was walking toward her apprentice. "The laws do not allow it. There are only two ways for a fifty-year sacrifice to be chosen. They volunteer, or all of the names of the elite are entered in a lottery. The first name taken is sacrificed."

"Interesting." Madeline could feel her muscles cool and stiffen. Skye seemed uninterested in further tormenting the victim. "You have elite and –?"

Skye turned as her apprentice wound red silk around her arms. "We have those who are able to do magic, and those who are not. The elite are the ones who can perform magic. You should prepare yourself for death."

"Not a chance. I've still got time," Madeline snapped.

She tried to think through the information she had. It seemed that Skye would have been willing to sacrifice anyone in the elite, but not this one. Her child? A parent? Her lover? How to find out? Since Skye was busy with her wardrobe change, Madeline walked to where Lee stood at the side of the temple.

"Is there anything you haven't told me? Anything I can use to make this work."

Lee licked her lips. Madeline had never seen her afraid before. It didn't feel as good as she hoped. Right now, Lee was a victim and Madeline couldn't feel anything but sorry for her.

"No," Lee started to say, then she had to clear her throat as her voice got lost in the fear. She swallowed, and then continued, "I don't know anything else. But I think I can guess. My courtroom instincts are still there."

Madeline refrained from saying that there may be more to it

than instinct here. She looked at the line of sunlight creeping across the sand. "We don't have much time. What do you think?"

Lee nodded toward Skye. "Look at her with that apprentice. I think there's more than a teacher to student relationship. They are lovers or I'm a fish. It was his name that came out in the lottery."

Madeline looked over her shoulder. The apprentice, Ophian, was wrapping Skye's body and Lee was right. His hands lingered on her waist in a way that told anyone willing to look that they were lovers. She whispered, "Oh yeah," to Lee and returned to the center of the temple.

Skye looked at Madeline and a smile curved her lips. "You have decided to accept your fate? Good, a willing sacrifice is better. That is how we are used to proceeding."

Madeline placed her knives on the ground and started stretching. If Skye was willing to take a break, Madeline would take advantage. "No, but if I don't keep my body warm, I won't be able to fight if I need to." She saw that hit home with Skye as the Choi woman tightened her jaw.

"You will not fight," she said, sweetly. "You will be... unable to fight."

Madeline ignored the tightening of her stomach, no need to be afraid. "Is that why you couldn't bring yourself to sacrifice the person whose name was drawn? Because they would have to lie there and just take it?"

Ophian was tucking the end of the red silk band into one of the folds at Skye's waist. He looked up and his expression was pure spite. He whispered something to Skye. She shook her head.

"Who was the name, Skye Greatmother? Why are you putting your people at risk by taking such an unknown course?"

Madeline looked at the crowd, they were all facing Skye. Madeline waited, but Skye simply dismissed the attention of the crowd and gestured to Ophian. "Continue. We do not have a lot of time."

He flicked a smile back at Madeline as he handed Skye a pair of crimson gloves. The material seemed to glow, as though the rising sun already shone from within it.

Madeline took his behavior as confirmation of Lee's assumption. Now she only had minutes to find a way to use that information. "Was it someone you loved?"

Skye's head snapped up. "I love all my people."

"Not as much as you love this person." Madeline saw a restless movement in the crowd. "You are putting the safety of your people at risk for one person."

Skye reached for a knife that Ophian held out. The knife was blue, and not metal. Madeline saw that it was a double blade, one that would pierce a vein and keep the wound open enough to drain the blood. Her pulse seemed to beat harder at the sight of the blade. She looked away and her pulse slowed. The knife was spelled to increase fear. That knowledge allowed her to minimize the effect.

"You haven't answered," Madeline shouted. "Who is it that you will save at the risk of your people?"

Muttering rose from the crowd. Madeline didn't wait for the answer. She knew how to draw sympathy and agreement from a jury. It was the same here. It just needed to stay below the level of a riot. "How long before you know if you were right? Will you know as soon as the ceremony is over?"

Skye hissed at the crowd then turned back to Madeline. "Do not press me, human. I have made the decision. We will save my people. If you fight the inevitable, the people who came with you will be used for their blood until I finally release them. If you go willingly, I will do as I promised and allow them free passage."

Madeline started to wonder if she had pushed too far and was about to change tactics when an old Choi woman called from behind Skye, "Yes, who are you protecting? Greatmother, we trust you but we would like to know."

"Yes," another Choi shouted. "We would like to know."

Skye spun to see the circle of watchers. She seemed shocked. The woman was not used to being questioned.

She pressed her advantage. "What harm can it do to tell them, Skye? They will probably figure it out afterward anyway."

The crowd echoed her question. It was getting close to the point that humans would be rioting. Madeline glanced at Jode. He nodded to her, and when she cast her gaze across the crowd, she saw curiosity, but no anger.

As she turned back to Skye, Madeline noticed that even though the torches were guttering, the sun was casting enough light to make up for it. Not much time left, maybe five minutes.

"I can guess," she said, looking at Ophian. "It is someone close to you."

Skye was controlled, although Madeline saw the fire in her eyes even over the distance of the temple floor. Ophian was not. Madeline saw the flush of pink in his cheeks. He straightened and seemed about to say something when Skye touched his shoulder.

"It is time." She strode toward the center of the temple floor.

Madeline took a step backward for every step Skye took forward, but she knew she would run out of space before Skye caught her.

"No, we have at least a few minutes." Madeline pointed at the line of light. "It is enough time to tell us who."

Skye stopped walking. She stood at the center of the floor, where the channels met in a dip. She looked at Madeline and crooked her finger. When Madeline did not step toward her, she flicked her fingers toward where Jode had been. Madeline looked and saw an archer aiming at her husband.

"You are right," Skye said. "But are you willing to sacrifice your own lover to be right?"

Madeline shook her head. "At one time, I would. I was like you. I saw only the goal and not the consequences. I will step willingly into the center if you name the person you are protecting."

SKYE FELT Ophian touch her shoulder. He should not have done that. He was not the level to be touching the Greatmother, at least not yet. This woman was damnably frustrating. She declared that she didn't want to kill Skye, but she would not simply stand still to be sacrificed.

"Do not tell her, my love," Ophian whispered.

The endearment did not raise warmth in Skye's heart as it usually did. She wanted to be focused and needed to be trusted. She ignored Ophian and glanced at the sun approaching the marker, only a few minutes to wait.

It could not hurt to tell the woman, quietly before the sacrificial blade sliced her veins. But then if the woman had a chance to speak it would be a pity to have Ophian's role in the ceremony tinged with suspicion.

He touched her again. The fool would give away the answer with his familiarity. His voice slid into her ear, "Please, my love. It is a trap. This woman will not honor her words."

Skye tried to ignore him, but he would not be quiet. She tried again to reassure him, "Hush, do not worry. I am in control of this."

Ophian tsked. "Do not judge her by our standards. She will not be willing to die."

He was probably right, but it was not acceptable that he would argue with her. This sacrifice was her job.

"Well," Madeline called from her place at the center of the temple. "Will you tell us?" She encompassed the Choi in her question with a wave of her arm. Skye saw their interest, and a few who stared directly at Ophian.

"It may be that our secret is not a secret anymore." She turned to Ophian to say more and looked directly into his blazing eyes.

"There will be no question when the ceremony is complete. Do not tell the woman about us." He was almost choking on the anger.

He has forgotten himself, Skye thought. Even after the ceremony, he would not be allowed to speak to her that way.

"There is no time to deal with this," she whispered. "When this ceremony is complete, we will talk about how you speak to me."

He reeled back in shock. "I... I am sorry." As the words came out, Skye noticed his eyes narrow. Perhaps he was less sorry than shocked.

"You will be, but now it is time to take the sacrifice." Skye took the blade in her left hand. "Do you have what you need to play your part?"

"Yes," he said, holding out the shallow bowl and bag of spices.

Madeline was standing patiently, but Skye knew she was trying to plan a way to escape. The power glowed from Madeline, more than from Lee Marshall. "This is the right thing to do. See how the power is already fading from the other woman." Skye waited for Ophian to comment but he was silent, sulking.

45

*M*adeline watched the interaction between Skye and Ophian, knowing she was right. Skye was protecting Ophian and her apprentice didn't seem happy about what was going on. The body language was very clear. Skye was annoyed and Ophian didn't care. This would be interesting.

She glanced up at the line of sunlight crawling toward them.

"Okay, Skye, we're burning darkness here." She figured that it was time to crank up the annoyance factor with Skye. The crowd wasn't reacting as much as she expected, so her only option was Skye.

The Greatmother approached, Ophian just behind her. Madeline smiled, now she could get at the apprentice too.

"There is no more time for you to avoid this." Skye's voice was regal.

Madeline could hear power vibrate in the air between them. Ophian smirked. Standing just to the side of Skye, he carried a deep basin in one hand and a small sack in the other.

A grinding noise drew Madeline's attention to the side of the temple. Two of the Choi who had accompanied Skye to the temple were attaching a stone vat to the end of the channel.

Skye stood in front of Madeline, and Ophian joined them. "The ceremony starts when the sunlight reaches that mark," she said, pointing to one of the columns which had a red smear a foot from the bottom. "It must end by the time it clears the top."

"So, it will be five minutes of bloodletting?" Madeline tried to see where Jode was standing, but he wasn't there. She could only hope he trusted her. But it was out of her control. "I'm not sure I have enough in me to keep it up."

"We will start with a small amount that we will use to light the power into the spell. Then your remaining blood will be gathered in the urn. We will use it to anoint all of the Choi."

Madeline looked at the crowd. "Well I know I don't have enough blood for that. How will you make it stretch?"

Skye laughed. "We will make do."

Madeline shrugged. "So how come you can't tell the rest of your tribe that Ophian was the sacrifice?"

Before Skye could speak, Ophian spat at her. "It is a mistake to tell her. Our people will know, and they will question you. Do not continue on this path."

"Ophian," Skye snarled. "Focus yourself on this moment. We are almost successful. It will be over soon. You will be able to become my lover openly."

Ophian's eyes widened. "Complete the sacrifice, Greatmother. Your people are waiting. I do not care about being your lover. I will be able to take younger and more beautiful mates when I am elevated to the council."

Skye's skin paled. Madeline saw the shock of realization that she'd been taken advantage of cross her face. "But that was our plan," Skye whispered. Then her eyes narrowed. "It is not too late."

Ophian dropped the sack from his hands and reached for the double-bladed knife. Madeline stepped in to defend Skye – not wanting to lose the bargain they had made about surviving.

As he reached for it, Skye moved the blade. And Ophian's jaw dropped as she slashed, slicing the vein in his reaching hand.

"Catch the blood, you fool." Skye shouted at him.

When he didn't move, Madeline grabbed the bowl from Ophian and caught the blood as it dripped from his elbow.

Ophian collapsed on his knees and his eyes rolled back.

Madeline looked at Skye for instructions before glancing at the column. The light from the sun had passed the line.

"Pick up the bag. It has spices." Skye bent to take the bowl. "Hurry we must complete this before I make the final cuts."

Madeline picked up the sack and pulled open the strings at the neck. Skye motioned for her to sprinkle the contents on the blood.

Skye was stanching the blood, ensuring none of it dripped to the temple floor.

When the sack was empty, Skye motioned for her to bring the bowl closer. When Madeline placed it before her, the Choi woman traced a pattern over the surface with her fingernail. The spices caught fire and Madeline felt a surge of power flow past, engulfing Skye and the moaning Ophian.

Skye then sliced Ophian down all the major arteries. Blood gushed across the temple, seeming to leap into the channel.

Sounds came back to Madeline as the final drips of blood slid from Ophian's body and down the channel. The Choi were cheering, and Skye was crying.

"I'm sorry, Skye." Madeline was surprised to find she meant it. Skye was betrayed by her lover and then had to take his life. It couldn't be easy.

"Do not be," Skye answered. "It is my fault for trying to avoid what must be done. There is great power in his blood; that is why the fates chose his name. My people will thrive."

"I am still sorry. It is hard to be betrayed by someone you love."

Skye sighed. "You and your party must join us for our celebratory meal and then you need to be on your way and leave the Choi to me."

$\mathcal{A}$ n hour later, Madeline and the rest of her party were sitting in Skye's multicolored tent finishing a hearty breakfast.

"I am glad you didn't attack," Madeline said to Jode for the tenth time.

He put down his tea and looked at her. "I came very close to doing that, but I trusted you. And I was right to do that. I will always trust you."

Madeline smiled; she was still in a bit of a daze over the ceremony. Having taken part, she now knew why blood magic could be seductive; the power generated was warm and silky against her senses. She felt relief that she was not able to do any more than feel the results. Her own magic tingled, anywhere from a slight frisson to a burning flash, depending on what she was doing. It was much different from the caress of blood power. It would be interesting to add this feeling to the information she compiled about the different magic in the world. She must remember to ask someone if it felt the same to them; someone not of the Choi.

"I was worried there at the end," Madeline confessed. "If

Ophian had just had enough self-control to make it through the first part of the ceremony, I would not be here."

Jode caressed her cheek. "But he did not. I saw what you did not. He was worried from the minute you started goading the Greatmother. You had worked him up to such a state of fear that it was surprising he did not react sooner. Now put this subject aside. I refuse to talk about what might have been. I am more than happy to live with what happened." He looked across the circle. "It seems that Skye Greatmother is going to speak. It would be polite to listen."

Madeline followed his gaze. Skye was waving away her attendants. Then she drew herself up and seemed to shake off the last of her sadness as she donned the regal leader demeanor.

"I am grateful that we were able to complete our ceremony with such success. We have assessed the power that Ophian's blood provided and the Choi will survive to multiply again. I am sad that his power was used because it cost his life. With such magical potential, he would have been a great leader." She paused for a moment. "But such is fate. Now I would speak with Lady Madeline alone. Then you may all depart in peace back to your land."

Jode looked at Madeline. "I can insist on staying if you wish."

"No. I will be fine. She is not happy to be in my debt as it is, let us give her some sense of privacy." She patted his hand. "You know I'll tell you everything I can when we are away from here anyway."

He kissed her and rose. Simon and Callisra walked out hand in hand. Lee strode out of the tent behind them, her usual superior attitude back in place.

Skye beckoned Madeline to her side. "I am obligated to you for two things. You helped me complete the ceremony and you showed me the foolish way I gave my power to the wrong man."

Madeline shook her head. "You would have seen that sooner or later."

"Yes, but later might have been at the expense of my people." Skye reached under the cushion beside her. "I wish to give you this."

Madeline felt her curiosity leap; a new scroll.

Skye smiled. "I see you are a scholar at heart. My people and yours will never be allies, but perhaps sharing knowledge will make the rift between us narrower." She placed the scroll in Madeline's hand. "To repay my first debt, I honor our agreement to let you and your companions leave. As to the second debt, I give you this scroll of our knowledge of the beings of the land." She seemed about to say something else. Madeline waited while Skye wrestled with whatever was stopping her.

After a few moments, Skye continued, "You will find more information in the scroll, but I feel I must tell you about the Tryll, so that you will find safe passage across the mountain."

Madeline raised an eyebrow. "Where I come from, that's called abiding by the spirit of the agreement not just the letter."

"Hmm, this is what we call honor. It is sometimes hard to tell where honor obligations extend the meaning of the agreement."

"That was the basis of my whole life before I came here." Madeline realized she didn't really miss anything about being a lawyer. She had no interest in explaining the distinction Skye described. "Tell me about these Tryll. Are they the reason the pass is avoided? Did they tear those people apart?"

Skye nodded. "It has been convenient for us to have the pass private. Tell me how you avoided them on the way here."

Madeline described the concealment spell and remembered the hiss she heard as it settled. "It must have been the Tryll. It is good to know magic can stop them," she said.

Surprise showed on Skye's face. "It may not always work. We bring them food. A live animal we butcher on site. They like the meat fresh. We do not like the way they kill, so we do it for them."

Madeline started to wonder where they would find an animal to offer.

"We will send a goat with you, so that you will pass. Be careful that you give them the sacrifice before you settle for the night."

Madeline put aside her queasiness and told herself it was just like any other meal. Meat always came from animals no matter whether you watched the butchering or not. "What else can you tell me about them?"

Skye shook her head. "You can read about it. If you do not leave soon, you will not be at the summit before night. And the pass holds more mundane dangers than the Tryll."

Madeline slid the scroll into her pocket, already planning on how to use the information it contained.

47

*L*ee stood watching the disgusting ceremony being performed in front of her. Yes, she understood that animals needed to be butchered to provide meat, but really, did it have to be so bloody? She pushed up the sleeves of her borrowed tunic and started to move away from the circle of people. Then as Mirial finished disconnecting the last of the joints, the ground seemed to heave.

Four creatures shimmered into being. One second they were shimmers in the ground and the next they were stark white. They had four limbs, but their joints seemed wrong somehow, like a lizard. Then they stood on their back legs and reached for the meat. One of them turned looking at the crowd and finally spoke, its voice seeming to come from a tunnel.

"Magic woman?"

Madeline stepped forward. Lee couldn't believe she was a witch, a bitch, yes, but a witch?

The creature tucked its share of the meat under its arms and then leaned toward Madeline, bending at the hips so that its body was parallel to the ground.

"Safe passage." It howled. "Be past the first turn in the path before one hour after sunrise."

Madeline nodded and then held up a hand to stop the creature leaving. That was typical of Madeline, keeping the spotlight. Lee wanted the creature out of sight and hopefully she could scour the experience from her mind.

"What is your name?"

"No names, woman."

Madeline didn't seem to care. "We had an accident on the way up, did you cause it?"

"No, we do not go below the first turn." The creature snarled at Madeline and shimmered back into the colors of the ground.

Madeline thanked Mirial and started to help set up a camp. Lee felt annoyed. She wasn't going to look lazy in front of Madeline so she walked over and started rolling out the pads as people untied them from their horses.

"Keep them closer together, please. I will cast a concealment spell just in case," Madeline said as Lee started.

"I thought we had an agreement with those things," Lee said, pulling the bedrolls closer. "Why do you always have to be the big hero?"

"I'm not, this is just practical. Those things are people, Lee. And they might not be the only ones up here."

"So, are you the only witch here?" Lee tried to pick up a saddle so it could be used as a pillow.

"I'm not a witch." Madeline reached to help with the saddle. "Here you can do magic or you can't. I can."

Lee struggled to heave the saddle by herself, pulling against Madeline's help. "I'm fine, I can do this myself."

"No, you aren't fine. I can see you're in pain. Callisra is a healer; let her ease your bruises."

Lee's eyes narrowed. "No. I don't trust anyone who thinks they can do magic. I saw what it meant to that Greatmother woman. And I saw those creatures. Leave me be."

"Lee, stop fighting me. Believe me, I know how overwhelming this can be and it can't be easy to realize you might have been a sacrifice, but you need to calm down a bit and try to get along with people."

"Don't tell me what I need. You might have saved my life, but you still think you are better than you really are. Let me do this." She yanked the saddle out of Madeline's grip and almost fell on her backside.

Madeline sighed. "Look, Lee. You may not like it, but I put all these people into danger because I thought I had to rescue you. I'm cutting you some slack, but don't push it. I won't take your shit anymore. I think you should just be quiet for a while. We'll figure out what to do with you when we get out of the mountains."

Then Madeline walked away. Lee couldn't think of what to say. That was the first time Madeline had told her off. Usually she just argued or went into a snit.

All the pains of being tied to a barrel and bounced along with the Choi, then riding behind that guard, Ridern, started burning. Lee decided Madeline might be right about shutting up.

BEFORE MADELINE SET the concealment spell, she lifted the one she had placed on the wagon and supplies they had left behind. Was that less than two days ago? She took a deep breath and then joined the circle of people at the center of the camp.

Lee was curled up on a bedroll, Callisra talking quietly to her. Maybe Lee would take the offer of healing Callisra was making. But then she saw Lee shake her head. Callisra returned to the center.

"She seems determined to enjoy her misery," the healer murmured. "Is it all right for us to talk, it would be nice to enjoy the company and the peace."

Madeline nodded. "It should be fine as long as we are quiet. I am probably being overly cautious. The Tryll promised safe passage and I trust Skye's word that we have it."

Simon slipped in next to Callisra and handed Madeline a stick of dried meat. "It's the last of it, we can hunt tomorrow. So, if the Tryll didn't saw the wagon axle, who do you think did?"

"I don't know," Madeline answered. "It worries me. We still have to take the second wagon down." She turned to Barsh. "Do you have any ideas about how we do that?"

Barsh looked at the wagon. "I've checked out every inch of it. There's no damage. We should be fine. I'll take it and no one else will ride. If something goes wrong, I can jump free."

"Do that. We can do without the wagon, but I don't want you hurt." Madeline bit off a piece of the meat.

"I had an idea about the damage to my wagon," Barsh said.

Madeline made an encouraging sound and kept chewing.

"I was with that wagon all the time. Hard to believe anyone got at it without me knowing."

Jode was wiping oil onto his sword. "I gather you don't remember seeing anything suspicious?"

"No, but I had no reason to pay special attention. I would be willing to have Lady Madeline search my mind with a spell if she has one."

Taking a sip of the water Skye had filled their wine skins with, Madeline said, "I don't know a spell. I appreciate your trust, but I would not go into your mind unless I was very sure of my skill."

"Perhaps we will have Blu try when we return to Arabela's home." Jode returned to his oiling.

Madeline waved her hand to dismiss that idea. "I do have something we can try. It's not magic but it might work. I would rather know right away if there is anything."

Barsh straightened and said, "I am ready."

"Give me a minute." Madeline took a long drink of water to

clear the spices from her throat. She needed to keep her voice soothing to make this work.

She settled across from Barsh and spoke quietly. "Close your eyes and we'll try to figure it out."

Barsh closed his eyes.

"We'll start by thinking of what opportunities there might be." Madeline tried to make her voice warm and bland, just like a therapist she's seen work on a client when she was a lawyer. Keeping that tone he'd said, helps draw the person into a state of semi-hypnosis. It releases medium and long term memories.

She asked a series of questions and Barsh's answers became more calm and reflective after each one. They determined that the only time someone might have had the opportunity was at night. In daylight, there were too many people around for anyone to saw through the wood.

"Let's start at the first night, on the road to Arabela's. Think what might have happened."

There was a pause. Madeline saw Barsh's expression change as he thought through the night.

"I do not think it could have happened then. There were people talking all night, and there was no opportunity to spend time at the wagon with no reason."

Madeline said, "The next night at Arabela's."

A longer pause this time. "I saw something. A shadow. At the time, I thought it might be a groom ducking out to see a woman. But I had not been as alert because we were in Lady Arabela's home; a safe place."

Madeline held her breath, but Barsh did not say anything else. "I think we have what we need," she said. "Why don't you rest now, Barsh? We need you alert tomorrow."

"I hope it was helpful," he said, yawning. "Good night."

Barsh crawled over to his bedroll, leaving Madeline to talk to Jode, Simon, and Callisra. "When we get to Arabela's we need to find out more about the people who left."

"Yes," Callisra said. "First, we have Tadric made ill, now our wagon damaged."

As much as she wanted to solve this tonight, Madeline realized she was exhausted. "We can't do anything more until we talk to Blu. I would rather spend our energy in getting there than scrying. Let's get some sleep."

48

"Thank the fates that's over." Madeline rolled her shoulders to release the tension.

The trip down the side of the mountain had not been as disastrous as the trip up, but it had been tense. Just as they rounded the last turn, the wagon slipped on the rough surface of the path and one of the horses had skidded into the side of the mountain, giving itself a deep gouge along its flank and its rider, Wint, a broken leg.

They were at the bottom of the mountain and sorting out how to carry all the equipment they had left there. Jode and Keegan had gone hunting and Callisra was tending to Wint. He would be riding in the wagon because she was only able to make him comfortable, not heal the break. Barsh had covered the horse's wound after applying an ointment.

Madeline looked for a task, but weariness overwhelmed her. No one wanted her and she needed rest. She found a place to sit against a boulder. It was still midafternoon but there was shade to be had here.

Simon joined her. "You did great."

"Thanks." Madeline pulled her knees up and wrapped her

arms around them. "It's not over yet, but it feels like we aren't under so much pressure. Like we have some time to breathe."

"Yeah. Lee's been quiet since you yelled at her." He nodded over to where Lee was helping sort supplies. "I almost cheered when you finally stood up to her."

"I shouldn't have yelled. She has been through more than anyone should have to, to survive. I'll talk to her later. I want to make sure she knows what her options are."

"And what are you giving her as options?"

Madeline looked at him. "What do you mean? The options are simple. She can go back, or she can stay. They aren't my options; they are the only options."

He patted her knee and rose. "Not so simple. If she wants to stay, she will need to have something to do. I'll leave you to think about it."

Madeline groaned. "Go make kissy faces with Callisra."

Simon laughed and went toward the wagon where Callisra was tying off the binding on Wint's splint.

Madeline laid her head on her knees and tried to wipe all thoughts from her mind. The only way she was going to be able to solve the next crisis was if she could get some sleep, some peace.

SHE WOKE after the sun was down. She'd curled up on her side at some point in her nap and her arm was asleep. Shaking out the pins and needles, Madeline sniffed; roasting meat and baking bread, so the hunt had been a success. A loud rumble from her stomach scared the rest of the sleep from her mind.

Walking over to the fire she noticed the wagon was loaded and there was nothing left of the pile of supplies.

"How did you get it all in the wagon?" She sat between Lee and Jode, trying not to feel like Lee was moving in on her husband. She trusted him.

Jode passed her a slice of bread with gravy on it. "The barrels weren't all full. Lee here figured out how to pack everything in the seven barrels that would fit in the wagon. The fire took care of the empty ones."

Madeline ate the bread to quiet her stomach, trying not to feel irritated that Jode thought Lee was useful.

Jode nudged her. "You need to make peace with Lee." He whispered in her ear.

"I know," she answered. "After we eat."

They ate as a group and chattered about what each of them would do when they got home. All five musicians practiced some new music after the meal, slow and gentle. Madeline shook herself out of a doze, realizing she had to talk to Lee now before either of them fell asleep.

She leaned over and said, "Lee, I'm sorry I yelled."

"Yeah you surprised me." Lee grinned. "I think this world has given you a backbone."

Madeline chuckled. "Yes, it did. We need to talk. Come. Let's go a bit away from the fire. Some privacy might help. And a little cooler air will keep me awake."

They moved, but not so far that they lost the light of the fire. The ground was hard, so Madeline pulled a bedroll over. "Just give me a second. I want to check that nothing dangerous is paying any attention."

Lee sat quietly while Madeline sent her senses out into the darkness. Nothing was within range other than some night animals.

"I think you need to know what your options are," Madeline said when she was sure they were safe.

"Okay," Lee said and waited.

Surprised and a bit suspicious that Lee was being so compliant, Madeline continued, "You can go home." Madeline smothered the little voice that said, *maybe* and *I hope Blu knows how.* "Or you can stay."

"What if I stay? Is there room for two lawyers here?"

Madeline thought back to her own struggles to understand what she could contribute in this world. "No need for lawyers here." She laughed at Lee's expression. "Yeah that's how I felt."

"But you found something to do." Lee looked over to where Simon sat with his arms around Callisra, talking to Urr. "And Simon is flourishing."

"You need to think about what you might do here." Madeline stifled a sigh. "We'll be traveling for a day or two. If you ask people nicely, maybe they'll give you some ideas."

"I don't know it seems pretty primitive."

Madeline wanted to say, *yes, it's really primitive, no TV, no movies, no internet.* But she said, "It's not really. You've seen what might be the worst of it. I can't guarantee it is actually the worst, but I can guarantee there's a lot of good stuff here. And you helped organize the wagon, maybe you can be the court organizer." Madeline paused. "For Arabela."

Lee shivered. "I'll try to be nice to people, but you know me."

"I'm sure you can do it." Madeline rose and held out her hand to help Lee to her feet. "Let's get back to the warmth and see if we can't get a full night's sleep before we hit the road again."

49

*S*imon returned to Callisra as the night grew quiet. Most of their companions were sleeping, or pretending to sleep. Callisra was checking on Wint one more time. Simon didn't feel like sleeping just then and convinced himself it was a good idea for someone to keep watch.

He waited until she turned away from Wint before saying, "Are you tired, or could we talk while we have some privacy?"

She smiled, the firelight bringing a warm glow to her skin, and an ache in Simon's body he had never felt before.

"I am as rested as I can be without a roof over my head, and a real bed under my bones." She took his arm. "Let us sit by the wagon. Wint is asleep and won't wake. I gave him some herbs to help him rest through the pain."

Simon led her to the front of the wagon. Its tongue braced on a saddle to keep it from moving. The horses were corralled in a circle to one side of it. If anyone approached, the horses would be the first to warn them.

Callisra leaned against the seat and looked at him. Her gaze so intent that Simon forgot what he was going to say. He closed his eyes and searched his memory. There it was, he was going to ask about where their relationship was going. Who would have thought he would be the one to start a relationship conversation?

He cleared his throat and wished for a beer, but here, just like in the old world, wishes didn't come true. "I think we need to talk about what we are planning."

Callisra smiled again and Simon wondered if that smile would always make him want to grab her and kiss her. She finally responded, "I don't know that we have planned anything. It is very early to be making plans. Or has Zora offered to split his winnings with you?"

He rolled his eyes. "I have nothing to do with that pool. I am so sorry they are embarrassing you like that."

"I am not embarrassed, Simon. It seems that you are, though." She touched his arm and warmth flowed when he felt her fingers. "Do not worry. It is harmless fun."

"Okay, as long as it doesn't bother you." Simon knew he was stalling, but really wished that Callisra would help him out by making a suggestion. "We've been under a lot of stress the last couple of days and that can make people feel differently."

"I know how I feel, Simon." She looked down and paused. "If your feelings were affected, I will understand. It is best to gain understanding before things progress too far."

Simon groaned. He was trying to give her an out, not find one for himself. "No, you don't understand. When I thought you were dead... when I realized how I felt." He sighed. "I am not such a great catch. I was giving you a chance to end whatever this is."

Callisra kept her gaze on the ground, leaving Simon to wonder what she was thinking. He was surprised to realize that her opinion meant everything to him. So much that he was holding his breath. The fire was burning low and its light was fading. Simon left the wagon to find another piece of broken barrel to toss on it. As he turned back, he could see Callisra was shaking. He hurried to her and put his arm on her shoulder.

"Don't cry. It's okay. Whatever it is we'll work it out. What's —"

"Oh, Simon," Callisra choked out through her laughter. "I am sorry to laugh. But you were so serious."

"Why would that make you laugh?" His pride was bruised but he was not going to start a fight. At least not right now.

"It must be this stress you mentioned. I have not changed how I feel." She started to get control of her giggles. "You are a wonderful catch for any woman. When I first heard of you, I was intrigued by the idea of your music."

"Well, the women usually go for the musicians not the managers." He stood in front of her and held her arms. "I have been here for a year, but I realize I don't know the conventions for courting."

She stepped into his arms and laid her head against his chest. "Did you not see how Sir Jode wooed Lady Madeline?"

"He just didn't go away." Simon remembered how Madeline resisted Jode because she wasn't sure she would stay. "Is it just persistence?"

"Well, there really aren't any rules unless you are marrying for political reasons." She snuggled in closer.

Simon kissed the top of her head. "You know I'll be away from home for long periods with the band?"

"Yes, but I can come with you."

"But don't you want to keep working with Madeline?"

Callisra sighed. "She does not need me. There are any number of people who can act as her secretary. Are you going to kiss me?" She wiggled in his arms before he could answer. Her lips warm against his. Simon took his time; he wanted this kiss to be wonderful and set the tone for all future kisses.

A world of time later, they separated.

Simon smoothed her hair back and kissed her nose, then her forehead. "How do we arrange a marriage? I don't care if Zora wins the pool. I just want to get started on our life."

"It is simple, at least for you and me. My family is small. My father will have no objections to me forming my own household. I think he was happy when I left him to his own devices."

"Where would you like to live?" Simon pictured a small cottage in a country setting.

She pulled away, and then drew him closer to the fire. "We do not have to solve every question tonight. It is enough that we are committed to marry. Until we decide where to build our home, I am sure we can continue to live in Jode and Madeline's house. Come, it is late and we need to rest."

50

*T*hree days later, Madeline sat with Blu in Arabela's library. They read the spell again. This time Madeline closed her eyes and said it from memory. When she opened her eyes, Blu nodded. "You are as prepared as we can be. This spell is new to me, also."

"If I had wanted to go back, would you have used it to send me?" she asked.

"I was confident that I could reverse my spell. But it was not my spell that brought your friend here."

"She's not my... Well, I guess we can call her my friend." Madeline stopped the kneejerk response. Lee would be gone soon, and then it wouldn't matter. "How can we make sure she goes? I don't want her here against her will. And neither will anyone else, believe me."

Blu stood and beckoned Madeline to the window. "What do you see when you look through this window?"

Madeline ran her eyes over the beautiful lawn outside. It led to a lake that she could see reflecting the sunlight. The trees were starting to turn color and the yellow contrasted with the dark bark of the trunks. She took in a deep breath of the cool air, and comfort flooded her veins. "Home. I see home."

Blu nodded. "Even though this is Arabela's land, you feel at home in Cartref. This whole world is home to you."

Madeline turned from the window. "How does this relate to sending Lee back?"

"When we cast this spell, it will be important for her to want to go back. If there is anything in her heart that stops her, we will not succeed."

"I talked to her," Madeline said. "She doesn't want to stay."

Blu reached for his box of ribbons. "Let us hope she is honest with herself. Now, this part of the spell requires her to answer some questions. When you spoke to her, did she say whether she wanted to remember her experience here?"

Madeline looked at the list of questions. "Maybe we should bring her in and get the answers. I don't want to guess at any of this."

Blu looked up from the paper. "A good idea, where is she at this time?"

Probably in the most awkward place possible, if I know her at all.

Madeline opened the door, hoping to find a servant she could send to find Lee. Instead she saw Lee talking to Jode. They were close together, and Jode was touching Lee's arm in a way that made Madeline seethe. Then Jode looked at her as though he had felt her presence. His smile pushed away her anger. No matter what Lee was up to, Jode was her husband, and she trusted him to be true.

Jode brought Lee's attention to Madeline and gave her a slight push. Madeline suppressed a smile then called, "Lee, we need you in here." She would find out from Jode later what they were so cozily chatting about.

As Lee made her way down the hall, Madeline was struck by how uncomfortable the woman was in the dress Arabela's seamstress had created for her. The periwinkle blue of the silk made

Lee's ash blond hair shimmer with light. But Lee seemed to march along as though she was wearing hiking boots and khakis. It wasn't like Lee didn't know how to wear a dress. She'd shown up in some beautiful designer gowns at office events. Madeline figured she was doing it on purpose to show she didn't belong here.

"Okay, what do you need?" Lee's temper had hardened in the few days on the road.

Madeline ushered her into the library. "The spell needs some information from you," she said. "When we have that, we are ready to go. We'll get you into your old clothes and send you back."

Lee rolled her eyes. "I can't wait. I feel like I'm at some weird Renaissance fair. How can you stand to walk in these skirts?" She held out the fabric and Madeline admired the way it draped. Her skirts were fabulous, but she was so much shorter, and elegance needed height.

"I like it, but I guess it's a matter of taste." She gestured to a stool beside the table. "Blu will ask you the questions and I'll make notes."

Lee sat beside Blu and smiled at the tiny monk. "I am ready. Please ask what you need."

"There are only three questions." Blu tapped the paper. "First, we need to know if you wish to remember your experience here."

"Oh, that's not what I thought. I expected you to want to know where I lived and who might be around when you dropped me back." She sat for a few minutes before asking, "If I say no, will I have this hole in my memory?"

Blu cocked his head in interest. "I do not know; it may be that you will simply fill in something from other memories."

Lee turned to Madeline. "What would you do?"

Madeline tapped her lip with the pen. The old Lee would never have asked for advice from Madeline – well the old Madeline anyway. "It doesn't matter what I would do, but I know you and if there was a hole in your memory you would not rest until it was filled. I suggest you keep the memory." She smiled. "Maybe you can write a book and make a million dollars on movie rights."

"Okay, I'll keep the memories. It will be good to know you and Simon are okay anyway. I missed fighting with you." Lee looked back to Blu.

He nodded to Madeline to make that note. "Is there anything of your possessions that may be left that you would regret?"

"That's easy," Lee said. "My bracelet and my Hermes scarf."

Madeline pushed aside the feeling that this was too easy. This cooperative attitude was probably just because she was about to leave. "We have them both."

Lee perked up. "Then no, nothing."

Madeline wrote it down, knowing that during casting she couldn't question what Lee had said.

"And finally," Blu said, looking directly into Lee's eyes. "Is there anything of your heart that is left here?"

"No," Lee said.

Madeline and Blu looked at each other. Madeline spoke first. "That was too fast. You need to think. Will you miss anyone? If you are hiding something from us, or yourself, it could make a difference."

Lee shook her head. "I hardly know anyone here. You and Simon have been gone for a long time and we were hardly friends."

"So, you are sure." Madeline poised her pen over the paper.

"I am sure."

TWO HOURS LATER, Lee was dressed in her old clothes, Hermes scarf tied perfectly around her neck. She looked comfortable, Madeline thought, going back was the right thing for her.

They were sitting in the middle of the courtyard. The sun was still up, so they didn't need to worry about setting special wards, just about getting the spell right.

Blu was going to cast the spell with Madeline. They had practiced it over and over, so she felt comfortable — well as comfortable as she could feel with something this unknown.

"Please, sit on the center cushion," Blu said to Lee. "Madeline and I will sit on either side of you."

Madeline waited until Lee was sitting cross legged on the cushion, and then sat facing her. When Blu sat, she unrolled the paper.

Blu took his ribbons out of the box and started to lay them across Lee's lap.

"Will I show up in my world with these all over me?" Lee asked.

"The ribbons are of this world. They will stay here." Blu kept working as he spoke. "Please, let us focus."

Madeline started the chant as she felt Blu imbue the ribbons with power. She could feel warmth radiate from her core through to the end of her fingertips. She continued chanting, running her finger across the paper so that she didn't stumble with the cadence. Cold replaced the heat as her power flowed to the ribbons.

All she could hear was her own voice summoning the power so she could add it to Blu's.

He finished with the last ribbon and Madeline slowed her chant. When she looked up from the paper, Lee was sitting in a cage of power lines that glowed in shades of blue and red. It was time to send her back.

Madeline looked at the paper again. "Are you Lee Marshall?"

"Yes, I am." Lee answered.

"Do you wish to return to your own land?" Madeline read.

"Yes, I do."

Madeline continued, "Do you hold all of your possessions?"

"I do."

"And is your heart free to leave?"

Lee didn't answer. Madeline looked up and saw that Lee was fading. Madeline flicked her eyes at Blu, but he was focused on controlling the power.

"And is your heart free to leave?" Madeline raised her voice this time, thinking Lee couldn't hear her.

"Yes," Lee's voice came as though from down a long tunnel.

Madeline sighed. The spell was over. Lee was on her way home and Madeline could get back to her own problems. One of which was this saboteur the other was deciding whether she wanted a baby now.

Lee faded a little more. Madeline raised her eyes to look at Blu, he was frowning, but he still poured power into the spell.

Then his eyes flew open. Madeline felt a crack of power across her skin. She looked at Lee and saw her snap back into full focus, the ribbons flying and landing in a circle around them.

ee was just about to step out into her living room when the courtyard reappeared. She looked from Blu to Madeline and saw the disbelief on their faces. "What the hell happened?"

Madeline looked at Blu, but he simply stood up and started gathering his ribbons again.

"How did you manage to screw this up?" Lee snapped at Madeline. They both stood facing each other. Lee had to look down at Madeline as usual. "I was almost there. Am I stuck here now?"

"We did everything right according to the spell." Madeline didn't snap or fight with her. She just spoke calmly. "You are sure you don't have any reason to want to stay?"

"No, and I haven't left anything here." Lee tried to loom over Madeline, to intimidate her, but Madeline refused to be intimidated.

"That leaves only your decision to remember your experience. I can't believe that would snap you back when you were almost there." Madeline turned to give Blu the ribbons she held in her hand. "Lee, calm down. We'll figure it out."

"Calm down? Look you might want to stay here, but I don't." Lee felt herself trembling, but she couldn't tell if it was in anger, or the creeping fear that she was stuck in a land where she wasn't needed, and everyone seemed to be on Madeline's side.

Blu touched her arm. "Madeline is correct. We will discover the cause. Please be sure we are doing everything we can to send you back."

Madeline sighed, and then said, "Why don't you go back inside. I'm sure the kitchen can put something together for you. A nice tea. And we'll let you know when we are ready to try again."

"Oh, no. I'm staying right here. I want to hear everything."

Blu gestured for them to follow him to a bench in the shade of a fountain. "Good, we may have questions for you. But I must ask that you do not interrupt our discussion. It is possible we will find the solution from the most unlikely question."

"Fine," Lee said settling on the bench, Blu on one side Madeline on the other. "Let's get started."

The little monk started talking to Madeline, and Lee quickly felt like they had forgotten her.

Blu's first question was, "Are you certain you read the words correctly?"

"Yes, I felt the energy flowing, and it was working all the way up to the last second. It is like we're missing the step that pushes her out of the spell into her world."

"That is what I felt as well." Blu was sorting his ribbons as he talked. Lee found it calming to watch his deliberate movements.

Madeline was reading the paper that held the spell. "Are you sure that this spell should work? Is it possible that only blood magic can send her back?"

Lee broke out of her lulled state when she heard that. "I can't go back to that woman. I don't trust that she'll send me home."

Blu patted her hand. "No, magic does not work that way here. Perhaps it does elsewhere, but no one can cast an irreversible spell. The closest they can come is to make the spell so complex that it takes a very long time to undo."

Lee heard Madeline muttering over the spell. It got on her nerves. "Is reading the spell over and over likely to solve this?"

Madeline's gaze was enough to kill, and Lee feared that it might be possible here to kill with a look.

"Blu asked you not to interrupt," Madeline said. "It might, but I think we should start from the beginning and try to re-craft the spell."

Blu took their hands. "Anger is not the way to find the answer. I think the matter is one of intent. The spell is failing not because it is wrong, but because one of you is not sure they want it to work."

Lee pulled her hand away and started talking, "Well, it's not me. I want to be home."

"And I am eager for you to be there." Madeline rolled her eyes. "And I know I keep messing up because I don't believe I can do it, but that's not what's going on. The spell isn't going wrong, something is missing. If Blu is right, either you have unfinished business here, or... or, I don't know what."

"Madeline, please bring us something cool to drink. I will talk to Lee and we will try to get to the bottom of it."

Lee waited for Madeline to protest, to say she wasn't a servant, but she just nodded and walked toward the house.

"Now, Miss Lee," Blu said. "Let us get to the bottom of this problem. If you are sure that you really wish to leave us, it maybe that something truly is getting in the way. Did you receive anything when you were with the Choi?"

Lee thought through the nightmare of the days on the road. "They mostly just kept me tied up." She shivered with the memory of feeling alone and threatened. "I tried to escape, but they just tied me up tighter."

"What do you remember of your arrival?"

Blu's calm questions drained the anger from Lee. "I was in my favorite bar and then I was in the middle of a clearing surrounded by rosy colored skinny giants. Oh my god, how am I going to explain disappearing off the face of the earth? Never mind, I'll figure something out." She closed her eyes to help her visualize the scene. "They grabbed me, and I only had a second to drop my scarf. I figured it would help anyone coming to find me. Then my bracelet got broken. Then I was tied up and we were on the move."

Blu nodded and hmmd.

Lee saw Madeline approach with a tray of drinks. Blu followed her gaze and said, "She is trying to help. It would be useful if you could keep your temper under control. If Madeline is occupied with arguing with you, she cannot help solve the problem."

"I know. I'll stop fighting." Lee pressed down on a feeling of annoyance, telling herself that Madeline had saved her life. She took the tea Madeline offered, and threw in a smile to avoid apologizing.

"Let me see the scarf and bracelet," Madeline said when Blu told her what they had discussed.

Lee handed them over and watched Madeline turn the scarf over in her fingers. "I don't think it's here. I've had this in my possession most of the time. There's nothing sewn in and no stains." She handed the scarf back and started turning the bracelet and charm over in her fingers. "This feels hot."

Lee reached out her hand, "Let me see. If there's anything different I might notice."

Madeline shook her head. "Give me a minute." She passed the links through her fingers slowly then turned her attention to the pendant.

As she ran her fingertip over the tiny diamond, Madeline jerked back. "Shit, that burned." She handed the charm to Blu. "It's in the diamond. Can you extract it? If not, how will we send Lee back and leave this here?"

"I can't leave it here." Lee pictured her mother's reaction if she thought Lee had lost the charm. "If it can't come, I can't go back."

Madeline glared at her and Lee felt a blush rise. "Sorry. I guess I can put up with my mother's disappointment."

Blu reached into his pocket and pulled out a thin black thread. He laid it on the diamond and started whispering words as he slowly drew it away. As the thread cleared the gem, harsh laughter ricocheted off the garden walls and the image of Skye Greatmother flickered above the stone.

"It seems the Choi leader had plans for you, Lee." Blu passed her the charm. "Let us hope that was the only gift she left."

Madeline stood. "Okay, Lee, let's give this another try."

MADELINE SET the protections around Lee and saw them glow to life. Sitting with her back to the setting sun, Madeline met Blu's gaze. He held the ribbons in his hands and nodded for her to begin.

Taking a deep breath Madeline started the chant. The power started to flow from her belly outward. She noticed Blu start his part and then dismissed everything but the words in front of her. Time disappeared and all she felt was the power flowing. Then suddenly, a surge of power thrust forth and then came back to knock her over.

"Well, done Madeline," Blu's voice cut through the shock. "She is gone."

Madeline blinked and sat up. Where Lee had sat was only a scattered pile of ribbons.

"Thank god. I was going to strangle her."

Blu chuckled. "I was also going to do her damage. I have never encountered someone so unwilling to accept the need to thank the person who saved their life. I commend you on your self-control." He started to pick up his ribbons.

Madeline stooped to help. "What had Skye done to the diamond?"

"A small drop of blood in the side of the setting. I was able to remove it with a little power."

She handed him the ribbons she'd collected. "Why? I mean what good would it do Skye to keep Lee here?"

"I do not know for certain. She must have done it immediately after Lee arrived. I think the bracelet was left for us to find."

"Do you think it was related to the sabotage, and the attack on Tadric?"

Blu started toward the house. "It may, or it may not. The timing is suspicious though, is it not?"

Madeline followed Blu. "It is very suspicious, but that doesn't mean it is connected. She struck me as someone who would do something like this just to cause problems."

"That is true. I will attempt to scry her later tonight and ask."

"Do you think she'll tell you, or will you be able to cast a spell? That would be a good skill, spell casting through a scrying surface."

Blu laughed and took her arm as they entered the door to Arabela's great hall. "It may be that she will explain. She knows we released her spell, so it will not come as a surprise. But I will be able to tell from what she says, and what she doesn't say, what her intent was. We will go from there."

52

*L*ater that evening, Madeline sat with Blu in front of the fireplace in Arabela's great room. Dinner had been a small affair. Madeline felt the tension of the last two weeks drain from her as the warmth of her new family surrounded her. Jode and Simon were with the other musicians. The sound of their session floating through the house.

Callisra and Arabela were in the kitchen discussing the details of the wedding feast. Since Simon realized he was going to marry, he had pushed the date up as close as possible.

"I guess Zora is going to win a lot of money." Madeline sipped her wine.

"Zora was not the winner," Blu said. "I invested in the pool. I chose one month."

Madeline laughed and the rest of her tension flew out on the sound. "Congratulations. Ah, it is good to have a breathing space."

Blu took a sip of tea before speaking, "Yes. I fear we have a much bigger adventure ahead of us."

Madeline wondered when she would next see her home. Starting a family was going to be hard if they didn't have peace and time. "Yes, we have the Tryll, the saboteur, whoever is trying to hurt Tadric, Skye's motives for that little spell on Lee. Am I forgetting something?"

"No, I think you have named all of the challenges we face, for now at least. Let us start with these Tryll. I am truly intrigued by the idea we have unknown beings among us. And you have the scroll from Skye."

"Yes. I haven't done more than glance at it. Given what she did to Lee, do you think we can trust the contents?"

Blu nodded. "She gave you that in gratitude for your work in the ceremony. If she did not give it in good intent, that would taint the magic. We will see why she tried to keep Lee Marshall here later when I scry."

"I have been thinking about researching all the magic of Cartref. It would benefit everyone if we had some way of understanding the magic we can't cast. The book in Arabela's library was a good start, but I would put more detail in it."

"I agree." Blu added a few small sticks to the fire. "And it would be most helpful if it was in a more modern language. It will mean you must deal with some very difficult beings. It will mean a lot of travel."

"I thought I would start with the friendly beings first." Madeline paused before speaking again, glad that Blu was always patient. "About the travel, I have been thinking about something else."

"And what is that?" Blu turned his gaze on her. "You are worried about something that is clear. Just tell me. I am happy to help."

"I have been thinking about babies. I don't know why it hasn't already happened, but I think it is getting time for me to have a child." She stared at the fire, not wanting to see his reaction.

"I think Jode would like to have children to raise. What is it you are worried about?"

Madeline tried to pinpoint exactly why she was worried. "It's been a year and I haven't fallen pregnant yet. If I am going to be trying to catalog the magic, and save Tadric, how will I ever get pregnant?"

"I am sure Sir Jode will be traveling with you, so the opportunity will present itself."

"But what about the magic? Do I have to stop so the baby will be healthy?"

"Magic will not harm your child. Nor will it harm you to be carrying a child while you work magic."

Realizing she was holding back the one thing that really worried her, Madeline asked, "What if we can't have children?"

Blu raised an eyebrow. "You must speak to Callisra about that. As a healer she will be able to tell you. What if you cannot, or if Sir Jode cannot? What difference will it make to your life, your happiness?"

"I will get over it. But what if Jode can't get over it?" Madeline hated the sound of fear in her voice.

Blu patted her knee. "This is something you will have to talk to your husband about. I cannot advise you on your marriage. But I do know he loves you."

Yes, but how long will that be true if I can't give him children?

53

"*M*adeline, don't be angry with me. You were worried about the same thing." Jode strode along beside Madeline who was almost running, as though she could run away from the answer she didn't want to give.

"Yes, I was. But I didn't ask Lee why my wife wasn't bearing children." The image of Lee laughing at Madeline's situation brought tears of frustration to her eyes.

Jode took her elbow and gently pulled her to a stop. "I thought you might be angry, but I still had to ask her. Would you have preferred I answered with a lie when you ask such questions? You did ask me what we were talking about, after all."

Madeline wrenched her arm out of his grasp but stayed where she was. "No, my preference would have been for you not to have asked her. But you are right in one thing. I am relieved that you told me the truth."

She had been trying to broach the subject of children as they dressed in the morning. Jode had been evasive, which was very unlike him. Then the memory of Lee and Jode whispering in the hall had risen. When she asked, Jode had said, 'I inquired if she knew of any reason you would not be able to carry a child.'

Red fury had filled Madeline and before she could do something she would regret she had stormed out of their bedroom. Jode had simply followed. Now they were standing at the top of the stairs and Madeline was afraid they were about to have a very public, very loud fight.

She turned back to the bedroom. "I will not discuss this here. Come back to the room."

"Yes, madam." Jode's voice carried a chuckle that irritated her even more than the words.

She tried not to react. She was being bossy, but it was better than spouting the invective that she felt push at her throat.

When they were behind closed doors, she turned to tell Jode why he shouldn't have asked Lee of all people when he said, "Do you wish to know what she said?"

Madeline stopped cold. Lee had given information? "I suppose it was some kind of lie but go ahead."

"Before I tell you, will you tell me what Callisra or Blu said when you asked them?"

Madeline's anger deflated a little. Jode's voice was curious, not accusatory.

"It's not the same as asking Lee. Callisra is a healer and Blu is my teacher. Lee is my nemesis, or she was."

"Yes, I understand the distinction. I only asked her because she is from your world. I thought she might have an insight that Simon would not."

"You asked Simon?" Madeline's cheeks burned.

"Is he your nemesis now?"

She shook her head. "No, but it's personal and embarrassing."

Jode chuckled. "Well you will be happy to know I did not speak with Simon. I assumed that he would have no answers for me. You do know that I love you and if there are no children it would not end our marriage."

The embarrassment didn't fade with Jode's words, but more

of her anger did. "I do, but it is nice to hear. Anyway, both Callisra and Blu said it was probably nothing to worry about."

"Lee was more helpful. She said you were probably taking contraceptive medications before you came."

"I was," Madeline said.

Jode smiled. "She said that it is often true that this medication continues to prevent pregnancy for one year after you stop taking it."

A wave of forgiveness flowed through Madeline. Forgiveness for Jode's indiscreet question and for everything that Lee had ever done to her. "Yes, she's right. And it's been almost a year." She threw herself at Jode. "There is nothing to worry about yet."

He caught her and spun her like a child in his arms. "I think we should continue to keep our energy up and a baby will eventually come of all our trying."

She kissed him and wiggled out of his arms. "Let's get to that trying."

54

That afternoon, Madeline and Blu sat in the library preparing to reset protections on Arabela's home. Tadric was healthy again and they wanted to keep him that way.

"I had a conversation with Skye last night," Blu said, handing her a ribbon. "Here take this and place it on the window ledge."

Madeline placed the yellow ribbon where Blu pointed. "And what did she have to say about the blood on Lee's ring."

"She was worried that Lee would escape. The blood would have been able to draw her back to Skye. She says she forgot about it. But I am not sure I believe her."

They draped the rest of the room and sat at the center preparing to cast the spell. "Well whether she is lying or not, Lee is gone. And I hope she stays there." Madeline suddenly had an awful thought. "She is going to stay there, right?"

Blu motioned for her to prepare for the spell. "We cannot know what will happen. I believe she is there permanently, but she was brought here once."

Madeline groaned. "I will not worry about it." She pushed everything away except her image of the happy peaceful beach.

She relaxed in the feel of the sand beneath her feet and the sun on her skin. The gentle lapping of the waves against the shore took her further into the light trance needed to allow Blu into the scene. "When you are ready," she said her voice low and calm.

Blu appeared on the shore walking toward her. "Now send your thoughts with mine. We will place a dome of protection over the land here. Should something try to attack from outside, we will know."

Madeline felt Blu guide her power and then a rainbow dome appeared in her vision.

"Very good. Now we must turn it inward to ensure any danger inside the dome is also prevented."

The dome flexed and Madeline struggled to keep her control over the power. "Is there something wrong?" she asked.

"It seems that the dome is already preventing attacks." Blu's voice was strained. "Let us leave it and withdraw to place a different internal protection."

She let go of the power she held in her mind. The rainbow of the dome darkened then settled. Madeline opened her eyes to the library. "Are you all right?" She asked as Blu swayed in his chair. He looked up and his face was gray. "No, clearly you are not." She ran to get a blanket that had been laid across the other chair in the room.

Blu accepted it and wrapped the warm fabric around his shoulders. "It will pass." His voice was thready and weak. "Ask for food to be brought and we will soon finish our work."

Madeline called one of the servants from the hall and asked for broth or some other hearty meal.

It took an hour, but Blu was finally looking healthy again. "We must create another spell to protect us from attack inside the dome," he said.

Madeline reached for the spell book, and said, "Take my power this time. You gave too much the first time. I can recover."

"Thank you, Madeline. I will take what I need. When we are finished here, I will rest."

The second spell manifested as a fine yellow mesh that covered the ground. There were no fluctuations in the color, no flexing in the coverage. Madeline relaxed again. For now, everyone was safe.

When Blu withdrew this time, he was pale but not as ashen as the last time.

Madeline called for more tea and they sat in companionable silence until the pot was drunk.

"So, the attack continues," she finally said.

"It seems so." Blu pressed his lips together. "I think we will need to abide here for some time to ensure the health of Tadric and Arabela. In time, we may identify the attacker."

Madeline hoped they would solve this problem soon so she could get back home where she and Jode could start working on a baby.

WANT MORE?

A new threat to the heir to the Summer Lands pulls Madeline away from her lessons. Use the QR code to grab your copy of A Twist of Power to ride with Madeline to the mysterious City.

CHAPTER 1

*M*adeline held the yellow ribbon and stared at Blu. The little monk was sitting across from her, a matching ribbon laid across his upturned palms. He was muttering so quietly that she had to strain to hear the words he spoke. Her responses to his statements were the only things keeping the spell intact until they finished.

"The net holds against all forces." Blu's voice held no sign of the effort he was pouring into the spell.

"Against all forces, the net flexes to hold," Madeline whispered. She tried to keep her fingers light on the ribbon, because it represented the net of protective spells they held over Arabela's house. If she held the ribbon too tightly, the net would become rigid and, with enough force, shatter rather than flex.

Three days ago, when she'd returned from the Choi temple with her friends, Madeline had hoped that the threats against Arabela's son would fade away. Until her best friend was safe, she wasn't going to return home. Until she returned home, Madeline feared she would never be able to have her own child. The life she'd been living on the road was too stressful. Unfortunately, the threat was still active and growing worse.

It was getting more difficult as time passed to not push back on the attacks. What she really wanted to do was blast all the power back down the line and fry the magic of whoever was on the other end. Blu had considered it when she announced the idea, but quickly said that it wasn't possible.

Madeline watched the golden protective net shudder one more time, and then settle, like Jell-O when it was turned out of a bowl. She breathed out a long shuddering lungful of air and waited until Blu told her to stop feeding power to the spell.

"It is enough for now," Blu said after a moment. "Let us rest and eat. I am afraid that each attack is meant to drain us of power until we are unable to repel even a child's effort."

Madeline stretched and felt the knots in her shoulders relax. She took his ribbon and placed both of them in the small travel chest beside the table. "I was almost convinced that this was a peaceful world – well peaceful enough given the way the Scree behave... and the Choi..." She snorted a laugh. "Where did I get that idea? Since you brought me here, I've spent most of my time fighting off one or another of the species of the world." *And killing too many beings to save the people she loved.* In her old life, she defended people in court not in battle. There no one had died.

Blu stood, only coming up to her shoulder, and took her arm. *He must be shrinking. We used to be closer to the same height. Now he must be only about four feet tall.*

He led her to the door. "Perhaps the months you spent at your home, with your husband were peaceful enough to make you forget that few living beings are satisfied with what they have in life. With dissatisfaction comes conflict."

Madeline pulled open the heavy wooden door to the room. Arabela's home reminded her of Renaissance chateaux in France – solid and safe. The walls warmed with rich, intricate tapestry, and the floors with bright rugs. "Perhaps, but these last few weeks have pushed those memories to the back of my mind."

"Well, we are safe for now," Blu said pulling her toward the stairs. "I smell pastry. Let us join whoever is baking and hope for a taste."

Madeline inhaled the aroma of butter and cinnamon; the intensity made her stomach rumble. Magic took a lot out of her. It also allowed her to eat whatever she wanted. Practicing spells was better than any boot camp program – and usually more fun. "Good idea, and maybe Callisra will be there and we can help to organize the wedding. Anything will be more interesting than casting protection spells." *Who would have guessed I'd become tired of magic?*

Blu started down the staircase. "Indeed; a happy occasion is just what we need to refresh our spirits." He turned toward her, a sly smile on his face. "I am surprised at Simon's hurry to perform the ceremony. He has not shown himself to be comfortable with committing to one woman. Is this normal for men from your world?"

When Madeline was transported to Cartref, Simon came with her. In their old world, he'd been her assistant. When they arrived here, he'd started a rock band within a few days. That band had been the distraction when the attack on Sayer Goddard had happened. Now he was managing the music business for what seemed like the whole world.

Madeline laughed; the last of the weight of the worry she'd been carrying since this morning's attack started lifting from her shoulders. "I suspect you are behind the haste. I thought you won that pool the goblins started. Didn't you pick a date in the next couple of weeks?"

"Perhaps I have counseled him to hasten the date. But no one has won until the wedding takes place." Blu's smile was all innocence, and it made Madeline laugh again.

"I think you're right. With these attacks, it's probably a good idea to get the formalities over with in case…well let's not guess what might happen."

Crossing the great hall with its fireplace and scattered chairs, they entered the kitchen. As they stepped through the archway, a warm blanket of belonging wrapped around Madeline, something she'd never felt back in her world of lawyers, and career momentum, and frozen dinners. The room was large, hot, and full of savory aromas. The chatter of the kitchen staff was a counterpoint to the sound of crackling logs in the ovens.

Simon, dressed in a white tunic over forest green trousers, was charming a tray of cinnamon buns from the cook. Callisra, raven hair pulled into a simple braid, was sitting beside Arabela, their heads bent over a gurgling bundle in Arabela's arms. Tadric, heir to the Summer Lands, and the target of these attacks. The child shared his mother's green eyes, but his curly hair was dark brown.

Madeline left Blu and poured mugs of caf. Before she filled the last one, Jode joined her at the counter. Even after a year, her breath caught when he was near. Tall, blond, and romance-novel handsome, he had captured her heart despite her reservations. "I missed you," he whispered in her ear. "I will be glad to have you to myself again when this threat is over."

"Come and see what my son has learned," Arabela called before Madeline could answer him.

Arabela sat Tadric on the floor and the child remained upright without support. "You see, how strong he is?" She caught him as he started to flop onto his side. "Well, for a short time anyway."

Madeline reached for Tadric and the child held out his arms for her. She settled him on her lap, wondering if her first-born would be a boy.

"You are pale," Jode said as he put a plate of tidbits in front of her. "Are you resting yourself enough? I do not wish to lose you."

She kissed the top of Tadric's head, feeling the tickle of his fine hair against her cheek. Then, smiling up at Jode, she reached for a pastry filled with minced and spiced pork. "We are being careful, maybe too careful. I think we need to talk to Blu again about going on the offensive. If we only repel the attacks as they come, we will eventually fail."

Jode glanced at the boy in Madeline's arms. "The Summer Lands have already lost Alric. If they lose his son, it will leave them open for anyone to take control. There will be bloodshed."

Arabela reached for her son. "If there were other heirs, we would know who was attacking. But Alric was an only child of an only child. And now Tadric is following the tradition."

Madeline took a bite of the pastry before speaking. "Then there must be a way to do something."

"It is too risky to change tactics," Blu said. "If we lose the defense, we lose everything. Neither of us has the power to hold the net alone. Neither of us has the power to attack alone."

Madeline knew her teacher was right, but being right was not going to be good enough if this kept up longer. "There must be a way," she said. "I'm not going to give up so easily."

"YOU CAN SLEEP," Blu said as Madeline jerked out of a doze hours later. "In fact, we should both sleep. No attacks have happened at night yet. I imagine our enemy is as wary of night spells as we are."

Madeline rubbed her eyes to force herself to alertness. She believed Blu but didn't think she would be able to sleep properly knowing she would be woken if... no, when an attack came. "I can nap here. You go to your bed. I'll be able to hold off anything that comes long enough to wake you."

Blu shook his head. "It is not your responsibility alone to keep the wards. But I do not know that I will rest with this threat hanging over us either. Let us talk, perhaps that will soothe us enough to rest."

Madeline felt Blu's touch on the protective net withdraw until it was only a single thread of contact. She followed suit and felt her energy rise slightly with the change. He was right, people here did not do magic at night. She was not sure why. Jode had tried to explain, but she still didn't understand. It didn't matter. Apparently, spells could continue through the night, they just couldn't be cast in safety. So, the net would survive until dawn when they would have to refresh the power.

"Let me get someone to bring us warm tea," she said, rising from the chair to open the door. "It will help us to relax."

A servant was waiting in a chair outside the door. Madeline knew everyone in the household was prepared to support them, but she still felt guilty that this maid was losing her sleep on the off chance they needed something. "Mary, can you bring us some tea. And then you can go to your bed. We won't need anything more tonight."

The girl nodded and slipped away toward the stairs. Madeline returned to the room and moved the throw cushions from the two upholstered chairs so they could curl up. That way, if they fell asleep, at least they would be comfortable. Mary returned with tea and two bowls of oatmeal, rich with cream and dried fruit. "Cook said this will help you sleep."

When they were alone again, Madeline settled into one of the chairs and waited until Blu did the same.

"I think we need a plan." She poked the spoon into the porridge but didn't feel like eating. Her nerves were shredded from just waiting and waiting. "Whoever is attacking isn't going to get bored and just stop."

Blu didn't answer for a few minutes. Only the fact he sipped his tea let Madeline know he was still awake. She knew better than to interrupt his thoughts. Even if she had a plan, he would know something that would improve it. That is if she could convince him to go on the attack.

Finally, he placed his cup on the wide arm of his chair. "You think I am willing to outwait our attacker, but I have been thinking the same thing. We are at a disadvantage. It is taking all of our power to hold the protections, and we will fail if that does not change."

Madeline rose to get the teapot. Topping off both cups, she said, "Is there someone we can trust to help us?" There were no others capable of magic in Arabela's household as far as Madeline knew, and they couldn't spare the energy or time to call someone from far away.

"There is someone. I have not asked him yet, because I thought we would have solved this problem by now."

Attacks on Tadric were more than a problem, but Blu was the master of the understatement, so Madeline didn't argue. "Who? I thought I knew everyone here. Has someone come in the last few days?"

"You forget about the musicians. Zora is an Eldman as well as a talented entertainer." Blu reached for his oatmeal and started picking out the fruit and eating it.

In the silence, Madeline thought about how Zora could help. "As far as I remember, Eldmen can only do small magic. And their spells take a long time because of all the chanting."

Blu nodded and continued to pick out the fruit. Madeline handed him her bowl. "Here, you might as well enjoy mine too. So, are you telling me they have more power than it seems? Or am I missing something?"

"No, they use all of their power. Are you sure you do not want any of the fruit?" Blu's question was polite, but he already had a slice of apple in his fingers.

Madeline shook her head and went back to thinking out the answer. Blu rarely told her what she needed to know, so she'd become used to puzzling it out. "So, that means he can't take my place, or yours." She didn't look at Blu. He knew she needed to talk it through before she came to her conclusion. "Can you use him as a battery?"

"What is that?"

"You store power in one and use it later." Madeline had an

ethical twinge about using someone that way; it didn't seem right. "They give you control over their power."

"An interesting idea." Blu placed the bowl on the floor beside his chair. "I have spells that will allow the caster to channel another's power, but it does not require relinquishing control. I do not know if anyone would be willing, or desperate enough, to agree. And I do not know of a spell that will allow you to store magic for use later."

That would have been too easy. Madeline tried to think a path through the growing fog of exhaustion. "He can do another spell. Yes! He can find us help, or he can seek a clue to the identity of whoever is attacking us."

Blu smiled at her excitement. "I think we can try both. If we sleep, perhaps one of us can spare some power to his spell and allow him to reach as far as the mountains."

Madeline nodded, the thoughts coming quickly. "We should also send the goblins out to find help from other humans, or perhaps from a Fay? They could even go past the mountains. I hope I can eventually find a spell that will remove that restriction."

Blu curled up in his chair. "Another very good idea. Now sleep. I fear we will be tested again in the morning."

Madeline watched her teacher slide quickly into sleep. Her mind was still churning, and she needed to let it slow down. If Zora could call someone, she'd suggest a Fay, because they can see at a distance. Blu was certain that the attacks were coming in from the Northeast. Tomorrow she'd ask Jode to show her what was on the map there, other than just mountains.

Tomorrow they would talk to Zora about helping. And to the goblins. They could move fast, not magic, but it seemed like it sometimes.

She blinked and felt her cup slipping from her hand. Placing it on the floor beside her chair, Madeline pulled her shawl around her and curled up to let sleep take her.

Tomorrow, she thought, it will all work out. Tomorrow, they would save the world.

WHEN ZORA JOINED them the next morning, Madeline let Blu talk. She monitored the protective net while they spoke. It left her able to listen, but most of her concentration stayed with the magic. The little she had left was used to worry about how they would channel the Eldmen magic.

"So, it seems if we do not act to identify this attacker, we will soon be too tired to maintain the safely of the household. We need your help," Blue finished.

Zora nodded and walked to the window, his stocky figure blocking most of the light from the opening. "I can lend you my power for a short time. One of you can try to trace the attacks." He returned to the table. "Also, I can ask Urr to go to the Fay."

As she was about to ask more about borrowing magic, Madeline felt a touch from outside the protections. Not an attack, but a gentle test of the strength. "Blu." She beckoned them over.

Blu reached out with his power and felt the spells. "This is not the same person."

Madeline reached for Zora's hand to bring him into their magic loop. She saw his presence in the net as red streaks against the golden glow. So, power was power. As long as Zora accessed his own magic, she could channel it.

"Strong magic," Zora said. "Take what you need of my power. I will not need my magic anytime soon."

Madeline felt power surge through her connection to the Eldman. The net glowed brightly, then settled back to a glimmer. Zora's magic, now a pale-yellow mist, wove itself around the ribbons of her own. The press from the outside came again, gentle but persistent.

"Is there any way we can reach through to find out who this is without weakening the spell?" The touch was so different from the slamming attack that she couldn't imagine it was a trap. This was like a child tugging at a mother's sleeve for attention. The attacks were as brutal as a battering ram on a screen door.

"It will be difficult," Blu said. "Any breach of the dome will open the way for attack. We will have to be very careful."

Zora shifted toward Madeline and slipped his hand to her shoulder. "I can stay in the link and still leave you with your hands free to work the ribbons with Blu," he whispered. Madeline glanced at him. His eyes were shut, and his lips were moving. Eldmen chanted their magic and Madeline knew that Zora would keep his chant going until they told him to stop, no matter how long it took.

She turned to Blu, leaving only a thread of concentration on the protections. "We could ignore this. Perhaps it is a trap."

Blu simply looked at her until she sighed and admitted, "I don't feel any threat. But it could still be a trap. How can we take a chance?"

Instead of answering, Blu opened his chest of ribbons and started picking through them.

Madeline thought about the possibilities. "If you and Zora were ready to deal with anything that happened, I could reach through and connect with whoever this is."

Blu handed her a green ribbon. "Yes, that is how we do it. But I will be the one to reach through. You are linked to Zora already. I will not allow you to be in such danger."

He handed her several more ribbons. Madeline laid them across her lap. "Are you sure I am capable of pulling you back fast enough?"

"It will all be in the ribbons. If you feel any danger, pull them toward you and I will follow."

Blu interrupted Zora's silent chant to explain what they were doing. The Eldman nodded and moved to sit behind Madeline, placing a hand on each of her shoulders. "You will be able to draw from me as quickly as if it was your own power now. Do not speak to me until you are finished, or it will break my access to the magic."

They settled down and Madeline focused on the net. She saw a golden thread snake toward the center of the spell dome. The questioning pressure tapped again. The thread of Blu's power zipped to the dent and wiggled through the weave of the net. Madeline tightened her grip on the ribbons, ready to yank Blu back.

His probe extended through the mesh and stopped. Madeline waited, feeling Zora's power fill her veins, warm and reassuring.

Suddenly a familiar heat rushed toward the net. Attack! Madeline yanked the ribbons into her lap and winced as the flash of gold scored across her senses. She flooded the net with Zora's power.

The attacker flashed away from the net and left.

"It's done," Madeline said, bringing her focus back to the room.

Zora's hands slipped from her shoulders as he stopped muttering. "That was exhilarating. I have never used so much power at one time." He shook himself and reached for one of the breakfast sandwiches.

Blu was wiping his face with a corner of his robe. He was pale but Madeline thought he looked unhurt.

"Did you learn anything before the attack? Was it a trick? Have some tea." Madeline reached for the pot that was warming on the hearth.

Blu accepted a cup, and then motioned for her to sit. "I am fine, Madeline. Keep calm. I believe we have done some damage to our enemy. But, no, it was not a trick. I was able to make contact, but we were torn apart with the attack." He reached to take a muffin from the tray.

"And?"

"Yes, Blu, stop tormenting us," Zora said around a mouthful of sandwich. "What did you learn?"

"I learned that we hurt the attacker. I think we will have some time of peace today at least."

Madeline restrained herself. Blu would string this out as long as he could. It was a good sign. If it was bad news, he would have told them straight out. "That is a relief. I think Zora will have to rest and rebuild his energy. So, was it worth the risk?"

"Our visitor told me that the answer lies in The City, and a stranger who is not a stranger."

"That's not much. Was there anything else?"

"The presence was male; that is all I can tell you."

Madeline reached for her own breakfast as she suppressed the urge to press harder for information. She reminded herself that nothing here was simple. "Where is The City?"

Zora pointed toward the mountains. "North, over the mountains. In the Mariai Lands. Two days, if you go by horse. And not too many of you."

Heat rushed through Madeline's body, and then drained away leaving her feeling dizzy and nauseated. She pushed aside her plate and said, "I think we need to go tomorrow."

Blu nodded as he picked fruit from the muffin. "It will be good to have those attacks come to an end."

The nausea passed, leaving behind a ravenous hunger. She watched the two men as she devoured a muffin; Blu, tiny and deceptively fragile, looking serene as usual; Zora, solid and stern, his movements deliberate as he chose his food from the plate.

"How will we know you are safe?" she asked, hoping for some kind of magical cell phone.

Blu smiled at her, "You must have faith, Madeline. We will endure until we no longer need to." When she opened her mouth to ask for something more concrete, he chuckled. "And I think we will send you a message if anything changes."

CHAPTER 2

*T*he last time she'd traveled toward the mountains, Madeline had tried her best to keep the group small. A futile effort as their party had grown to almost twenty people in the end. And all of them had proven useful.

This time, only three people accompanied Madeline. Jode who would never have stayed behind, Simon, and Callisra. In the rushed hours of preparation, someone had managed to find a few minutes to hold the wedding ceremony. Simon had promised a celebration party when they returned, but neither wanted to leave on this mission with their vows unsaid.

Now they rode across the rolling grassland to the north of Arabela's home. In the distance, a forest stood between them and the line of mountains on the horizon.

"We will be at the pass by nightfall," Jode said. "The way through is easy; if we do it in the light. In the dark, it can be treacherous, so we will camp before crossing."

They traveled at a fast walk. The horses would go a long way at that pace and still be rested enough for a speedy journey to The City. Madeline tried to imagine what a city – or rather The

City – in Cartref would be like. Probably no skyscrapers like she was used to, maybe she wouldn't call it a city at all.

"Callisra," Madeline called over her shoulder to the couple. "Tell me again what you remember of The City."

"I'm not sure my memories will be useful," she answered. "I was only a child."

Madeline smiled. "At least you have some memory."

Callisra was quiet for a moment. Then she answered in a voice that seemed still stuck in the memory. "So many people. I remember clinging to my father's hand, worried that I would get lost. And the streets were narrow, and it was hot."

"Anything good?" Simon asked.

"It was peaceful. Even with all the people, everyone kept the rule of peace within the walls." Callisra added laughing, "And the food and candy were delicious."

Madeline joined the laughter but wished there was something else she could use to make a plan. She hated going in blind. They only had one contact and that was not even the person who sent the message. The touch of the messenger was torn away before Blu could identify their ally.

"You are quiet, my love," Jode's voice broke through her musing. "Are you fretting about what we might find?"

"You know me too well. I'm not really fretting. It's hard to worry about a plan being successful when you don't have one. All we know is that Blu's friend Zerenia might be able to tell us something about our mystery man."

Callisra nosed her horse between them. "I don't think Blu would have sent us to her otherwise. The Mariai visions usually turn out to be right. The trick is to interpret them correctly."

"Isn't that always the problem?" Simon asked. "Prophecies, visions, messages from beyond… they are all a hundred percent right in hindsight."

Madeline laughed, deciding to enjoy the ride rather than do her usual worrying about controlling the future. "I guess I'm missing the old days when I would take the time to prepare for court. No, not that kind of court," she added at the confused look on Jode's face. "Anyway, why is it called The City? I mean we've seen small towns and villages, but nothing like what I would call a city."

Jode moved his horse off the path so that they could ride together. He increased the pace slightly before answering, "It is the only port on this part of the world. Because of that, it attracts people who wish to travel, or set up business. Ports have a lot of visitors and they need places to stay, goods to buy."

Ports were the same from world to world, Madeline reflected. "How many people live there?"

"Four or five thousand, I expect. No one has counted," Jode answered. "Most are Mariai, but I expect we will find elves, and goblins, and even some Scree. Most beings have some residence or business in The City."

Elves? From what little she'd heard they weren't the Tolkien version – or any of the Tolkien versions to be accurate. Something between a scholar and a berserker was as close as anyone came to describing them.

"Maybe after we find and stop whoever is attacking, we can spend some time exploring The City?" She mentally crossed her fingers that it would be that simple. She was getting tired of rushing around the countryside rescuing people. It felt like forever since she'd been in her own home, not just two weeks. A few days to deal with this problem and maybe she could go home to the Lower Plains.

"I imagine we will see most of it in our search for the culprit," Jode said. "But it would be pleasant to have time with my wife with nothing to do but explore and…" He grinned at her in a way that made her blush.

Callisra giggled. "It is nice to know that, even after almost a year, you can behave like newlyweds."

. . .

HOURS LATER, Madeline was getting tired of the sameness of the grasslands. The rolling landscape lulled her mind and she shook her head again to wake herself up. There was enough breeze to move the grass in gentle waves, which added to the soporific effect.

The edge of the forest beckoned with the promise of coolness and variety of scenery. The sun was not so hot it burned, but it was hot enough to drain her energy. They rode more or less side by side, but from what she could see of the path through the trees, they would have a road to travel soon. Perhaps they would be able to move faster on firmer ground.

She kneed Thunder to a trot and said, "Let's pick up some speed. If I'm going to fall asleep, I'd rather do it when I have my bedroll beneath me."

Looking back, she saw the grin on Jode's face as he urged Ice Storm to race her. Simon and Callisra laughed and joined the scramble for the tree line.

"Last one there is a rotten—" her challenge died on her lips as an arrow slapped into the ground ahead of her. She turned to see who had shot it.

"Madeline, get down and find cover," Jode's voice cut through her confusion.

She spurred Thunder to a gallop and glanced around to see Simon join Jode in scanning the grassland behind them as their horses raced forward. Callisra matched Madeline's pace as they crossed into the shaded canopy of the forest onto a well-packed dirt road just ahead of their husbands.

"Into the trees," Jode shouted.

Madeline kneed her horse and veered off the road praying that Simon and Callisra would split up. Whoever was behind that arrow would be taking aim again, and if they could present more targets, they could make it harder to do too much damage. And, perhaps, find way to figure out who was attacking.

A few feet into the forest there was enough cover, so Madeline pulled on the reins. She could hear brush snapping and swishing off to her right, one of the others in her party barreling along to safety. There were no sounds coming from behind.

She brought her horse to a halt and turned him in a space between two giant trees. Jode wouldn't like it, but she had to investigate. Not so long ago, they were attacked when they ascended Severed Pass. That time, it was with a sawed through axle and this time an arrow. Two very different approaches. She hoped that didn't mean more than one person was out to kill one of them.

She slid off the horse and looped the reins over a branch. Then she started back to the road on foot, taking care to put her lessons in tracking to good use. Slipping from tree to tree, Madeline backtracked. There was still no sound coming from behind where they had left the road. Madeline glanced at the trees, wondering if someone was approaching through the tight canopy. No flicker of movement caught her eye. The noise of the horses would have frightened away the birds. Crouching low, she approached the packed earth of the road, stopping only when a low bush covered her.

No one was standing there arrows in hand searching for victims. Madeline slowed her breathing and sent her senses down the road. There were the small touches of animals, but nothing that was big enough to draw a bow. The animals were calm, which indicated whoever had shot the arrow was gone.

Turning her attention around her, Madeline checked to make sure that the attackers hadn't passed them in the rush to escape. The golden glow she knew to be her husband was the only sign of anything larger than a rabbit in the woods. Jode was behind her, and she would have to face his disapproval before they continued to the pass. Before turning to greet him, she sent her senses quickly out ahead, only Simon and Callisra, and it looked like they were back on the road and headed for the pass. Darn! If they had doubled back, maybe she could have deflected the lecture.

"They are gone," Jode said when she met him at the tree where her horse stood placidly waiting to be released. "Our attackers have retreated."

"How did you get there so quickly?" Madeline reached up and tossed the end of the reins over the branch to release her horse. "And how do you know they haven't moved ahead?"

Jode mounted and waited for Madeline to do the same. Then he led her to the road at an angle. When they were trotting toward the pass, he finally answered, "I turned back as soon as I had cover. Ice Storm is trained to move quietly through the woods. When we hunt, I do not always wish to be on foot as I come to my prey."

Madeline wondered if it would be worth investing time to train her horse to do the same but dismissed the idea. She didn't want to take part in the hunt and hoped to eventually live a quiet life. "I know the attackers are gone, but how do you know they aren't running ahead to set a trap."

Jode turned to look at her and Madeline sensed the lecture on her behavior was about to start. Jode never yelled at her, but his disappointment hurt. Although not enough for her to be a meek obedient wife. Fortunately that wasn't what Jode wanted, and he was smart enough to know it. "If we had time, I would take you back and teach you the finer points of tracking. I saw evidence that only one person was on the attack. Others came, and the tracks lead back to the grasslands. It is no guarantee that we will not be troubled again, but we have some time to travel in peace."

"It's like the wagon axle." Madeline urged her horse into a faster gait. Short bursts of speed would not harm the animal. "An attack with no follow up."

"I am confused as to the approach as well." Jode glanced behind as he spoke. "I have not heard of this type of attack. I wonder if it is simply uncoordinated, or if they are attempting to frighten us until they finally close in."

Madeline considered what she knew about terrorism, and guerrilla fighting, neither seemed to fit this situation. "If we are safe for now, let's catch up to the newlyweds and get to the pass."

Jode kept his eyes on the path ahead. "Now, perhaps, we can talk about your risky behavior."

Madeline saw that the trees were thinning out ahead. "Are we almost out of the forest?"

"No, but there are clearings. We will stop in one for a rest soon." He glanced at her. "If you are killed, we will not be successful on this task. I do not think we will be able to solve this without magic, and you are the only one in our party with anything other than healing talent. Will you allow me to protect you?"

She wanted to say yes. She knew it would be impossible for her to stick to that agreement. Before she could answer, Jode continued, "No. That is not a fair request. Will you at least allow me to help?"

A bird called from a bush to the side of them, its mate replied from a neighboring shrub. "Yes. I promise. If there is time, I will always ask you to help me."

"Always. Regardless of how much time is available, Madeline." Jode pulled closer. "Promise me that you will not leave me behind to avoid asking."

Madeline stared into his eyes, the blue darkened with worry. "I promise."

FOUR HOURS LATER, the forest was thinning, and Madeline hoped they were close to the pass where they would stop for the night. Her muscles felt like she had been in the saddle for days, sore and bruised.

Other than the aborted attack earlier, nothing had happened

to break the monotony of the ride. Conversation had dried up after the last stop where the horses had rested, and the humans had walked off the stiffness.

"Tell me about this pass," Madeline said, hoping to restart some discussion – if only to move time along. It already felt like she was taking too long to stop the attacks.

They were riding two abreast, Madeline and Callisra behind the two men. Jode turned to look at them and said, "I have been told that the pass is more like a break in the foothills. The mountain range is almost at its end this far east. I only have second-hand information. Callisra, how did you travel when you came here?"

"As I said, I was just child. We came in a wagon," she said. "We did go over the pass in the morning, but that is all I remember. But I'm not sure we came this way. Is the pass wide enough for a wagon?"

"Barely," Jode said. "It is unusual for wagons to travel any other way but along the coast. A small pass farther that way." He pointed to the right.

Madeline waited but no one said anything more. The buzz of insects the only sound that accompanied their horses' dull clump on the packed earth. Finally, she asked, "Why can't we go over before morning? I can cast light, if that's the problem."

Simon groaned. "Are you serious? My bones were looking forward to the rest before we went on."

"Wouldn't you rather get to a real bed faster?" Madeline knew that the morning would bring different pains, and she knew that Simon knew that too. She really just wanted to keep talking to push away the anxiety that had ridden with her since the attack. "Isn't it only a few hours from the pass to the entrance to The City? If we could get through when we arrive, we could be eating a real breakfast after a night in a real bed instead of jerky and grains."

The road widened and the men nudged their horses to the side so Madeline and Callisra could ride with them.

Madeline watched Jode. He had on his thinking face. He knew that if he chose the wrong words, she would continue to argue, or perhaps he was used to her arguing for the sake of it. She smiled. It had only been a year and she felt like they knew each other as if they were an old married couple.

He finally said, "In the daylight, we can cross the pass in an hour or so. Your magical light casts odd shadows, which will slow us down and make us jumpy. The City is, indeed, only two hour's hard ride. I do not want to travel at night in an unknown place. If we are attacked again, I want to be able to see what is coming."

Madeline gave up on her halfhearted pressure to move on. Jode was right, unknown terrain was hazardous enough without potential attacks. She was about to voice her capitulation, when her heart stopped beating at the sound of flapping and a loud squawk as a group of birds broke through the underbrush behind them. Jode and Madeline turned their horses and drew weapons before realizing it was only birds.

"Well, that woke me up," Madeline said, sliding her throwing knife back into the sheath on her thigh. "It has been too quiet up to now."

Simon looked at Jode and said, "I think you were right."

"About what?" Madeline looked between Simon and Jode. "Right about what?"

"Have you noticed how quiet it's been?" Simon asked.

Callisra answered, "I just thought it was because the animals are nocturnal."

"Keep moving." Jode shook the reins and his horse stepped forward. "We are being followed."

Madeline flicked a glance around but didn't see anyone. As her horse started after the others, she sent out her senses. Something tickled at the very edge of her reach. How had she missed the clues? Whoever was following was too far behind for her to get more than an impression of anger, hatred, and something else. Far enough behind that she couldn't tell how many, or what kind of being.

"How much farther?" she asked, moving a little closer to the other three.

"To the pass?" Jode asked

"Or at least out of the forest."

Jode looked up as though he could see the sun. Madeline followed his gaze and saw that the canopy had thinned enough to allow them to see where the sun was, low and behind them. The afternoon was slipping away.

"At this speed, we will be out of the trees in a half hour. Then there are several miles of rolling lands before we reach the camp." He glanced back. "When we are out of the forest, it will be difficult for them to follow without being seen."

Madeline nodded and urged Thunder to a faster gait. "Then let's not give them the advantage any longer than we have to."

MADELINE COULD FEEL EYES – or arrows – aiming at her back. "The horses can take a lot more speed, right?" She knew that if push came to shove, the horses were expendable. No matter how much she loved Thunder, if anyone in her party was in danger of being killed, the horses would come in second to the humans. "If we hurry to the pass, I can hide us under a protective spell like I did before, on Severed Pass." *Where it had saved everyone.*

No one took the trouble to answer; they all urged their horses to a trot, then a gallop.

They emerged from the last line of trees and Jode signaled for them to slow back to a trot. "The horses cannot continue at a gallop and still bring us to the pass. We do not want to walk from the pass to The City."

Madeline reluctantly obeyed; the itch of eyes on her back

almost overwhelming. Even at their slower pace, the trees faded into a green line behind them in only a few minutes. All of them rode side by side in grass that was up to the withers of the horses. Looking back, Madeline saw the grass ripple just at the edge of her sight.

"Someone is following, and they are closer than they were," she said, keeping her voice low. "Not a lot of people."

Jode didn't turn. "I saw them exit the forest. I should say I saw the effect of them leaving. I do not know who it is."

She glanced back again. "They are falling behind now. On foot, not that fast. Any clues?"

Simon drew closer. "Can't you use some magic to see them or something?"

"Not and stay on my horse. We just need to keep going and hope we can gain enough lead to set our spell tonight."

The ground started to rise, and Madeline saw that what she had taken for low-lying clouds was the foothills they had to cross.

Callisra rode ahead to the top and waited for them to catch up. When they gathered, Jode staring back the way they had come, Callisra said, "The hills are not an easy ride. Look, there's a path, but there is very little cover."

Madeline surveyed the road as far as she could see. A track wide enough for two horses, a broad shoulder on one side, and a rock face on the other. This path had been cut out of the rock. If it continued this way, they could go fast enough to gain more time on their pursuers. If it didn't stay this way, maybe she could cast the spell, and they could travel slowly. No, even if it got rougher, they needed to travel fast. "There will be no point in casting a concealment if our pursuers are able to see me do it. We need to get as far ahead as possible before stopping."

Jode turned his horse to face them. "They are perhaps a half hour behind us. Is there anything we can do to protect ourselves, or the horses, for this?"

"Yes, can you do that invisible spell again, like when we rescued Lee?" Simon automatically took over the job of watching their trail as he spoke.

Madeline sighed. They seemed to think she could solve everything with magic. "It doesn't work that way. I could cast it, but it would be too easy for someone to wander too far out of the spell. Any dust we raised would become visible. The spell isn't meant for this kind of situation." She glanced again, not seeing any movement. "We need to just go, but we have a few minutes. Callisra, can you check to see if any of the horses are hurt?"

She nodded and dismounted to start running her hands over the legs of the mounts.

Madeline glanced behind them. "I'll try to see what is happening behind us while we wait."

She slipped into a trance and threw her senses toward the grasslands. At first, she couldn't quite cast far enough. Her power resisted her commands, as if it had a plan, as if it were sentient. Then it flowed as easily as usual. She felt the distance in her mind, a mile or two back, something was there. But it was a void, and it was moving. She probed gently at what felt like a bubble, to no avail. Taking a quick assessment of the size of the bubble, she drew her consciousness back to the group. "No luck. They have something that bars my magic from details. From the size of the blankness, it's probably a party of four or five people." *At least it's not an army.*

"No injuries," Callisra reported.

"Then we go," Jode said. "Simon, take the lead. I will guard the rear. Madeline and Callisra, stay between us."

They started forward at a working trot. As fast as the horses could go and maintain the gait for long enough to make a difference.

The sun was setting as they pulled up for a rest at the entrance to the pass. "Do you have any idea where they are?" she asked as Jode joined them. "Do we have time for a quick rest?"

He rose in his seat and scanned the area before answering. "I lost sight of them. It could be that they have given up, or –"

"Or, they have found a way to catch up," Madeline finished his statement. "Let me check."

Not waiting for agreement, Madeline sent her power out in a circle as far as she could reach. This time her power answered immediately. She sensed nothing more than a few field animals, and what felt like a ten-foot snake. She rolled her shoulders to take the creepiness of the snake essence out of her mind. She pushed out another wave of power, now reaching for the sense of some other magic; still nothing.

"I think we're safe for now, but I don't want to chance it much longer." She returned her gaze to the road ahead. "If we had light, would it make a difference?" Her question was barely audible, she was thinking out loud more than making a plan, so Simon's voice startled her.

"I think we should try," he said. "Light or not, staying here feels like a really stupid idea."

Madeline laughed at the image that came to her mind. "Like a teen slasher movie? The power is out, and the bimbo goes into the basement."

Jode and Callisra gave her the look she was getting used to. It said, '*I don't know what you mean, but please don't try to explain'*.

Simon dismounted before saying, "Yeah. I'm having a difficult time finding it funny though." He grinned and Madeline realized he wasn't taking a jab at her. He continued, "I need to walk for a while, or I might never recover from the saddle."

"I can heal you," Callisra dismounted to stand beside him.

Simon shook his head. "The horses need the rest as much as I do, and you must be as saddle weary as I am. If we walk for a bit, it won't make that much difference. Besides we can eat and drink on the road to make up the time."

Jode also dismounted and held his hand to assist Madeline. "I hear water. The horses need that more than rest. We can stop long enough for the horses and humans to eat and drink, but I think we should be in the saddle as we travel the pass."

Madeline felt her muscles seize up as she tried to walk. Grimacing in pain, she continued, one step at a time, as Jode led them to the river.

A HALF HOUR LATER, Madeline cast the glow spell in front of the horse so that she could lead them through the pass. Jode kept to the rear, alert for the mystery attackers. All of them rode with reins in one hand and the other holding a weapon. Madeline's nerves were vibrating at every skitter of falling pebbles and swoop of night bird. It took all of her concentration to keep the light steady.

Despite the urgency, Jode worried about the horses, so he made them go at a walk to minimize the risk of an injury. The path inclined steadily but the surface deteriorated into ruts and loose rubble. Madeline had to keep reminding herself to breathe. The glow of her spell cast harsh shadows on the walls that rose on either side of them. More than once she raised her throwing knife only to realize it was a shadow of a horse not an attacker.

"If this goes on much longer, I'm going to explode," she said.

A chuckle came from behind her. Callisra was clearly not as wound up. "Madeline, it is not that dire, you can relax a little. There are four of us here. You are not the only one responsible for our safety."

The words caused her to turn in the saddle to see the rest of her party. They followed, arms relaxed, almost lounging on their horses. "Maybe if someone had mentioned that earlier ..." then the tension flowed out and she snorted a laugh at herself. "I guess I was taking the lead a little too seriously. It's not often I'm up here in the front."

It took two hours of careful stepping to get through the pass. As they exited, Madeline's spell spread out to show the terrain ahead. Golden sand dunes rose on each side of a path that curved out of sight.

She moved her horse to the side as the others made it through the narrow opening. As she waited, she sent the light out as far as she could. Nothing changed. Still only sand carved into patterns by the wind.

The sight was enough to take her mind off the immediate danger. "If The City is the only port, how do they send goods to the rest of the land?"

"They go the long way around," Callisra answered. "The wagons don't cross here. Either they travel along the coast and cross through Ale's pass, or they travel the other way and cross at the Narrows pass. I think we must have come through Narrows pass when I came with my parents."

Madeline nodded and looked across the sand. "Can we rely on this path? Does it lead all the way to The City?"

Jode dismounted and tested the sand with his feet. "Yes. But we will have to wait for light to be sure we don't wander off into the dunes."

Simon twisted to look through the gap they had just passed. "Could someone come through a different way?"

"No. The other crossings are at least a day away. And you saw how steep the sides were. No one can come over the mountains. Only one person at a time can come through, so I think we can safely rest here. I will take the first turn at guard."

Madeline couldn't shake the feeling that they were in danger. "I think we should try to leave. I know it will be hard, but even if we go slowly it will get us away from whoever is following us."

Jode wrapped an arm around her and kissed her forehead. "If you can sense the danger, we should go, but I worry that we are tired and that means we may make mistakes. If we rest for a few hours, it will mean a safer passage."

His embrace chased the fears to the edge of her consciousness. "A couple of hours' rest is fine."

. . .

MADELINE SHOOK SIMON AWAKE. "It's time. We'll be in The City by morning, even if we travel slowly. Wake the others while I get the horses fed and saddled."

It had only been a couple of hours, but she felt encouraged that no one attacked. Even such a short shift at watch had been difficult for Madeline. Staying alert in such silence after a long day in the saddle was a skill she didn't possess. Her leg would be black and blue from the number of times she'd pinched herself to stop falling asleep. The thought of a bath, and a meal of something other than trail food, almost drowned out the fear that they would be too late. That the attacks on Arabela's home had succeeded.

As she saddled the horses, the others joined her, passing a snack of dried meat, dried fruit, and the last of the water. "What about the horses?" she asked before biting into a dried fig.

"I watered them before I woke you for your shift," Callisra said. "They will be fine as long as we do not push them too hard."

Madeline looked at the sand just beyond the packed earth of their camp. Nothing but dunes curving away, backs shaped by the wind. Everything was a gradient of shadow arranged around a darker line. "Is that the trail?"

Jode nodded. "I am told it will widen as we leave the shadow of the mountains."

Madeline hoped that was soon. Going single file made it too easy to pick them off if an attack came.

"We should travel quickly," Jode said. "I will lead today, perhaps that will save my wife's nerves."

"Thank you," Madeline said without a trace of the sarcasm she would have used at any other time. "I'll take the rear. Throwing knives will do a better job at keeping attackers off us, so we won't have to use our close weapons."

When they mounted, Jode started for the thread of trail.

"Trust your horses. They will not step off the track unless you make them."

HOURS LATER, Madeline wished they had kept a few sips of water in the canteens. She swallowed against the thirst that was threatening to overwhelm her and sent her power out to seek again. Still no presences. The sun was barely over the horizon and she found herself imagining waterfalls and cool baths. No one should travel in this abominable heat.

"Is that The City?" Callisra's voice broke through Madeline's doze.

Looking up she saw a line in the distance, the gold of the sand fading into a darker red.

"It must be," Jode answered. "It is still a long way, but it is nice to see evidence that our journey will eventually be over."

Madeline squinted into the distance, feeling the buzz of faint thoughts along the power thread she'd thrown toward their destination. "Yes, there are people there, lots of them." Hope for shade and water made her almost faint. "Jode is right. It is much farther than it looks. I think, maybe, a couple more hours." How was it possible that this was only two hours of hard riding normally?

Simon's groan sufficed for all of them. Then he cheered a little. "I'm with Jode. At least we know we are going to make it. I've been thinking this track might be going in circles. It's a wonder anyone travels this way."

"Most don't," Jode answered. "And those who use the pass travel at night, crossing the pass in late afternoon and then resting. But they are not worried about pursuit. I did not expect us to travel so slowly and now we are too worn down by the heat to move faster. Perhaps we should have risked injury when it was still dark and cool."

"And perhaps we would be walking now if we had. Don't

second guess yourself, my love." Not having the energy to add anything else, Madeline returned to her half doze. Perhaps when they got closer, they could go faster.

IT TOOK ALMOST four hours for them to approach close enough to see more than just shapes. Jode pointed to the gate. "I was expecting to approach from an angle. It would make sense for protecting The City, but the trail goes directly to the gate." He leaned forward in the saddle. "Look, is that really a fountain I see?"

Madeline started to ask if they could speed up their pace without killing the horses, but as she opened her mouth, Simon fell from his mount.

She reined her horse and leapt to the ground. As she reached to see how badly he was hurt, something whined past her ear.

"Stay down," Jode called, spinning his horse to find the attacker. "Is he harmed?"

Callisra joined Madeline beside Simon, pulling their horses around to form a shield. "No, he will be fine. It is just a bruise."

Madeline glanced up at her husband. "Jode, don't make yourself a target. Ouch." A sharp splinter of stone deflected off Simon's saddle, clipping her ear as it passed. She spun around. "Where are they? Who are they?"

Another stone landed in a puff of dust a foot from where they crouched.

"I cannot see who they are," Jode said as he slipped from his horse. "They are off to the north, but there is magic concealing them. Madeline, can you find them?"

"Forget spending energy to find them. They aren't between us and the gate," Simon said, pulling himself up from the ground. "We can run for it, before they get closer, or cut us off."

Madeline didn't feel good about mounting again and presenting a clear target. "Will the horses make it?"

"Just," Callisra said, running a hand across each mount's flank. "And they will have time to recover fully while we search The City."

"Mount low in the saddle and don't worry about anything but clearing the gate," Jode said. "No matter who they are, they will not risk breaking the peace of The City."

"Okay, together then." Madeline grabbed the pommel of Thunder's saddle and mounted, then dropped low just as an arrow screamed past. The stones were bad enough, but arrows tended to do more damage than a shard of flint.

Jode slapped her horse's rump and the beast took off at a gallop for the gates. Madeline clung to the saddle and listened for other arrows, and other horses. The only hoof beats she could hear were her friends' and they were just behind her. As they sped to the safety of The City, arrows started to stab into the sand to either side of them.

"Are they bad shots, or are we being driven somewhere?" she muttered. Looking ahead, she saw a clear run to the gates, only a hundred feet away. Then an arrow thocked as it pierced the saddlebag, an inch from her leg. Anger flared and she tore the shaft out, holding it in her fist as she crossed through the carved stone gates of The City. Safe.

She reined her horse and spun to watch the others come through. Callisra came first, Simon right behind leaning to cover his wife's back. Jode rode still farther behind, as though he had delayed on purpose.

Madeline's grip on the arrow tightened until she heard a snap as the shaft broke. She could see that the attack was still going on, as Jode raced for the safety of the shade beyond the gates. Arrows followed him, falling to the sand as his horse's rear hooves lifted. Too close.

His horse's head entered The City. He was clear. She started to yell in victory. Then one final arrow found its mark in Jode's shoulder. He slumped in the saddle as Ice Storm took the final steps into the shade.

The world shrank to the shaft of light in the gate. Sounds dropped away to only the beat of Thunder's hooves as Madeline kneed her horse forward. She rode past Jode, instinct holding her in the saddle, knowing that Callisra would make sure he was taken care of.

Thunder managed a gallop all the way back into the sun toward the attackers. Voices called her name, but they sounded miles away. All she saw was a red haze flowing around her like a veil.

Without conscious effort, she sent her magic shooting out on her fury. Seeking revenge on whoever had let that arrow fly.

She heard screaming, and forced her magic farther seeking blood. But nothing was there.

Then someone grabbed her from her saddle and carried her back to The City. Voices came through the screaming, but she couldn't make out any words.

Then someone was shaking her.

"Madeline," Simon's voice cut through the haze. "Stop it. He's going to be okay. Stop screaming."

* * *

A NEW THREAT to the heir to the Summer Lands pulls Madeline away from her lessons. Use the QR code to grab your copy of A Twist of Power to ride with Madeline to the mysterious City.

FREE EBOOK

Claim your copy of Obstacles of Magic when you use the QR code to sign up for my newsletter and learn more about Madeline's history with magic.

ALSO BY P A WILSON

For more books by P A Wilson

Use the QR code below or go to pawilson.ca

ABOUT THE AUTHOR

Perry Wilson is a Canadian author based in Vancouver, BC who has big ideas and an itch to tell stories. Having spent some time on university, a career, and life in general, she returned to writing in 2008 and hasn't looked back since (well, maybe a little, but only while parallel parking).

She is a member of the Vancouver Writers Social Group, The Royal City Literary Arts Society, and The Surrey Writing Workshop. Perry has self-published several novels. She writes the Madeline Journeys, a fantasy series about a high-powered lawyer who finds herself trapped in a magical world, the Quinn Larson Quests, which follows the adventures of a wizard named Quinn who must contend with volatile fae in the heart of Vancouver, and the Charity Deacon Investigations, a mystery thriller series about a private eye who tends to fall into serious trouble with her cases, and The Riverton Romances, a series based in a small town in Oregon, one of her favorite states. Her stand-alone novels are Breaking the Bonds, Closing the Circle, and The Dragon at The Edge of The Map.

For more information
www.pawilson.ca
pawilson@pawilson.ca

 X

ACKNOWLEDGMENTS

People think that the process of writing is solitary. That's not the case for me. I have help from so many people it would be hard to acknowledge everyone, but I'll give it a try.

The support and inspiration I get from my writer's groups is incalculable. The Vancouver Writers Social Group opens my mind to other ways of telling a story. The Royal City Literary Arts Society gives me the opportunity to meet and share with other writers who have more knowledge than I do. The Other 11 Months group is where I learn about getting the words on the page. And my critique group who helps me find the best parts of the story I want to tell. Thanks to all of the members of these great groups.

Last of all, but definitely a huge part of the process, my beta readers. These are the people who love stories and are willing, and more than able, to tell me if my finished story is ready for you, my readers.